Books by B. V

STAR FORCE SERIES
Swarm
Extinction
Rebellion
Conquest
Battle Station
Empire
Annihilation
Storm Assault
The Dead Sun
Outcast
Exile
Gauntlet
Demon Star

REBEL FLEET SERIES
Rebel Fleet
Orion Fleet
Alpha Fleet
Earth Fleet

Visit BVLarson.com for more information.

Red Company: First Strike!

(Red Company Series #1)
by
B. V. Larson

Red Company Series:

Red Company: First Strike!
Red Company: Discovery
Red Company: Contact

Copyright © 2023 by Iron Tower Press.

This book is a work of fiction. Names, characters, places and incidents are either products of the author's imagination or used fictitiously. Any resemblance to actual events, locales or persons, living or dead, is entirely coincidental. All rights reserved. No part of this publication can be reproduced or transmitted in any form or by any means, without permission in writing from the author.

ISBN-13: 979-8395325648
BISAC: Fiction / Science Fiction / Military

Chapter 1: The Rock-Rat

A group of four Red Company marines marched by. "Marched" was possibly the wrong word, as under the low-gravitational pull of an asteroid, they appeared to be taking a series of leaps. Each step took them farther than an Olympic jumper could fly back on Earth.

My eyes were drawn to them and away from my drill-bot. That was a dangerous thing to do, but I couldn't help it.

The marines were patrolling the perimeter around the mining rig, looking for danger. They carried stubby laser carbines and wore bulky armored vests. They seemed so superior to me, so organized, well-trained—and above all, dangerous.

Their flying steps soon took them over the horizon of the asteroid and out of sight.

"Starn? Dammit, Starn! Are you listening to me?" It was the foreman. A mean man with a quick temper.

"I'm here, boss," I said, keying my helmet's comms. "I'm moving my drill-bot to—"

"Shut up. Get your bot over to pit #3, on the sun-side. There's a good vein over there. Move your ass."

"On my way, boss!"

Moving my drill-bot when it was in the middle of a run was easier said than done. I had to practically lift the thing bodily out of the trench it was making. The laser head burned a smoking gash in the rock between my boots before I could get it to shut down. The AI on these things was stubborn.

As I drove the bot toward the new pit the foreman had identified, I had time to ponder my life with all its ups and downs—and it seemed to me that the downs dominated the story.

I'd been born with the cool-sounding name of Devin Starn—and that's where my luck had ended. I'd spent my childhood navigating the labyrinthine streets of Earth's sprawling giga-slums, never suspecting that I would one day find myself in the cold expanse of deep space. Yet, here I was today, an indentured, D-Contract rock-rat.

This difficult, dangerous work had begun when I'd been confiscated as an asset related to a long overdue debt. When the state had sold me off as a partial payment, my contract had been snatched up at a bargain price by the shrewd Captain Hansen.

She commanded the mining rig *Borag*, an aging but formidable vessel that prowled the darkest, most remote corners of the Solar System in pursuit of rare elements. *Borag*, with her patchwork exterior and mismatched components, had long endured the harsh realities of space mining, but she was our joint ticket to fortune—or so I hoped.

I toiled away during my so-called "days"—a term that felt out of place when the sun's light was no more intense than a full moon back on Earth—drilling and blasting through the rocky terrain of low-gravity asteroids. My goal wasn't gold or silver, the metals that had captivated the imaginations of treasure hunters of the past, but rather metals like titanium and beryllium. These elements were far more precious in the unforgiving vacuum of space.

The work was grueling and unrelenting. I alternated between sweating and freezing, as the temperatures swung wildly. The stale air I breathed was a stench accumulating within my solitary spacesuit, an ever-present companion.

Each day, I couldn't help but think of the steep price I'd paid for my parents' unknown transgressions. Earth-Gov had never bothered to enlighten me about the nature of their crimes, but the consequences weighed heavily upon my shoulders.

On the positive side, I'd been born on a real planet. That simple fact set me apart from most of the other miners whose contracts were purchased to work aboard *Borag*. Most of them had elongated bones with muscles like rubber bands. My stocky build was a gift from the gravity I'd grown up with, but it also made me slower and less agile than my colleagues in low-gravity conditions.

As I drove my drill-bot to the brighter side of our chosen rock, I descended into pit #3 with the usual sense of foreboding. The constant danger of ice-slides and cave-ins weighed heavily on my mind. The hum of machinery came through my boots and into my scratched helmet, making it hard to think.

Hours passed uneventfully. I took a deep breath and endured the itching sweat on my brow until the sun finally went to the other side of the rock, at which point I began to shiver. Still, it was ninth-hour, and my shift was winding down. I kept thinking about the four-minute shower I'd allow myself to purchase when it was over.

As I glided my bot over a new hotspot—which glowed like lava after the drill-head was done—I noticed a fellow rock-rat sidling up close on my left.

Charley was working nearby. I didn't really know him well, but he seemed like an okay guy. I nodded in greeting and Charley returned the gesture.

"Long day, huh?" I said, deciding to break the silence.

"Always is," Charley replied. "But it beats the alternative, I suppose. It's the end of the shift, and that always gets a man to thinking."

I turned my faceplate in his direction and raised an eyebrow, prompting Charley to continue.

"I'm thinking about how I got here," he continued. "I was young and dumb... fell into gambling and ended up in debt. This was the only way out."

I nodded in understanding, but I couldn't help feeling a burning sense of resentment toward the system that had cast us both into this slice of Hell.

"I was different," I said, "I was a free-loader, a man of the streets."

Charley laughed at that. "Most homeless losers have cool names to describe themselves," he said.

"Yeah, well... I thought I was an orphan—but the computers schooled me about that. Apparently, my parents were infamous criminals. When I was arrested by a robo for vagrancy, the state sold me off as a child-asset to pay for the crimes of my parents. Then Captain Hansen bought me cheap, and here I am."

"Ooooh," Charley said, squinting warily. "Criminal parents?"

"That's what I was told. I don't recall ever having met them in person."

Charley took a side-step away from me. I knew what that meant. He was thinking about ditching me.

I was used to it. Everyone knew it was a bad idea to associate with dissidents.

He seemed to reconsider, and he paused to speak again. "You're one of those, huh? Well... I'm sorry to hear that. Guys like us have got to make the best of it, you know?"

I adjusted my drill-bot and kicked it in the side until it started buzzing again. I couldn't help but wonder if there was an easier way out of this life. A way to break free from the chains that bound me to this remote corner of the Solar System.

When my muscles ached and my eyelids were heavy with exhaustion, the grueling hours in the mines had come down to the final twelfth-hour. My shift was ending, and I hesitantly checked my profit-margins. I found my metered accounts had dropped slightly. That was depressing.

Each month, I was charged an exorbitant amount for the oxygen, heat, water and food I needed to survive. The expenses often left me owing more each paycheck than I could earn from my work. My debt kept moving up and down, but not really going anywhere decisively.

I'd tried all the tricks, of course. Breathing shallowly, skipping meals and showers. I tried to ignore the gnawing hunger in my stomach, the dryness in my throat, and the dull ache in my chest that came with each breath. But the feeling of suffocation was ever-present, a grim reminder of my parents' mistakes.

These thoughts were interrupted when I heard some indistinct shouts of alarm over my suit radio. I looked up to see one of the mining robots malfunctioning, its arms flailing wildly as it careened toward Charley. The machine rammed into him, but I was spared the awful crunch since there wasn't any air around us to transmit the sound.

Without a second thought, I rushed toward Charley. I managed to reach him before the robot could finish him. I grabbed hold of the robot's arm and strained against its wild motion, my muscles screaming in protest.

Charley lay on the spiny rocks, his leg trapped under a slab that would have weighed more than a truck on Earth. The robot's treads were still moving, pressing down on his chest. His eyes were closed, and he looked pale and cold inside his cracked helmet.

I gritted my teeth and strained against the robot's motors. My muscles burned with the effort. I could feel the metal threatening to cut into my suit, but I refused to let go. With a final burst of strength, I lifted the robot off Charley's injured body and tossed it into a spin. It almost reached orbit, still flailing and casting weird shadows and flashing reflections from our distant sun.

Charley gasped for air, and his eyes fluttered open. "Thanks," he croaked.

I nodded, with my heart racing from the adrenaline. I could feel the sweat pouring down my face.

Charley peered up at the robot, which was still flying higher. "A normal rock-rat couldn't have done that," he said. "Too much inertia—and those bots have magnets and other tricks to get traction, you know."

He coughed and wheezed, and I told him to take it easy. The other miners rushed over to see what had happened, and I couldn't help but feel a sense of pride. Despite the odds, I'd managed to save Charley's life.

I watched as the other miners gathered around me, their expressions a mixture of appreciation and worry—but the moment was short-lived. The foreman approached, and his expression was grim.

"What the fuck is this? A twelfth-hour strike?"

"No, sir!" the miners all replied in unison, and they did their best to melt away and return to work. Strikes were illegal, and the punishments were harsh if the charges were upheld by an AI judge.

"You two are way behind on your quotas of ore," the foreman said, checking our numbers.

We apologized and assured him we'd work harder. He was about to let us off with a write-up and a warning—when he caught sight of the drill-bot spinning overhead.

At that point, his voice became wrathful. My heart sank. I'd been working harder than ever, but it never seemed to be enough.

"That's company property, Starn. I know Charley didn't throw that thing up there—he's no dirt-kicking Earther like you are. You know the punishment."

"Yes, boss."

The foreman pulled out a shock-rod. I gritted my teeth as he jabbed the crackling stick into my side, sending a surge of electricity through my body. I fell to my knees, gasping for air. The other miners scuttled away to safety.

But I knew the routine. After six or seven zaps—I lost count along the way—I got up, ignoring the pain, and returned to my work. The foreman hauled Charley onto his back like a sack of rocks and carried the groaning, injured man back to the hulking ship.

After I'd corralled the drill-bot, I penetrated deeper into the surface of the asteroid, and I actually found a rich vein of titanium. That was something, at least.

My thoughts turned to Charley. I figured I knew what would happen to him. Charley would be hauled back to the lowest hold on *Borag* for processing. I'd seen it happen to others before, and I knew no miner wanted to endure that.

Despite the danger and the uncertainty, I continued to work, my mind consumed with hopes of riches. I knew that was the only way to break free from the chains that bound me to this life.

When my shift was nearly done, the titanium had really come in. I'd paid for at least three days of my own upkeep. That was a big win to my way of thinking. This new rock was a bonanza. If we spent a month or more here, and the metals didn't run out…

My thoughts snapped back to the here and now when I caught a glimpse of *Borag's* captain, a no-nonsense woman named Captain Elsa Hansen. She looked stern and unapproachable, and she had a reputation for being tough on her crew.

Next to her was Oswald Blackwood, the ship's chief accountant. Blackwood was a tall, spare, stick of a man. They said his splayed feet had never touched the dirt of a real planet, and from the look of him, I believed the rumors.

"Devin Starn?" Blackwood said.

"That's me, sir."

"It's come to our attention that you were involved in a work-related accident."

I felt the sweat break out on my stubbly temples despite the cold in my half-heated suit. "Not exactly, Mr. Accountant, sir. I tried to—"

Blackwood threw up a webwork of overly-long fingers, and I instantly stopped my stammered response. The accountant flipped open a computer that glowed blue light into his faceplate. His eyes ran over the numbers as did his fingers. He shook his head grimly.

"The company has experienced a loss, today. Unscheduled maintenance on a drill-bot. Spare parts are required, plus labor costs incurred. I'm putting you down as accountable."

"What?" I squawked. "It was an accident, sir. All I did was try to save Charley."

Captain Hansen watched all this quietly. She was listening without interrupting on anyone's behalf.

Blackwood pursed his lips. "Are you expecting us to eat this entire charge?" he said, shaking the computer at me. "It's more than you're likely to earn in a lifetime, but you're going to do your best!"

With that, he turned away from me. I was desperate, so I called him back. "It wasn't my fault, sir. The machine malfunctioned. All I did was try to help save a man's life."

Slowly, the accountant turned back to face me. "Is that right? Are you aware that the man in question is also in a state of insurmountable debt? You're both liabilities on every cell of my spreadsheets!"

"But sir, can't you see your way to handling this differently? I can't take on more debt—I just can't."

The man narrowed his eyes, and he opened his mouth to shout "no" but another man stepped forward. It was my own foreman.

"There is a way…" he said, looking slightly excited. "He can take punishment instead."

"That won't pay for anything!" Blackwood raged.

"No, but if we mark this down as an act of defiance and violence, instead of an accident, it'll go into a different category, won't it?"

The accountant thought that over, and he brightened. "You're right. A different category… with a different source of funding… we'll call it vandalism. I like the way you think, Foreman."

Blackwood turned back to me, and his face had a predatory cast to it. "Mr. Starn, you will be disciplined for your gross acts of violence directed toward company property. When do you choose to take your medicine?"

I shrugged. "My shift is over—and I've had a good day as far as ore goes. Let's do it now."

With a grim expression, the foreman glanced at Captain Hansen. She'd been quiet all this time, but she was listening closely. She nodded her head to the foreman.

The man lifted his shock-rod, and he turned up the power all the way—then he jabbed me in the ribs with it.

The pain was indescribable. The shocks I'd received earlier were nothing like this. It was like comparing tiny arcs of static to shoving a wet finger into a light socket. My eyes blinked on their own, and my body folded up. My legs were water. I fell gently due to the low gravity.

"Again," said the accountant, and the foreman obliged.

He gave me another one, and I could taste metal and blood in my mouth. I'd bitten my tongue.

"Again."

This time, I blacked out for a moment—at least, I thought it was only a moment.

"He's aware again," Blackwood said in a bored tone. "What an obstinate brute… keep going."

I grunted in fear and almost pissed myself—but the next shock never came.

To my surprise, I heard Captain Hansen's voice speak for the first time today. "Enough," she said firmly. "That's an order."

I couldn't believe what I was hearing. The foreman had always been merciless, punishing miners until they fell unconscious—or worse. But here was the captain of the *Borag* rig, ordering him to stop.

Blackwood complained that I hadn't yet fallen unconscious. "Insurance might reject our claim!"

But Captain Hansen insisted. "We don't need any more deaths on this ship," she said, "not on this shift, anyway."

Her voice left no room for argument. They walked back to the dark mass which was *Borag*. I lay there, gasping on the rocks for a time, with my entire body aching.

For the first time in a long while, I felt a glimmer of hope. Sure, I'd suffered a bit. But I'd kept my gains today. Maybe, just maybe, there was a way out of this life, a way to escape the brutal cycle of debt and servitude.

As I lay there, looking up at the starry sky, my thoughts turned to Captain Hansen. She had shown me mercy, something that was all too rare in the harsh universe of asteroid mining.

Chapter 2: The Claim-Jumpers

Another work cycle began. I was sent out to operate the drill-bots again, my body still aching from the beating I'd endured despite the brief rest in a bunk.

Borag still crouched on the same nameless rock. All the other rock-rats were there alongside me, drilling relentlessly. Like a swarm of metallic leeches, we surrounded the immense ship's underbelly and labored around the clock.

Glancing up, I eyeballed the sharp lines of the vessel's hull. Monstrous engines that propelled her through the void stuck out from the fantail, and the rows of yellow windows lined her waist. Gazing at the ship's towering mass, I could make out the silhouettes of crew members scurrying within. Their forms were minuscule in comparison to the vastness of the spacecraft overall.

As my shift dragged on, my thoughts couldn't help but stray to my fellow miner, Charley. I inquired about him to the other miners, but no one could provide a definitive answer. They averted their gazes and muttered something about him being "processed."

My heart sank. I figured I knew what had happened. Charley had likely been deemed a worthless asset and terminated.

I felt a pang of guilt. I'd been so focused on my own survival that I'd forgotten about everyone else. Charley had been as innocent as I was when the drill-bot malfunctioned, and I'd failed to save him. Now he was being processed, and there was nothing I could do to help him.

As I drilled deeper into the thorny rock, hitting a fresh vein of metal, my thoughts turned to getting out of my predicament. I knew that I had to find a way out of this life, a way to break free from the chains that bound me to this remote corner of the Solar System. But the odds were against me. Even if I mined a rich vein every day for the next month, I'd still fall back into the red as charges for breathing accumulated on the long haul back to Mars.

Like a thousand other contracts before me, I pondered escape. Defaulting on your debts and disappearing wasn't unheard of—but it was pretty much impossible on a mining rig. There simply wasn't anywhere to run.

But I refused to give up. I was a survivor, a fighter, and I would do whatever it took to achieve my freedom. Earning my way out, that was the only path that made sense. I assured myself it could be done.

As I chipped away at the rocks, I noticed Captain Hansen marching by with two of her marines in tow.

I tried to avoid making eye contact with the captain, but I couldn't help but feel a sense of curiosity. What was she doing out here? Was she checking up on the miners? Or was there something else going on?

Just then, I noticed something odd. Charley was walking toward me, but he was limping and holding his side. I rushed over to him, my heart racing with concern.

"Hey, man! I thought you were a goner!"

"I'm… functional," Charley said, his voice strained. "Some of my parts are plastic, now—but I can work."

"That's great to hear. What's the captain doing out here?"

Charley cast a worried look sunward. The asteroid we were mining was in a slow spin, faster than Earth but slower than some of the others we mined. It took about three hours to do a full rotation. He pointed after the captain and her two marines.

"I heard there are claim-jumpers on the far side of this rock. Their captain asked ours to come out to talk to him."

I frowned inside my helmet. Claim-jumpers were a scourge of the asteroid mining industry, ruthless scavengers who would stop at nothing to steal the precious minerals that D-Contract rock-rats like me had risked our lives to mine.

"You think…" Charley said, "you think maybe we should have a look?"

There he went again, seeking his second beating in a week. I could see why Charley wasn't topping the list of hard workers who might yet earn out their contracts.

"I can't afford the time, man," I told him.

"I can. I'm screwed anyway. If these claim-jumpers kick us off this fat rock, or they take half the metal… well, I want to see what's happening."

I shook my head. "It's your funeral."

Charley hobbled away into the light of the sun. Our local star was smaller than it was supposed to be, but with no atmosphere to interfere with the light, it was still kicking out plenty of radiation.

I looked after him skeptically. I'd seen the fire in Charley's eyes.

Part of me admired him, and after a few minutes, I set my drill-bot to idle, and I walked after him.

"You're not on break yet, Starn!" the foreman called after me.

I waved to him. "Sometimes a man has to go, sir," I called back, waving. "I'll be right back."

The foreman snarled and made some notes on his tablet. No doubt he was looking for a way to tack on a surcharge, but I knew that we were all allotted eight minutes a shift for unscheduled breaks. That would have to be enough.

I followed Charley over a rocky rise. On an asteroid, you didn't have to wander far to be out of sight of one another. The curvature of these tiny planetoids placed every horizon only a hundred yards off. Sometimes, it was less than that.

As I hopped toward the far side of the asteroid, I could hear a commotion and shouting in my local radio range. I'd already figured out the discussion of claims between the two captains had gone badly by the time I topped a jagged blade of nickel-iron.

There they were: a group of claim-jumpers, armed to the teeth and planning to take what they wanted.

Captain Hansen and her marines were outnumbered and outgunned. She was racing toward me—toward the safety of *Borag*. Her face was etched with a mix of fear and determination.

Then I spotted Charley. He was clawing his way over the rocks, too. His new plastic feet had to be slow-moving, because he was crawling, using his gloved hands to grab onto every handhold he could and propel himself in my direction.

Hansen had one of her marines with her, and he was firing wildly at the claim-jumpers. But then he was hit, and I watched in horror as he fell to the ground, his blood spraying out in a hot gassy plume. It froze a moment later in the cold vacuum of space.

Captain Hansen made a sound of rage and fired her weapon, hitting one of the claim-jumpers in the chest. But then more of the bandits appeared and fired wild laser-shots at her. I saw her go down, and I knew that we were in trouble. The bandit that had shot her whooped and rushed close, batting aside her weapon. He grabbed her arms and began to haul her away.

What was his plan? Capture and ransom? Something worse?

I didn't know, but I rushed forward, my muscles straining with the effort. Unlike a man born in null-G, I wasn't graceful and quick—but I was strong.

The claim-jumper turned to face me, surprised. He lifted his pistol, but I smashed it down. He wasn't ready for my strength. I hit him with everything I had, my fists connecting with his ribs, and I felt the satisfying crunch of thin bones giving way.

He went down, and I knew that I had him. I could feel the adrenaline pumping through my veins, and I knew that I was stronger than he was.

I crushed him, my muscles bulging with the effort. And then, as I stood there panting, I realized that we'd won. Charley was gone—but so were the claim-jumpers. They'd run off the moment they'd seen the guy I'd knocked flat go limp. He had an officer's markings on his shoulders, and I figured he was their leader.

We had emerged victorious.

Captain Hansen lay on the ground, her arm bubbling blood which boiled then froze as it left her suit. Her eyes were filled with a mix of pain and anger. Perhaps she was somewhat ashamed, too.

I'd barely caught my breath after the fight when I heard the sound of more *Borag* marines approaching. The foreman was leading them. They looked angry, and I knew what that meant.

I'd been so focused on the fight that I had forgotten about my work. I was supposed to be mining, but instead, I'd been fighting claim-jumpers. Now, they were here to make me pay for it.

They grabbed me roughly, and I winced in pain as they hit me with their shock-rods. They didn't even bother to tell me why—but I knew the answer. I was away from my work and way over the limits of my break-time.

I was soon on my belly, crawling over the rocks and gasping for air, but they didn't stop. They kept zapping me, over and over, until I thought I would pass out.

But then I heard a familiar voice. It was Captain Hansen, and she was ordering them to stop. I looked up, and I saw her standing there, holding a patch to her arm. She returned my gaze evenly.

"He's a tough one, isn't he?" she asked.

"That he is, Captain. A beast of a miner—but disobedient. There's almost no point to beating on him. He doesn't learn. I don't think he even really feels it."

The captain studied me. She was the only one there who wasn't glaring and full of anger.

"I'm short one fighter, Starn," she said at last. "Will you take the job?"

I was stunned. Could I really serve as a security man, or better yet, a marine on her ship? That was dangerous work—but it meant I'd be free from the mines, free from the endless cycle of debt and servitude. Marines didn't have to work for air and food. Such things were provided in their contracts.

I looked at her, my heart racing with excitement and fear. Could I do it? Could I really become a security man, a member of her crew?

Then I looked at my workmates surrounding us, and I knew that I didn't have a choice. They were scowling and angry—the foreman was the worst of all. His face was twisted up into a mask of rage. I had to take the job, or I would be back in the mines, beaten and broken.

I nodded, feeling a sense of hope rising up inside me. As I climbed to my feet and stood, my muscles still ached from the beatings—but I didn't care. I was free—or at least, I was on my way to freedom.

Captain Hansen looked at me, her eyes full of careful calculation. She knew I would serve her well out of gratitude, if nothing else.

Daring to smile, I reached out to shake her hand. She allowed it. In that moment, I knew I'd made the right decision. I had taken a step toward freedom, toward a life that was no longer completely controlled by others.

Sure, marines tended to live even shorter lives than rock-rats, but at least it was a life that provided a level of pride.

Chapter 3: The Recruit

The year was 2125, and Earth-Gov ran most of our Solar System. They did so not through a politicians and nation-states, but rather through conglomerates known as mega-corporations. These conglomerates had no regional identity. They were instead interconnected through various nexus-points of power.

However, beneath this level, many smaller companies existed. Among them, independent space-faring vessels functioned as companies in their own right.

The planets, moons, and the asteroid belt had all been explored in the latter decades of the twenty-first century. The exploitation of this vast source of mineral wealth was the focus of countless one-ship operations.

The exploratory vessel *Borag* was just such an independent company. *Borag* was a combination patrol ship and mining rig. Our captain had a reputation for efficiency and cost-effectiveness. It was her duty to enforce contracts and search for unauthorized pirate vessels owned by competing conglomerates. At the same time, she was on an endless quest for rich veins of minerals among the countless rocks that floated in the far-flung corners of the Solar System.

I felt a sense of excitement and trepidation as I stepped onto *Borag's* mid-decks. As a miner, I'd never made it above the ship's waistline before. It was a heady feeling, knowing I'd just been promoted into the ship's security forces.

I was no longer a D-Class rock-rat, no longer trapped in the mines. I was now a member of Captain Hansen's crew. From now on, my job was to keep the ship and her crew safe.

But as I made my way to the marine's quarters, I was stopped by *Borag's* executive officer, Commander Kaine. He was a formidable presence. His stern expression gave him an air of authority and power. He was a tall man, with chiseled features and piercing blue eyes that seemed to bore into your soul.

Despite his imposing appearance, there was a hint of weariness in his eyes, as if he had seen more than his fair share of danger and hardship. He had served aboard *Borag* for years, and his experience showed in the way he carried himself.

As the ship's executive officer, Kaine was responsible for the safety and well-being of the crew, and he took that responsibility seriously. He was a man of action, always willing to lead from the front and put himself in harm's way for the good of the mission.

Kaine looked at me with disdain as he perused my documents online. The more he examined them, the more his look of disapproval grew, as if I were nothing more than a worthless asset.

"You can't join security," he said finally, his voice filled with contempt. "You owe too much on your contract."

I gaped like a fish. I felt a sense of panic rising up inside me. I'd thought I was free—but now it seemed that I was still trapped. The foreman was going to be in a terrible mood if I returned to my bunk on the lowest decks.

But then I heard Captain Hansen's voice. She had followed me, and she looked determined.

"It's my decision, Commander," she said, her voice cold and hard, "I'll pay the difference myself."

My jaw sagged low. Captain Hansen was willing to pay off my debt? I couldn't believe what I was hearing.

"Thank you, Captain," I said with disbelief in my voice.

She twisted up her lips, and I did my best to think straight. I cleared my throat and turned back to the exec again. Commander Kaine was red-faced, but he controlled himself. I got the feeling he didn't want me joining his security contingent—but that was just too damned bad for him.

"All right, then," Kaine said. "I've got no further objections. Put your biometrics right here, Contract."

I stared at the tablet he held up. A confusing legal document was displayed, and I knew I wasn't expected to read it. Reading it would probably enrage everyone as it would be a rude waste of their time.

It was time to make a decision. Did I want to join the security teams, or did I want to go back to the mines? I wasn't a trained fighter, and fresh security recruits died even more often than rock-rats did. It was a serious choice, but I knew what I had to do.

"Are you brain-dead or something?" the exec demanded. "Press your frigging digits down here or go back to your drill-bots!"

Jolted into action, I pressed each finger down on the tablet, one after the other. Then I let the device scan my retina.

Just like that, I'd signed up with ship's security. Feeling a sense of sick excitement and floating unreality, I realized I was no longer a D-Contract rock-rat. I was no longer a victim of the mining company's greed.

I was now a member of *Borag's* crew. Officially, I was a C-Contract—a special breed.

The exec spun around and stalked off. I barely had the brains to follow him. The captain, for her part, had disappeared during the lengthy signing process.

One nice thing about serving on the mid-decks was immediately obvious: they had windows up here. These apertures were open for viewing whenever the ship was far from dangerous particles.

Looking out through *Borag's* windows at the asteroid belt, I was struck by the vastness of deep space. The blackness of the void stretched out endlessly in all directions, broken only by the occasional glint of starlight or the jagged shape of a nearby asteroid.

Around us, the asteroids loomed like giant monoliths, their rough surfaces pockmarked by countless craters and fissures.

They were silent and still, like ancient sentinels standing guard over the secrets of the universe.

But even in the midst of this stillness, there was a sense of motion and energy. The stars seemed to sparkle with a life of their own, and the asteroids shimmered with the reflected light of distant suns.

At the start of the next shift, I was introduced to the other marines—and I could immediately feel their disdain for me. I was still an outsider, a former rock-rat trying to shoulder my way into a world of better men.

They were in the middle of a training exercise, a grueling series of drills designed to test their physical and mental strength. Without being given any time to catch up, I was tossed into join them. I pushed myself harder than I'd ever done before, determined to show that I was worthy of being a marine.

But as I struggled to complete the drills, I could feel their eyes on me. They were watching, waiting for me to fail. I was particularly poor at marksmanship, as I'd never held a gun in my hands before.

"Come on, Starn," Private Ledbetter sneered. "Is that all you've got? Maybe you should go back to drilling on those fat rocks instead of trying to hit one with your rifle."

I gritted my teeth, not wanting to show any weakness. "Fuck you guys," I said, my voice filled with frustration.

They laughed, and I could feel my anger rising.

"You think this is a joke?" I said, my voice full of bitterness. "I'm out here giving everything I have, and you're just laughing at me."

"Look, kid," another marine said. It was Corporal Tench, and his voice was as cold and hard as space itself. "You weren't born to this life, and I can tell already you'll never be one of us."

I felt a sense of rage boiling up inside me, and I could feel my fists clenching. "You want to arm-wrestle?" I asked. "No? How about any of the rest of you?"

But they just laughed again, and I could feel my anger deepening.

"You may be strong, kid," Tench told me. "But an ox is strong. That doesn't mean you have what it takes to be a marine. Let's kick things up a notch."

Then, in the middle of the drill, everything changed. The holo-environment transformed from a featureless shooting range into a battlefield. The simulator had been designed to model a combat situation—and suddenly, we were under attack.

I could feel my heart racing as we scrambled to take cover, our weapons at the ready. We didn't have real rifles, just mock ones that fired low-powered lasers to score hits, but they felt real enough in your hands.

The simulated enemy soldiers were suddenly all around us, and I could hear the sounds of gunfire and explosions coming from every direction.

I raised my weapon, my fingers trembling with fear and anticipation—and then I fired.

An enemy soldier hit the ground, his body twitching on the dust. As I looked around, I saw the other marines looking at me with a newfound respect.

"Who hit that?" Corporal Tench demanded.

"The scorecard says it was Starn."

Tench showed his teeth. "Bullshit. He couldn't hit a bull's balls much less a bull's eye. The computer is off—or Starn is cheating. Are you a cheater, Starn?"

"Nope."

Tench went over the data, and he shook his head. "Okay, so you nailed one," he admitted at last. "A clean kill. But every noob gets lucky now and then—don't let it go to your head."

We finished the exercise, and as we gathered our things and headed back to the ship, I felt a sense of pride and satisfaction. I might be able to get the hang of this before I died on my first mission.

As *Borag* drew closer to Mars, I began to feel a sense of pride and accomplishment. I hadn't yet proven myself to the other marines, but I felt I had a clue as to what it took to be one of them.

After another exercise, during which I made an effort to charge the enemy lines first, Sergeant Cox came to talk to me personally.

"You think you're some kind of hero, don't you, Starn?" Sergeant Cox demanded, his voice filled with contempt. "Yeah, I'm talking to you, boy. You're some kind of head-case, right?"

"I don't think so, Sergeant."

Cox sneered at me. "I know how you weaseled your way in here, preying on the good and kindly nature of Captain Hansen—but that doesn't mean shit to me. You're just a D-class Contract. A rock-rat. A nobody who got lucky. You're going to be paste the first time we deploy—mark my words."

"Wooo!" Corporal Tench whooped. "Sarge called it! He's got an instinct for these things!"

The rest of the group laughed. I could feel my blood boiling again, but I knew that I had to keep my cool. "Sergeant, I think I showed that I have what it takes to carry this rifle."

Cox laughed, and I could feel my frustration growing. "You? A squaddie? Never. You're nothing but a liability, Starn. You don't have the training, the skills, or the experience to carry a real gun. You'll be issued a shock-rod after bootcamp is over with."

My mouth sagged open. "A shock-rod?"

"That's what I said. Is something wrong with your ears?"

"No, Sergeant, but—"

"Shut up. You're here because everyone in *Borag's* security force goes through some training days with Red Company. We're the only outfit that drills all the time. But you're destined to be zapping the gonads off one of your former coworkers—at best. Personally, I'd assign you to head-watch."

"What's that?"

The group laughed again. It was a mean laugh. Corporal Tench walked close and thumped a big hand down on my shoulder. "You know the head is the toilet on a ship, right?"

"Of course."

"Well then... you figure it out."

I frowned, and I did get the idea. These guys had no intention of letting me be a full-fledged marine. They wanted me to join one of the goon squads—enforcers and foremen. The guys who beat on any of the crewmen or contracts that got out of line.

I turned away, feeling a sense of crushing disappointment. Was I really going to become nothing more than another thug who beat down other men? A bully who cared for nothing but quotas and the ship's bylaws?

"Sergeant?" Private Ledbetter said. "With all due respect, I think Starn showed a lot of promise during the exercise. He was able to think on his feet, to make split-second decisions, and to fire accurately in a tough situation."

I was stunned. I hadn't expected any support from Ledbetter. He was a small, wiry fellow with the face of a hound dog and eyes that never seemed to open up all the way.

Sergeant Cox snorted. "All right, seeing as Ledbetter here is in love with you, I'm placing you in his masterful hands. You'll practice on targets as a team. If both of you don't hit the requisite number of kill-shots by next week, you'll receive demerits and lose a stripe."

Ledbetter looked pale. I glanced from him back to Cox.

"Sergeant..." I said, "I don't have any stripes to lose. Not yet, anyway. I've just got the one."

"Oh, that's right!" Cox said, slamming his palm into his forehead. "Well, as you can see, Ledbetter has three. He's a private, first class. We'll have to take two from him."

Ledbetter mumbled something, while Corporal Tench released a wicked howl. "Your ass is on the line, Ledbetter!" He laughed uproariously.

After the rest of the men left us alone at last, I turned toward Ledbetter. "Seems like we should stay late and practice."

"You think so, huh? This is what I get for sticking my fucking tongue out—it gets shredded."

I squinted, thinking about thanking him for speaking up. Given his mood, I passed on the idea. "Um... you can shoot straight, right?"

"Not straight enough to fix your score at long range. Come on, rock-rat."

Following him to the target room, I spent a few hours plinking away until my eyes were crossing. I got better, but not enough to satisfy Ledbetter's concerns.

I had to wonder about Cox and his tactics. Had he set me up with Ledbetter just to harass me—or was he honestly trying to transform me into a better marksman? I wasn't sure, but either way, it was working. I'd lost a possible buddy and gained an irritable teacher.

Chapter 4: The Marine

The marksmanship test was a critical part of our training, and the competition between Private Ledbetter and myself was intense. A short week later, we lined up at the firing range. Honestly, I figured I was going to kick his ass.

Sergeant Cox stood nearby, his eyes fixed on us as we took aim at the enemy targets. The sound of gunfire filled the air, and I could feel the heat of the laser rifle in my hands.

I took a deep breath and steadied my aim, squeezing the trigger with precision and care. The target exploded in a burst of sparks and smoke, and I felt a surge of satisfaction.

But as I looked over at Private Ledbetter, I saw that he had already hit several targets with deadly accuracy. His aim was true, and he moved with a speed and efficiency that left me in awe.

I gritted my teeth and focused on my own shooting, determined to keep up with him. But as the seconds ticked by, I could feel my focus waning. The pressure was getting to me, and I was struggling to keep up.

Suddenly, it was over. The sergeant called time, and we lowered our rifles, sweating and gritting our teeth. I looked over at Private Ledbetter, expecting to see him grinning in triumph.

But to my surprise, he looked just as worried as I did. As Sergeant Cox approached, I could see the look of disappointment in his eyes.

"Neither of you did well," he said, shaking his head. "Barely enough enemy targets went down to pass the test. You'll have to do better next time."

I felt a sense of relief wash over me. I hadn't been kicked out—not yet—and I hadn't let Ledbetter down. He wasn't going to be robbed of his hard-won stripes. Still, I knew I needed to work harder if I was going to be pass these performance tests.

After that day, I redoubled my efforts, training tirelessly and pushing myself to my limits. I was going to be the best marksman I could be.

After completing our training exercise, I headed for my bunk on the mid-decks. Along the way, I ran into a squad of Red Company regulars coming the other way.

"There he is," Corporal Tench growled, pointing at me. "I can't even believe it."

I stopped walking, and I looked at the group. They were sour-faced, one and all.

"What's up, guys?" I asked in a neutral tone.

"As if you don't know," Tench said, approaching me with his fists planted on his hips. "You've got some nerve. Do you realize how many security men want this post? How many of them have worked for months to earn it?"

I still had no idea what was going on, but I stood my ground as two privates walked up to stand too close to me. They had their arms folded, and they scowled from my left and my right.

"You suck at shooting," Tench said, poking a finger at me.

I felt like breaking it off—and I probably could have—but I didn't make a move. Not yet.

"You suck at everything, because you're new. Lots of guys have been working shock-rods forever, waiting to get into the marine attachment, and this is—"

"Wait a second," I said. "Are you saying I've been assigned to Red Company? Officially?"

Corporal Tench spat on the deck. "No," he said. "Not until you prove yourself in hand to hand."

"What?"

That's when the private on his left swung for my face, and the private on my right jabbed at my balls.

Taken by surprised, I grunted and absorbed both shots. Tench laughed. "Not so tough today, huh? I'm putting this down as a big fat, fail. You're a loser, Starn. You should just face facts now, and—"

He stopped his speech, because although my knees were buckling a little, I wasn't out of the fight. Not yet.

Both the privates were throwing punches—but you have to understand that the punch of a man born in low-grav feels kind of like when your sister clocks you one. Sure, it hurts, and it pisses you off—but it doesn't usually have the power behind it to put you out.

I reached up two thick hands and slammed them together. The two grunting men were so focused on thumping away at my ribcage, they didn't even see this coming.

Crack! Their unprotected skulls clacked together. It was an awful sound. Fortunately, I didn't actually fracture their craniums, but I did scramble their brains pretty good. They staggered back, gasping.

They wanted to fall to their knees, but I didn't let them. I reached out those same two ham hock hands of mine and gripped them by their skinny necks. I lifted them up some, and they snarled, ripping at my fingers with their scrawny stick-digits.

"You fucking animal!" Corporal Tench said, stepping closer. "You're not getting away with this line-jumping. Just because you diddled the Captain—"

"Is that what you jokers think?" I said, laughing. "I've been working the rocks, boys. Hansen doesn't go down to the lower decks and slum for the likes of me."

The two men in my hands were elbowing me now, and it was becoming uncomfortable, so I gave them a shaking until they stopped. Panting, they glared at me with hate, unable to break my grip on their scrawny chicken-necks.

Corporal Tench cocked back his fist for a hammer blow, but I stepped closer to him, dragging his two sidekicks. Their heels scraped on the deck.

"Oh," I said, "so this is a three-on-one deal, is it? I didn't understand that."

I glared at him, daring him to throw that punch he had simmering over his shoulder—but he never did.

Instead, he stepped back a pace and showed me his teeth. His hands lowered and straightened his uniform. "Stand down, men."

The sudden change of demeanor puzzled me, but then I noticed all three of the men were gazing past me, over my shoulder. I turned and saw Sergeant Cox walking up on my six.

"Is this some kind of a rescue practice, Corporal?" Cox asked.

"It's nothing, Sergeant. Just comradery and high spirits."

Cox nodded, unsurprised. "All right, then. Starn, follow me. We're late for a meeting."

I dropped the two squirming privates, who gasped and cursed on the deck in my wake. Brushing past Corporal Tench, I followed Sergeant Cox into his cubby-hole sized office.

"What can I do for you, Sergeant?"

Cox smiled at me from behind his desk. He offered me a hand, and I shook it.

"News travels fast. You've been placed under my command as part of Red Company, Starn—but I guess you already know that."

"There is a rumor to that effect going around on the decks, sir."

Cox whistled, long and low. "You're a serious piece of work, you know that? The moment Captain Hansen was informed that you'd completed your basic training with acceptable marks, she gave the order to place you under my command. I'm not sure how I feel about that right now."

"You're not going to regret her decision, Sergeant. I'll serve with distinction. I'll—"

"Yeah, yeah," he interrupted. "Listen, I don't know what kind of weird thing is going on between you and her—and I don't know to know. But whatever it is, you'd best be planning to prove yourself worthy of this amazing jump in position."

I tried not to grin, and I almost managed it. "I'll do my best, Sergeant."

He studied me with squinting eyes for a moment or two longer. I just stood at attention and stared straight ahead. I hadn't been trained to do much yet, but I'd learned that trick at least.

"All right," he sighed. "You're dismissed. Get the hell out here."

I turned to walk out, but Cox called me back.

"Technically, you're part of Red Company now, Starn. But that isn't real until the rest of these men accept you. Don't let those big muscles of yours go to your head. They won't save you when we're on deployment, and you catch a bolt with your spine."

His words made me blink. I left, thinking them over. Was he saying one of these men—possibly one of the privates I'd just humiliated—might have a targeting error at the worst possible moment?

Chewing that over, I found I didn't like the taste. We were going to be living and fighting together in space, after all. Space was all about killing a man. It had a thousand ways to do it, from freezing to roasting, from radiation to streaking meteors no bigger than a marble.

The last thing a marine needed in such a hostile environment were comrades who wanted to shoot you in the back.

Chapter 5: Pirates

After that fateful meeting with Sergeant Cox, I officially joined Red Company, the ship's marine attachment. It was a surprise to me and to everyone else that I'd been assigned directly to this group. Red Company did the real fighting when things got serious, performing missions such as ground ops and boarding actions. The other groups, including the security enforcers and the foremen, handled smaller matters, policing crewmen and contracts.

Red Company had dealt with the claim-jumpers we'd faced on the far side of this rich asteroid. It was strange to think that the fact two men had died in that action had greatly benefited me. Captain Hansen had ordered Red Company's commander to place me in his group precisely because they were down two men.

Privately, I figured she'd been impressed with the way I'd handled the bandits that had almost killed her. Sometimes, saving an officer's ass was worth decade of salutes and yessirs.

When *Borag* had mined out all the best minerals from the rock under her hull, Captain Hansen called us to a briefing to discuss our next destination.

I could feel a sense of excitement and anticipation building up inside me as we prepared for a new mission—one where I wasn't expected to jockey a drill-bot all day.

"Listen up, everyone," Captain Hansen said, her voice firm and commanding. "We've just received word that three raiders are on their way to these coordinates."

There was a lot of muttering at that. "Oh shit…" Sergeant Cox said, and Corporal Tench just went white.

"How bad is that?" I asked. "It's real bad, right?"

"Shut up, you fool," Ledbetter hissed at me. "Do the math. Three against one is never good."

I thought about my meeting with the three men in the passageway the other day, led by Corporal Tench. I guessed it wasn't like that when you were dealing with ships and counting cannons.

"That's right," Hansen continued. "We're in trouble. We're pulling up stakes and hauling ass out of here to deliver this load of ore. Be on alert and ready for anything. Captain out."

That was it. We were left grumbling and worrying. Corporal Tench was the most vocal complainer in the group. "Frigging crazy," he said. "Batshit."

"Do you have something constructive to say, Corporal?" Cox demanded.

"I certainly do, sir. We should dump this load of ore and run. It's only going to slow us down. What good is a hold full of metal if we're captured or destroyed?"

Sergeant Cox formed a tight line with his lips. "That's not our place to decide, Corporal. Now, kindly shut the hell up and listen to your instructions."

The sergeant gave us all posts and duties. They mostly amounted to standing watch at key sections of the ship. I didn't see what the point to all that was.

Ledbetter tried to explain it to me. "These ships on our tail—they're raiders. They'll try to catch up to us. If they can do it, they'll demand that we surrender."

"Why would we do that?" I laughed. "Isn't this ship bigger than some raider? Can't our boys down on the gunnery deck shoot straight?"

Ledbetter nodded thoughtfully. "Yes, we could fight, but once you start a shooting war in space, things get nasty very fast. We'll probably be disabled, while they'll lose one or two of their ships. Then, when they come aboard—they'll be pissed."

I thought about that, and I frowned deeply. "Motivated by revenge for their friends, huh?"

"Exactly. If had to guess, it will go one of two ways. Either we'll outrun them, or they'll get close, and we'll dump our ore. It's a rich load. The pirates will probably be tempted to stop and pick up the easy stuff."

My heart sank. I'd been counting on my share of that ore. I no longer had big debts to pay back—or at least, not as big, but I wasn't exactly rich, either. Everyone aboard *Borag* needed that payout.

"This sucks," I said, making Ledbetter smile.

"I can see you've got your head wrapped around the situation now."

Red Company wasn't headquartered anywhere close to *Borag's* bridge, but we did have an operations room where we could plan and witness events that were occurring outside the ship's thick hull in the cold vastness of space.

The three pirate spaceships were closing in fast, their engines flaring brightly as they pursued *Borag* through the vast emptiness of space. I could see the black silhouettes of the enemy ships growing larger and more menacing with each passing moment.

As the ship's executive officer, Commander Kaine barked out orders, his voice ringing out over the intercom. The crew sprang into action, racing to their battle stations and preparing for the inevitable boarding parties that would follow.

The marines of Red Company were particularly focused, their eyes sharp and their movements precise as they loaded their weapons and checked their gear. They knew that their skills and training would be put to the test, and they were ready to meet the challenge.

As the pirate ships closed in, I could see their weapon turrets rotating, targeting *Borag* with deadly accuracy. Captain Hansen calmly directed the ship's evasive maneuvers, her experience and skill evident as she navigated through the dangerous debris of the asteroid belt.

The chase was intense, with the pirate ships drawing ever closer to *Borag*. The crew worked together with a sense of urgency and purpose, each member playing their part in the frantic race to escape.

Finally, the pirates drew so close to *Borag*, Captain Hansen had to turn the ship about to bring her weapons to bear.

"That's it!" Cox said. "Feel that under your feet? She's swinging this big tub around. It's three dogs on one big bear now."

I did feel it. The big ship turned, and everything turned with her.

"Why are we turning around?" I asked, confused and little bit worried.

Cox glanced at me. "Because you can't shoot cannons out of your ass—at least, this ship can't. We've got only two guns on our fantail, and they aren't meant to do much more than knock out an incoming missile."

I gritted my teeth. Had it really come down to this? Had I worked so hard to escape drudgery, only to be blown up by pirates and a stubborn captain?

As I was considered the greenest of recruits, I'd been given the less than critical task of cleaning off the screens and taking out the trash in the ops chamber. The job would have been as humiliating as Corporal Tench meant it to be if I hadn't still been ecstatic about having escaped the ranks of the rock-rats. At least playing the office-boy in the ops chamber allowed me to watch the battle unfold.

Only a few members of Red Company were in ops at that moment, when the fateful call came in. On every viewscreen aboard the big ship, the image of a rat-faced pirate with elongated features filled the display. His beady eyes darted about, scanning the ship with a calculating gaze, while his thin lips curled into a sly, sinister grin.

"Corporate pig, *Borag*," his voice grated. "You will brake and prepare to be boarded."

The pirate wore a patchwork of mismatched armor, each piece scavenged from a different source and crudely welded together. His helmet had been modified to allow his elongated snout to protrude, giving him the appearance of a twisted rodent. Had he been mutated by radiation, or some accident? I didn't know, and I didn't care.

Despite his grotesque appearance, there was a dangerous intelligence in his eyes, a sense of cunning that made it clear he was not to be underestimated. His fingers were long and slender, ending in sharp nails that glinted in the dim light.

As he spoke, his voice was low and gravelly, tinged with a hint of sadistic pleasure at the prospect of having caught up with *Borag*. It was clear that this rat-faced pirate was every bit as ruthless and cunning as he was ugly.

"There will be no boarding of my ship," Captain Hansen said firmly. "That is out of the question."

The rat-pirate looked surprised. He lifted his long fingers and began to count on them, slowly folding up digits until he held up three of them.

"Have my eyes or my ears failed me?" he asked. "I see three wolves standing over one fat pig. How can these numbers be lying?"

He had an odd accent, one that came from the far reaches of the Solar System. Way out here, isolated from the rest of humanity, men like him had developed their own mannerisms and habits of speech.

"Our battle computers predict we can destroy two of you—but probably not three," Captain Hansen said. "That is the only reason you've not yet been destroyed."

Sergeant Cox laughed at that. "She's bluffing," he told the others. "She's good, isn't she boys?"

The others in the room flickered smiles back at him, including me. I wasn't so happy to hear that her words were a bluff.

The rat-man had a different reaction. He lifted his misshapen lip a fraction—the beginnings of a snarl. "This is no matter of debate, Captain. You will surrender your ship and cargo, or you will be destroyed. Prepare to be boarded. If you fire upon us, we will return fire, and the destruction of all our vessels will be assured."

The screen went dark, then the exterior view returned to focus. True to their word, the three pirate vessels split apart and began to close with *Borag* from three different trajectories.

That image soon faded, to be replaced by a worried face. It was Captain Hansen. "All hands, this is your captain speaking." All over the ship, we could hear her voice echoing loudly in every passageway. "We're about to be faced with boarders. We can and will resist this attempt to capture my ship."

"Oh shit…" Cox said. All humor had drained from his face. "Hansen's bluff has been called, and she's going for it!"

We all exchanged worried glances.

"Green Company will stand at the airlocks," Captain Hansen continued, "they'll try to burn their way in there first. Red Company will deploy to defend Engineering and the Bridge. Hansen out."

Green Company consisted of all the security forces that weren't marines. All over the ship, every foreman and passage-cop was issued a pistol from the armory and sent racing to the airlocks. There were three main airlocks, plus the big doors that led into the cargo hold.

"This is crazy," Corporal Tench said. "They might come at us from three directions at once! Why doesn't she just blast them out of space?"

"Because that would be suicide," Commander Kaine answered as he stepped onto the deck. We all wheeled and saluted him. "As long as we don't fire our cannons, they won't either. They want our ore and maybe our vessel, they don't want to destroy everything."

"But sir," Tench had the pluck to ask, "if we do beat them back from our decks, won't they just blast us out of space anyway—at point blank range?"

"Have faith in your officers, Corporal. Praying wouldn't hurt, either. Now Cox, I'm taking over this ops center. You'll deploy your squad on the bridge. If the enemy does breach one of our defensive lines at the airlocks, be prepared to rush to that deck and push them back."

"Sir, yes sir!" Sergeant Cox responded. He hustled for the door, and those of us from his squad followed close behind.

As I moved to follow Sergeant Cox and his squad, Corporal Tench glared at me and dared to put a hand in my path. "What about the greenie? Shouldn't we leave him here at ops? He can shine Kaine's shoes or something."

Cox hesitated, but only for a few seconds. He shook his head. "No. The commander's orders were clear. Quit bitching about Starn, he'll do okay."

We followed Cox into the passages. We checked our rifles and closed our helmets. If the ship suddenly lost pressure, a sealed suit would keep us breathing.

Corporal Tench grabbed my shoulder. My instinct was to shake him off, but I didn't.

"Don't screw this up, Starn," he said. "If you do, if you shoot just one of my men in the ass by accident, I will throw you out of an airlock without compunction."

I didn't answer him. I just glared back for a moment. Then he moved off.

I wasn't really rattled by his threats. After all, I've been a rock-rat for over a year now, and I'd received countless similar threats from the foreman. Hell, even my drill-bot was trying to kill me half the time. Corporal Tench was going to have to do better than that to scare me.

Still, I couldn't help but take his words under advisement. I was the least experienced man in this unit by far. If anybody was likely to accidentally get someone killed, it was me. Accordingly, I vowed to be careful with my aim.

I'd never faced a real battle before, except for that one time fighting with the claim-jumpers. I hoped I wouldn't freeze up or make a mistake. I steeled myself, telling myself to remember my last few weeks of training, and to keep my head no matter what happened.

I found myself really wishing that this boarding action had come a year from now—or preferably not at all. I was scheduled for a full, proper bootcamp training back on Mars the next time we returned to port, but that simply wasn't possible while spending months in deep space. For now, I was an emergency replacement and nothing more. I would have to do my best.

With Sergeant Cox in the lead and Corporal Tench in the rear, we raced through the passages. We negotiated ladders and the clanging metal stairways, sometimes pulling ourselves through holes in the ceiling or wall using metal loops. The fact that our bodies weighed much less than they should helped us sail through the ship to our destination.

"Move, Starn. Move!" I heard the corporal shout from behind me. He rammed me in the back with the butt of his rifle. "You're lagging. Get a move on!"

I might have turned on him angrily, but I knew he was right. My bulky, squat body, born and bred on Earth, was plenty strong, but it simply wasn't as agile or as natural-moving in low gravity. The other troops were like fish in water by comparison. I did my best to hustle and to keep up.

Chapter 6: The Bridge

When we finally reached the bridge, we were allowed to slow down and spread out. We didn't occupy the bridge itself, but rather the main passageway that led up to the ship's critical nerve center.

Borag's bridge was a large, circular room with walls covered in blinking, flashing screens displaying various information about the ship's status and the surrounding space. The room was dimly lit, with only a few small, circular lights casting eerie shadows across the faces of the crew. In the center of the room stood a raised platform where Captain Hansen and her top officers were stationed. The platform was surrounded by rows of consoles where crew members sat, monitoring the ship's systems and preparing for battle. Everyone was tense and sweating as the crew waited for the inevitable pirate attack.

The command deck officers eyed us coldly. Commander Kaine wasn't there, of course. He was back in the Security Ops Center, handling the defense of the entire ship. I didn't know the rest of the faces on the command deck. In fact, I'd never even seen the bridge before—not in person.

Putting our backs up against the curved passageway walls, we marines tried to make ourselves as unobtrusive as possible. Ensigns and midshipmen flew back and forth past us, ignoring us, shouting to one another. It was as if they didn't see us at all.

We were here to provide a final defense should everything else go to hell. Until that moment came, we were just in the way.

"Eyes front, Starn," Cox said.

I gave a guilty start, because I'd naturally been stealing glances into the command deck, taking a look around and seeing who was in there and what they were doing. They all seemed very professional, focused and worried.

I turned my helmeted head and stared at Private Ledbetter instead, who was directly across the passageway from me.

The private stared back. His face was almost emotionless. I don't think he was really looking at me. He was thinking about what was coming next.

I decided to listen as best I could, rather than stare.

"Keep those gun ports open but the turrets retracted," Captain Hansen said.

She proceeded after that to make quite a few references to our main armament, which consisted of several cannons.

Was she planning on firing? Or was she simply making sure the big guns did not threaten the pirates so greatly, that they got spooked and decided to fire first?

Space combat at point-blank range like this was highly lethal. In space, everything was about range, especially effective range. If a given target was only a few miles away from the weapon that was aiming at it, or better yet, just a few feet off your bow, hitting that target was a virtual certainty. But normally, ships were nowhere near so close to one another. And therefore, targeting was nowhere near as certain. Missiles could home in of course, but while they were in flight, there were obvious means for countermeasures. Guns and cannons, especially ones that shot in a straight line without any intelligent guidance, were highly inaccurate when shooting at moving targets over great distances. But now, the pirates and *Borag* were right on top of each other. There was no way anyone could miss.

"What's the response time?" Captain Hansen demanded. "What's their calculated response time? I want a number."

I could hear some people working screens. I could hear the computers quietly rattling out answers in fake voices.

"We're really not familiar with this raider design, sir," answered another officer, "not enough to make tight predictions like that. We have to assume their software is up to date, that their sensors and their AI is of a quality build. I would say the answer is unknown. If we fire right now, we may or may not inflict enough catastrophic damage to their systems to prevent them from retaliating and destroying us in turn."

"Give me a firing solution, Lieutenant," Captain Hansen said. "I'll make the decision."

"Holy shit," I heard one of our men whisper. "She's going to do it." He was obviously listening in to this conversation, the same as I was.

Glancing up and down the line of marines that were pressed up against the walls of the passageways, I saw a lot of pale faces. The men were swallowing inside their helmets with their eyes shut. One or two of them even seemed to be mumbling prayers to themselves.

Even I, a lowly rock-rat recently transformed into a marine, knew that Captain Hansen was contemplating the unthinkable: an ambush at point-blank range.

The situation was a standoff, the likes of which I hadn't seen since I was a kid back on Earth. In those days it had been gangsters pressing pistols into one another's bellies, each daring the other to fire. It was a game of chicken, of mutually assured destruction. Both sides were likely to die if either fired—but still, both were tempted. A surprise strike, perhaps in the moment of your opponent's distraction, could hand you an instant victory.

The trouble here was that we weren't talking about men facing one another, but rather computers. A smart battle computer operating a ship—any ship, even a raider—was scripted to automatically return fire when it sensed it had been fired upon. Even if one side ambushed the other, and every warhead struck home, there was no guarantee that some independent turret wouldn't lock on and fire back, even as the target ship died.

"What about missiles?" Captain Hansen demanded. "Dammit, give me all the numbers on the missiles!"

"There's no way we're going to win with a surprise missile strike, Captain," the weapons officer reported. "We're going to have to ride out this boarding assault and hope our marines can hold them. I don't think we have any choice."

"I don't want to hear your opinions, Lieutenant," Captain Hansen snapped. "I want to hear some facts. Tell me why the missiles won't work."

"It's a matter of range, sir. They're in too close now. We don't have any missiles loaded with low-yield warheads. A missile strike would destroy everything for a mile around—including us."

"Dammit!" Captain Hansen said. "We waited too long."

"No, sir, I don't think so," the lieutenant replied. "Missiles just aren't an effective option. Not once we were within effective cannon range. Once you fire missiles, everybody knows about it. Compared to our cannons, they would give the enemy's computers a lot longer response time before they ever got hit. Again, we should have been destroyed."

"All right then," she said, defeated. "It's all up to the marines. Stand down the missiles. Keep our gun ports open, but don't even let those turrets twitch. There's no point in setting this thing off unless we have to."

There was a lot of hustling and talk on the bridge after that. Everyone was breathing again. I felt both relieved and concerned. We weren't about to blow up—but there was some hard fighting in my near future.

"Crew," Hansen said a minute or so later, "let it be known: I have no intention of allowing any top-tier officers to be traded away to these rodents as slaves. You can set your minds at ease about that."

Ledbetter and I exchanged glances at that. We were both listening in—all the marines in the passageway outside the bridge had heard it. It was impossible not to. The captain had a microphone attached to her helmet, and when she keyed it and made a statement to everyone on the bridge, it was boomingly loud.

The critical point, the point that was sinking in for both Private Ledbetter and me, was that Captain Hansen had made a promise to her *upper echelon officers*. She had said nothing about the lowly enlisted, or the pathetic indentured contracts that worked on the lower decks. Could it be she was already considering trading away such assets on *Borag's* balance sheets in order to buy off these pirates?

It wasn't unthinkable. It had happened before.

At that moment, as if she'd suddenly realized what she was saying and who might be listening in, Captain Hansen ordered that the big, round doorway that led to the bridge to be closed. The heavy portal clanged shut, and thick bolts shot into the bulkhead, locking it. After that, we couldn't hear anything more from the officers and their fateful planning.

We were left in a tense silence, the only sound being the quiet whirring of the ship's engines and the distant hum of working systems. The weight of what had just been discussed hung heavy in the air. The possibility that we could be boarded by ruthless pirates and taken as prisoners was a terrifying thought.

Private Ledbetter was still standing across from me. His face was set in a grim line, and I could tell he was deep in thought. We were both relatively new to Red Company, and neither of us had faced a situation like this before. It was a sobering reminder of the dangers involved in signing a contract to serve as a space marine.

I took a deep breath and tried to push my fears aside. I had to focus on the task at hand and be ready to fight if necessary. It was our duty as marines to protect the ship and her crew, and I was going to do my part.

We waited in silence for what felt like an eternity, but was probably only a few minutes in reality. Finally, the intercom crackled to life, and Commander Kaine's voice boomed through the speakers.

"Red Company, prepare for possible boarding action. Check your weapons and gear, and get into position. We don't know what's going to happen, so be ready for anything."

I felt a surge of adrenaline as I checked my rifle and made sure my gear was secure. We all knew what was at stake, and we were prepared to fight to the death if necessary.

As we waited for the pirates to board, I couldn't help but think about what Commander Kaine had said earlier. We didn't know what kind of ship the pirates were flying, and we didn't know what kind of weapons they had. It was a gamble to hold our fire, but it was a risk we had to take.

We were like coiled springs, ready to unleash our fury on anyone who dared to threaten our ship and her crew.

Suddenly, the ship jolted as the raiding ships made contact. The intercom crackled again, and Commander Kaine's voice came through loud and clear.

"All front-line defenders, prepare to engage the enemy! Let's show these pricks what we're made of!"

Chapter 7: The Boarding Party

The pirate had a tall, lanky frame with elongated features that looked almost alien. His skin was a pale gray, and his eyes were large and black, almost insect-like. He wore a sleek, black jumpsuit that clung tightly to his body, emphasizing his thin, wiry frame. In his hand, he held a high-tech pistol that gleamed menacingly in the dim light of the cargo hold. The weapon appeared to be a fusion of organic and mechanical components, with pulsing blue lights and complex circuitry etched into the metal. The pirate's fingers curled around the grip of the pistol, and as he aimed it at his target, the weapon emitted a low hum, as if it were alive and eager to be fired.

It was kind of weird, seeing the pirate displayed on the wall. He and his kind weren't in combat with Red Company—not yet. They were invading the airlocks, breaking down our outermost defenses with ease.

To be fair, *Borag* had not been designed with the purpose of repelling boarding parties. The ship was primarily a mining rig. An exploratory vessel designed to find metals, leach them out of large rocks, and return them home to Earth.

As the human population of our home star system grew, free and easily available sources of rare minerals became harder to get. Someone along the way had figured out it was easier to steal from the hard labor of others than it was to go out and find your own claim and mine it to the fullest.

Over recent decades some mining ships had mutinied and become pirates. In addition, there were rival corporations that sometimes masqueraded as pirates to avoid prosecution back home on Earth. These rival ships—whether being true outlaws, or the competition in disguise—were ever increasing in number across the Solar System.

From the look of this rat-like fellow on the screen in front of me, I calculated that he was indeed an honest-to-God, outlaw pirate from the far corners of our star system. He didn't look like the kind of ruffian that would get hired by earthbound companies to perform this kind of theft. In addition to his appearance, his bold, almost desperate approach pegged him as a genuine pirate. *Borag* was an armed and capable rig in her own right. The fact these scumbags had dared to tangle with us proved they were truly desperate thieves.

Ships like *Borag* were thoroughly prepared for this kind of situation, but the outcome was still in doubt. Yes, *Borag* had marines. Yes, she had defensive guns. But no, we didn't have entrances built for combat, the way they built them on true warships. The airlocks on a cruiser from Earth's defense forces would be nearly impossible to break into with sheer brute force. Such vessels were armored and could be sealed with an external access that was so perfectly smooth and well-machined, it was difficult to even find the crack around the entrance hatch.

There were many other differences as well. *Borag* was designed to facilitate work, for the most part, to allow crew members and contracts easy access to the guts of the big vessel. There were emergency access buttons right on the outside of the hull, and even secondary methods of entry—such as pull levers and explosive bolts—all designed to make it easier to get in or out of the ship in the case of an emergency. So, unlike a true warship, *Borag* was rather easy to break into.

"Look at that freak! Just look at him!" Sergeant Cox urged us. "He's nothing. He's got a skinny pistol, and even skinnier arms—they're like toothpicks. Hell, I bet Starn over there could break him across his knee like a piece of graphite."

The marines flickered a smile and glanced at me. Obligingly, I flexed and grinned back. They laughed. Sergeant Cox was bolstering morale, and we all knew it, but it was still working.

A moment later however, the still shot of the pirate transformed, shifting into video. Our smiles faded as we watched a full-on firefight in the passages.

Our foreman and police troops looked more like sheltering civilians than soldiers. They hid behind a hastily erected barricade of tumbled containers and barrels, firing a shower of bolts from the laser pistols they'd been issued.

Flying in the opposite direction were dozens of return laser bolts. Splashes of energy and burn marks were all over the passageway walls. Lights were knocked out, and spots of molten metal sparked. Those hotspots burned and ran like wax until they hardened again to a deep reddish-gray color, with a fine coat of ash forming over each melted spot.

We watched, wincing and shouting encouragement. We dared to hope Green Company would hold despite their inexperience, lack of equipment, and obvious fear to expose themselves to enemy fire. For a while, they did fine.

"They should have given them rifles," Private Ledbetter exclaimed, holding his weapon up.

We all carried short-range laser carbines, the usual weapon used by Red Company recruits. The laser carbine was designed for ship defense. It was a compact, short-barreled weapon with a sleek and minimalist design. It worked best in tight corridors and cramped spaces, which were all normal environments on any spacecraft.

The weapon was made from lightweight alloys with reinforced composites used to reduce its overall weight. The grips were ergonomically designed to provide maximum comfort and control.

The gun emitted a focused beam of energy that could penetrate through armor and vaporize flesh on contact. It was highly accurate, with a targeting system that could lock onto moving targets with ease. With its built-in power cell and an additional port for extra juice, just one of these guns could fire several hundred shots before needing a recharge.

I'd been told about, but not yet practiced with, a variety of tactical attachments. These included a holographic sight for improved aiming, a suppressor for stealth operations, and a flashlight for low-light conditions. The weapon could also be fitted with a bayonet for close-quarters combat.

Ledbetter spoke up again. "Just think what Green Company could do with some real weapons."

"Weapons like ours cost money and require training, Ledbetter," Sergeant Cox admonished him. "Accounting always knows best, you know that. So shut the hell up—right now."

"Yes, Sergeant!"

As we prepared to defend our ship and our crew, I couldn't help but feel a sense of apprehension and unease, knowing that the next few moments would be critical in determining the outcome of this deadly encounter.

We gritted our teeth as more invasions were attempted at other airlocks. Our special mission now seemed more clear.

At first, I couldn't figure out why we'd been assigned to standing around outside the bridge. If the enemy were coming in the door, why not hit them right there with everything we had?

The problem was, *Borag* had many doors. Three of them were under heavy attack, right now. If one of those defensive lines crumbled, the boarders could race straight to the most critical regions and capture the ship. If we lost control of our weapons, helm or engines—the ship would be captured.

So, we bided our time, watching and cursing. In the end, it was the first defensive line to be hit that collapsed. Perhaps it was only a matter of time until they all did.

"Red Company, 1st Squad," Commander Kaine's voice sounded in my ears. "We've got a breach at airlock 11. Sergeant Cox, you are hereby ordered to reinforce the defenders and push back the intruders. Move out!"

Following our sergeant, it felt good to be moving at last. All of this waiting around and sweating had been nerve-wracking. At least now, we would be doing our part.

Sergeant Cox led the charge, yelling out orders and marking targets on our tactical displays. Inside my helmet, one of the advancing skinnies was lit up with a red triangle. I lifted my weapon—but before I could release a flurry of bolts, Corporal Tench shoved my barrel down.

"You're aiming too close to those Green-company wounded," he shouted at me. "Follow me, we'll go around to the cross-passage and hit them in the butt."

We flanked the pirates from the left, while Private Ledbetter covered the right side. The passageways were narrow, and the pirates had taken cover behind the cargo containers and makeshift barricades.

1st Squad was well-trained—with the exception of myself. Our laser carbines flooded the passages with hundreds of bolts. There was nowhere to hide, and what little cover they had was soon shredded and smoking.

The carbines definitely helped, proving to be superior to the pirates' pistols. We aimed carefully and fired in short bursts, taking out the enemy one by one. The pirates fought back fiercely, but they were clearly outmatched. They went down, only scoring a few glancing hits on our armored jackets.

Sergeant Cox led the final advance, shouting out a battle cry, and the rest of the marines followed his lead. We pushed the pirates back, step by step, until they were forced to retreat back through Airlock 11. We pursued them, firing and throwing a volley of grenades.

Finally, the last of the invaders were taken down. We surveyed the damage, our adrenaline still pumping. Private Ledbetter grinned and slapped me on the back.

"Good job, man," he said. "We really showed them what their guts look like, didn't we?"

Then Sergeant Cox gave him a shove from behind, and he stumbled. "Look alive, Ledbetter! We can't let our guard down just yet," he said. "We still have to make sure there aren't any more of them lurking around."

Our squad moved cautiously through the passageways, checking every nook and cranny for signs of danger. We found nothing other than a few wounded. We'd won this battle, but we knew there would be more to come.

Chapter 8: Stalemate

"Sergeant!"

It was Commander Kaine, and we all reacted as if stung. Sergeant Cox straightened up from where he'd been leaning against one wall, congratulating himself and his men, to answer our CO.

"I'm here, Commander. Go ahead."

"While you've been celebrating, the pirates have overwhelmed my defenders at Airlock #3. I swear, Green Company is worthless. All they can do is delay the enemy."

"Should we secure things here at #11, sir, before—?"

"No, dammit! I'll throw some more hopeless swabbies onto that duty. Move your ass to #3—no scratch that, they're moving deeper into the ship. They're halfway to Engineering—that must be their goal."

Sergeant Cox appeared visibly relieved. "That's good news, sir. Can't 2nd Squad take them out?"

"Maybe, but I want you to trap them. Get on their six, and slam into them right when they engage the defenders at Engineering. Then, we'll crush them between two hammers!"

Sergeant Cox gritted his teeth and nodded. "I'm on it, sir."

That was it, Kaine was gone. The sergeant began kicking our tails up and down the passageway, getting us up and running. A few of us were wounded, but none seriously. We'd been lucky so far.

"Move, move, move!" he shouted, and we obeyed.

Sergeant Cox quickly gathered his squad and began moving toward Airlock #3. As we made our way through the narrow passageways, we heard the sound of laser fire and the shouts of the pirate invaders growing louder.

"Get ready for a fight, marines," Cox shouted to his squad. "These pirates aren't going to take Engineering without going through us first."

As we approached Engineering, we could see that the pirates had already breached the bulkhead and were pushing forward. Corporal Tench took point, leading the way with his laser rifle at the ready. Private Ledbetter and I followed close behind, covering their flanks.

The pirates were caught off guard by the sudden appearance of the marines behind them. They were trapped between two squads and taking fire from every direction. My squad advanced eagerly, driving the invaders back into the defenders at Engineering.

As they were surrounded, the pirates regrouped and mounted a counterattack in our direction.

"They're trying to break out and get back to their ship," Cox said. "Don't let them go home, boys—no prisoners unless they surrender!"

We took cover behind crates and containers, exchanging fire with our carbines. The battle raged on for several tense minutes, but in the end, the marines of Red Company emerged victorious, having successfully crushed the boarding party to the last man.

"Well done, marines," Lt. Quinn said. He was the marine in charge of 2nd squad. Apparently, his sergeant had perished in the fighting.

Together, Cox and Quinn counted the dead. We'd lost two, while the pirates had lost nearly thirty. The battle had been a resounding success—but it wasn't over with yet.

Commander Kaine spoke to us over the intercom. "Well done, boys. Red Company has saved *Borag* from certain destruction. Now let's mop up the rest of these pirates and get back to business."

Sergeant Cox and Lt. Quinn led the charge, while I tried to lend supporting fire when I could. We found a few more pockets of resistance where the pirates had holed up. They tried to fight back, but they were overwhelmed and outmatched. It was a brutal and bloody battle, but in the end, the pirates were all destroyed.

As the smoke cleared, the Red Company marines looked around at the carnage. Bodies of pirates littered the passageway, and the walls were scorched and pitted from the intense firefight. Sergeant Cox gave the order to regroup and continue the sweep of the ship.

It was a hard-fought victory, but we had done it. Red company had successfully repelled the pirate invasion, and *Borag's* decks were clear of rebel scum once again.

Captain Hansen initiated communication with the pirate raiders, who were still locked onto our hull. They were like three angry insects working to break the skin of a larger animal. They were leeches—and I hated them all.

Captain Hansen spoke calmly but firmly, making it clear that any attempt to fire on *Borag* would result in mutual destruction. She explained that *Borag* had defensive measures in place that could easily take out their ship, and that they had no chance of winning a battle against the well-armed mining vessel.

"You owe us," the same rat-looking pirate said. "Your debt will never be forgotten. Dump your ore now, let us feast upon it, and you may go in peace."

The captain snorted in amusement. "You've tried to take our ship. You failed. Nurse your wounds, cannibalize your dead, and leave us."

It was an insult, suggesting that the pirates were cannibals. Sure, some of them were—but not all of them. They didn't like being reminded of this grim fact.

"You offer us nothing?" the pirate said in dismay. "That will never be understood by my crews. They will lose all respect for me."

There was a desperate, almost pleading look on his face. I didn't get it at first.

"Uh-oh," Corporal Tench said aloud.

Sergeant Cox looked at him in concern. "You don't think…?"

Tench nodded his head. He looked pale. To me, he looked more worried than he had when he was facing a shower of laser bolts from the pirates and their pistols.

"What's going on, Sarge?" Ledbetter asked, giving voice to what all of us greener men were thinking. No marine ever liked to see his superiors looking freaked out by anything.

Sergeant Cox showed his teeth. "It's like this, boys. If these raiders get nothing out of this, after having lost a lot of men… well, there's likely to be a mutiny on their decks when this is over and done with. That rat-looking captain—he's probably toast."

Ledbetter scoffed. "Good. Who cares if these savages tear each other apart?"

Tench and Cox exchanged glances. The sergeant nodded to the corporal, suggesting that he should explain.

"It's like this," Corporal Tench said. "That captain has nothing to lose, now. That means he'll order his ships to fire—even if it's suicide. What else can he do? He's dead anyway, so he might as well go for it."

Finally, I got it. If we backed this pirate leader into a corner, putting him into a no-win situation, he was likely to take huge risks.

Concerned, we all turned our attention back to the viewscreens. Captain Hansen had muted the channel while she talked things over with her bridge crew. Now, she turned back to face the pirate and began to speak again.

"We understand. We'll dump the contents of hold number seven. Three large containers of prime ore will be disbursed."

"Three?" demanded the pirate, irate all over again. "Only three? That's unprocessed excrement!"

"It will be prime materials, I assure you. Scan the asteroid we've just mined. It was a rich strike."

"Bah, we've already done that. Why do you think we're here? We were alerted to your presence by a friend who spotted you, and we raced to find you stealing our resources, just as was said."

Captain Hansen narrowed her eyes at this. So did I.

A *friend* had alerted the pirates? That must have been the claim-jumper ship we'd chased off. Had they done that out of sheer spite? It seemed to me that they must have. What a dirty trick. I was no longer feeling sorry for the man I'd killed back there and left to float forever on that rock.

"We'll make sure that the ore we release is of good quality," Captain Hansen assured the angry pirate.

At this, a howl of anguish was released from behind her, offscreen. I thought it sounded like the voice of the ship's chief accountant Blackwood.

Eventually, the pirates accepted our deal and several large bins of ore were released to float in space. Then, *Borag's* engines ignited again and the ship slid away from the pirates, who greedily swarmed the meager prize they'd garnered.

"All hands," Captain Hansen said over the ship's speakers. "Brace yourselves. We're going to full burn to exit this region."

"It's about damned time!" Sergeant Cox shouted, clapping his hands.

We all raced to flip-down our jump-seats and secure harnesses. The big ship trembled under our feet. We were all pressed back, feeling a full G of acceleration—maybe more. The others seemed like this was a burden to them, but I almost enjoyed the sensation.

"What do you think was in those crates?" I asked Ledbetter.

He shrugged. "I don't know. Spare socks, probably. Hansen and Blackwood—they don't give up on their loot easily."

I reflected on that statement. It seemed to me that Ledbetter had a point. Blackwood had had a fit... but had the captain really ordered him to dump the good stuff? It was a box without any labels. She'd only left it as breadcrumbs, not as an honest offering. We owed these pirates nothing but death.

Still, her move had allowed the enemy captain to exit the situation without killing all of us. It had been well-played, if you asked me.

The fact that we were racing away from the scene at this very moment, at maximum burn, seemed like the right move no matter what the final result was going to be.

Suddenly, however, a new alert sounded. It was a flashing blue, and I'd never seen it before.

We looked around at the ceiling of our ready room, gawking and reading displayed notices. They all said the same thing:

Missile launch detected.

Chapter 9: Three Missiles

As *Borag* raced through space, three missiles trailed close behind, each leaving a fiery trail in its wake. All three of the pirate raiders had launched a single missile after us, and they were all built with different home-brew designs.

The first missile was long and slender, with a pointed nose and sleek design. It seemed to be the fastest of the three, darting side-to-side as it attempted to catch up with the mining rig.

The second missile was a bulky and heavily armored model, with a square body and a pair of large, thruster engines. It moved more slowly than the first, but seemed to be more resilient, shaking off the debris that peppered its hull as it continued to pursue its target.

The third missile was the largest of the three, and the most terrifying to behold. It had a massive body and a thick, stubby nose, and seemed to be filled with enough explosives to blow a hole in the side of a planet. Its engines roared like a hurricane, propelling it forward with incredible force.

Despite their different designs, all three missiles shared one common goal: to destroy *Borag* and everyone aboard her. As they continued to chase the ship, their warheads primed and ready to detonate, the crew of our mining rig could only hold their breath and hope for a miracle.

"Holy shit…" Sergeant Cox said. "Looks like the pirates didn't like the gift boxes Captain Hansen packed for them."

"Yeah," Corporal Tench agreed. "She must have filled them with sewage from the miners' bilge."

The remarks were amusing, but no one laughed. Quite possibly, we were all doomed now.

I felt a flash of anger. Why hadn't they left the pirates something good? Something good enough to make them leave us alone, anyway.

It had to be that dick, Blackwood. He was the numbers man. The ship's accountant held onto every credit piece like it was dipped in gold and honey at the same time.

We were still accelerating, but as the effect was steady now, we were able to release our harnesses and walk around freely. I noticed the others—especially the thinnest of them—were having difficulty. Me, with my earth-grown body, felt good. Normal, in fact. For once, I could move around the ship more easily than anyone else in the squad.

"Attention! Commander on the deck!"

We all snapped to attention. Commander Kaine prowled in, and he walked among us. As he hadn't called for anyone to stand at ease, we maintained our rigid poses, swaying slightly as the big ship kept accelerating.

The deck was vibrating under our boots. Creaking sounds of stressed metal came from the hull now and then, sounding like whale calls.

Finally, Commander Kaine stopped in front of me and Ledbetter.

"You two—you're it. Follow me."

Bewildered, we fell into step behind the commander. I had to admit, the man must work out regularly. He could walk in full gravity without a qualm. Ledbetter did okay, but I could see he was sweating already.

Commander Kaine led us up to the bridge. He didn't tell us squat until we reached the big, closed hatch.

He put a hand on the wheel to open it, then paused and turned to us. "I've received a private text from the captain. She's asked for security forces on the bridge. She asked for me to send my two most discreet and capable men. I've chosen you two idiots for the job. Your mission is dead simple, boys. You're going to stand watch on this deck. You're not going to hear, see, or later on talk about anything that happens here. You got that?"

"Sir-yes-sir!" Ledbetter and I said in unison.

"Good. If I hear word one about you guys bragging or gossiping later, I'm going to cut off your dicks in slices. You got that?"

"Sir-yes-sir!"

Commander Kaine nodded. "All right. If Captain Hansen gives you an order—do it. No questions. No thoughts. No hesitation."

With that, he swung open the big door, and we stepped onto the bridge for the first time.

The moment we were inside, the big door clanged shut again. Commander Kaine was on the far side of it.

Not knowing what else to do, Ledbetter and I stood in front of the door, looking tough. The conversation in the chamber came to a halt when we arrived. A dozen pairs of eyes glanced our way.

No one seemed happy to see us—not even Captain Hansen bothered to smile or nod. For just a second her eyes met mine, however. Was that a flicker of recognition? I thought maybe it was. She had, after all, made a point of elevating me to the role of a ship's marine just weeks earlier.

Borag's bridge was a spacious, circular chamber located in the center of the ship's command deck. The room was brightly lit, with large view screens mounted on the walls that displayed various readouts and data feeds. In the center of the chamber was a circular command console, which could be raised or lowered to accommodate different crew members.

The crew of officers serving on *Borag's* bridge were a well-trained and highly skilled group of professionals. They were responsible for piloting the ship, monitoring its systems, and overseeing its operations.

At the head of the bridge was the captain's chair, a high-backed, leather seat that swiveled and tilted to provide a comfortable position for the ship's commanding officer. To the right of the captain's chair was the helm, where the ship's pilot sat, steering the vessel through space.

To the left of the captain's chair was the navigation console, where the navigator plotted the ship's course and monitored its progress. In front of the captain's chair was the communication's station, where the ship's communications officer watched all incoming and outgoing transmissions.

Other crew members worked at various stations throughout the bridge, monitoring different systems and keeping track of the ship's status. Despite the pressure and danger of their jobs, the officers on *Borag's* bridge remained calm and focused, carrying out their duties with skill and professionalism.

"The math is clear," the navigator said. "We'll be caught and destroyed before the missiles run out of fuel."

"What can we do?" Captain Hansen asked.

The officers all looked at each other warily. "There's only one option, sir," the Chief Engineer said. "And I think you know what it is. We can't increase our thrust, so we'll have to reduce our weight…"

The ship's accountant Blackwood flew into a sudden rage. He beat a skinny fist on a console. "No! No, not again! We're not dumping our payload—don't even think about it!"

Captain Hansen looked at him, then turned her eyes back to the engineer. "How much weight do we have to lose?"

The man did some quick calculations. "Sixty percent of the contents of the main hold—seventy to be sure."

"Seventy it is, then. Prioritize the value of the various ejections. Throw the cheap stuff out first."

"Dammit!" Blackwood said with mournful, helpless anger. "We were so close to profit this time…"

Captain Hansen eyed him coldly. "Maybe if you hadn't insisted that we stuff those crates with worthless shale, the pirates might not have fired upon us!"

Blackwood stood, lengthening his freakishly tall, thin frame to its maximum height. I knew that was quite an effort for him, now that we were under the stress of real gravity from *Borag's* engines. "I take no such responsibility. All final decisions lay with the captain—that's the rule on any ship. I'm just saying I don't think I can cover this kind of deficit, ma'am. Not this time, not again. You'll have my resignation by the time we reach Mars."

Hansen barely glanced at him. "So noted." She pointed at Blackwood and the engineer. "You two are dismissed, you've got a lot of dumping to do. Don't take your time."

The two men hustled out past us, and I dared to sneak a look at Ledbetter. He looked as freaked-out as I was feeling.

We were dumping our payload? What did that mean to the debts all the contracts had on their books? Were they going to get credit for their work, or were they going to be screwed over yet again?

I already knew the answer. Some clause in their contracts would erase everything, making it all seem like the miners themselves had something to do with this calamity. Hell, they'd be lucky if their debts weren't doubled in some "shared indemnity" plan to spread out the damage and make it look like the ship itself hadn't lost as much as it had.

Captain Hansen looked around the room at all the glum faces. "It should be obvious," she said, "that my decision wasn't made with any malice or relish. I stand to lose out just as much as the rest of you. It's time to dump most of our payload—or die. I'd rather breathe than enjoy profits. If any of you here feel differently, there's a garbage chute just down the main passageway on the left side. I'm sure Private Starn here would be glad to stuff anyone into it who needs some help. If your limbs don't fit, we'll edit those, too."

I was stunned to be called out. I felt the eyes of everyone on the bridge for a moment. I kind of felt like laughing, but I knew no one else was in that sort of mood, so I decided to play the thug Captain Hansen wanted me to be.

I stared straight ahead, face like stone. I lifted my rifle a bit higher, holding it across my chest plate, as if I was ready and willing to perform any heinous act the captain might order me to do. For emphasis, I snapped the bolt on my weapon. The metallic sound was loud in the sudden quiet.

The act worked. A few of them mumbled about brutes from Earth, but most simply sulked. Their eyes slid away from me again, and the officers all focused on one another.

They fell to talking over details. They bickered about what weight-to-value ratio items they should keep and which ones they shouldn't.

Down below, I could hear big doors chunking open and our ship went into a gentle spiral.

The navigator explained that flying in a slight spiral would spread the dumped matter into a field behind us. With luck, it might even destroy the missiles that were chasing us.

We were dumping our ore—all that hard work, all that money. Men had died to collect it all, and I felt sick about it.

I didn't let my despair show, of course. I maintained the broad-shouldered marine look, ready and able. No one dared to look me in the eye again.

It took several sweaty hours to play out, but at last the three missiles drew close. As *Borag* continued to accelerate away from the pursuing missiles, her cargo holds dumped a long stream of dust and debris in her wake.

This was a common tactic used by ships in space combat, as the debris could interfere with the guidance systems and actually destroy incoming missiles if they hit a chunk of rock at great speed.

The three missiles launched by the pirate ships were eventually caught up in the field of debris. Two collided with chunks of rock and metal, exploding in a shower of sparks and shrapnel.

Everyone on the bridge cheered when we saw this. Even Ledbetter and I pumped a fist in the air. We couldn't help it, but then, at a stern glance from the captain we went back to playing statues.

The last missile was smarter than the rest. Long and thin, the missile resembled a flying pencil. After appearing to spin out of control, it righted itself and kept on coming.

"That one is smart," the navigator said. She seemed to admire the thing's tiny electric brain. "It's recognized the danger and changed course."

"Unlimber the aft guns. Let the computers do the aiming."

The bridge fell silent again. The enemy missile was on our trail. When we changed course, it did the same. It was flying off to one side now, on a parallel course to avoid the debris. Once it got close enough, however…

"Let it get closer," Captain Hansen told the tactical weapons officer.

I could tell just by looking at him that he wanted to fire right now, but he obeyed his captain.

We all waited in relative quiet for about seven minutes—then the weapons man spoke up. "Sir, if let it get any closer, we might fall into the blast radius. We don't know what the yield will be on that warhead, and—"

"All right. Shoot it down—and don't miss."

The tactical officer made some final adjustments and double-tapped the kill command.

Borag shuddered as a long stream of tiny particles were fired into space. The missile was still thousands of miles off, but it was closing in on us fast. I could tell its tiny, artificial brain really wanted to finish us off.

"First volley is a miss," the tactical man said. "Reloading the magazine."

"Fire again," Captain Hansen said.

"But ma'am, we have to let the barrel cool down. All the accelerated—"

"I don't care about your gun's health! It's changing course. It's starting to evade us. Fire again!"

It was true. The smart missile was a sleek, silver bullet with a long tail of flame trailing behind it. As it approached *Borag*, it began to twist and turn, making erratic movements to avoid the ship's defensive fire. Its movements were fluid and almost organic, as if it were alive.

The missile's onboard computer was constantly analyzing the ship's movements and making adjustments to its flight path. It was programmed to evade defensive fire and find the weakest point in *Borag's* armor to strike.

As it got closer to the ship, the missile's movements became even more erratic. It would suddenly change direction, banking hard to the left or right, then darting back in the opposite direction. The ship's defensive systems were struggling to keep up, and several shots missed their mark.

The missile was getting dangerously close to *Borag*, but it still hadn't connected. The ship's crew could see it through the bridge windows, a bright silver dot moving rapidly across the blackness of space.

Suddenly, the missile made a sharp turn, banking hard to the left. It appeared to be heading straight for the ship's engines. The crew braced themselves for impact, but at the last second, the tactical officer's spraying projectiles connected. Mortally wounded, the missile veered off and exploded harmlessly in the empty void of space.

On the bridge of *Borag*, the officers had watched the spectacle unfold on their monitors. As the last of the missiles exploded, the tension on the bridge began to ease. Captain Hansen allowed herself a small smile before turning to her crew.

"Good work, everyone," she said. "Let's keep this up and get back to port in one piece." The crew nodded in agreement and got back to their stations, ready for whatever came next.

Chapter 10: Mars Colony

Borag reached safety at the Mars-One spaceport over a month later. The ship gradually docked at the cylindrical space station, which was made up of a series of concentric rings. The rings rotated around a central hub to create artificial gravity, allowing people and objects to move about as if they were on solid ground. There were docking ports evenly spaced along its circumference.

As the crew disembarked from *Borag*, we could see Mars City. It appeared as a multi-domed sprawling colony on the surface of Mars far below.

Beyond the cluster of domes, terraforming factories shaped like massive pyramids continuously chugged out gasses into the sky. These days the planet had clouds and even occasional rain. It would take decades more, however, before a human could walk on the surface without freezing or suffocating.

The domed colony nestled in a valley, with the surrounding hills and mountains rising up on all sides. The domes themselves weren't made of glass, but rather a thick, transparent polymer that allowed the red Martian landscape to be seen, but also kept the air inside.

Inside the domes, the enclosed regions were heated, pressurized, and the air was breathable. The interior was supposedly quite pleasant, but so far, I'd never been allowed to experience it. D-Contracts weren't given shore leave—not ever. The risk of them running off was deemed too great.

Today was a new day, however. As a C-Contract, I was free to roam. All the marines from Red Company, in particular, were encouraged to get off the decks and explore. I was really looking forward to it.

Disembarking onto the space station, we could see the surface below in greater detail. The domed city's buildings, streets, and parks, along with the various vehicles and machines that helped the colony function were so clean and well-designed. Earth's aging slums were, by comparison, filthy and ramshackle.

I was intrigued by the duty-free shops and bars in the spaceport lounge section, but Ledbetter put an arm around me, steering me away from these enticements.

"You don't want to get fleeced of every credit you have, do you? Those places are tourist-traps."

"What?" I asked, having never been anything like a tourist.

He rolled his eyes at me. "They're scams. You've got scams in the slums, right?"

"Plenty of them."

He led me toward a line of people. The line terminated in front of an imposing set of steel doors, beyond which was space elevator. "This thing will take us down to the surface."

"We can walk inside the domes?" I asked, incredulous.

"Yeah, sure. We're not citizens, or anything like that, but we're better than some D-class. That's one step from being in prison—no offense."

"None taken... since you're right."

After a long wait, we paid a few credits, and I followed Ledbetter onto a disk that kind of vibrated with a scary energy that was hard to describe. He told me the elevation effect was controlled with air pressure, heat and some tricks of physics he didn't understand.

I didn't argue, I just enjoyed the ride. At first, the sudden sickening lurch downward was enough to make me swallow hard a few times. My guts were coming up into my head. We descended at an increasing rate—then my feet lifted off the floor of the disk entirely.

"What the hell...?"

"Look out, greenie," Ledbetter said with a laugh. "You're going to ram your head into the furniture."

Gaping and looking up, I realized I was indeed floating slowly up to the ceiling—which, unlike the deck we'd been walking on, was furnished with chairs and tables. All of them were bolted down, of course, but it was a weird thing to see. I reached out my arms and made a half-assed crash landing on the roof.

Following Ledbetter's example, I got to my feet and stood up—upside down. The deck we'd been walking on a few minutes ago was now the ceiling.

"Freaky... what's the point of that?"

"You'd have to ask the engineering nerds. There's a few of them over there."

He pointed, and I saw a cluster of midshipmen. They did indeed look like nerds. One of them caught my eye, however. She *really* caught my eye.

"I think I'm going to do just that," I said, stepping toward the group.

"Careful, Starn. You're still just a contract."

I ignored his warning and walked closer to the group. Three smiling men surrounded one woman. When the three men noticed me, their expressions shifted. They looked like they smelled shit.

"There's nothing to shoot at here, Marine," one of the midshipmen said.

Glancing at the girl in their midst, I had to disagree, but I didn't want to argue with officers if I didn't have to. "Sorry, sirs. I was wondering if one of you could answer a technical question for me?"

The midshipman was just a cadet in training, but I felt it was a good idea to stay polite. The three men all shook their heads and looked like they wanted to spit and laugh at the same time.

"I'll help you out," the surrounded girl said.

Glancing at her in surprise, the others began to frown as she walked to me and flashed me a pretty smile.

"I'm Freya," she said. "Freya Carter."

"I'm Devin Starn, ma'am."

"Don't worry about ranks, we're on shore leave."

I smiled, and I couldn't help glancing over her briefly. She was a striking young woman with dark hair and bright blue eyes that seemed to sparkle in the light. While wearing spacesuits, women tended to look like short dudes with pretty faces—but she was in a casual uniform now. I had no doubt that was why she'd attracted all the attention.

Freya kept walking away from the other guys, and so I naturally followed her. We walked away to a safe distance, and I had to frown as we gazed down at the swelling vista of Mars laid out below us.

"Were those guys bothering you?"

"No, not really," she said. "They've all been cooped up aboard *Borag* for months so... they're a little edgy."

I nodded, and I glanced back at the trio, who were muttering bitterly among themselves. I'd probably ruffled some feathers by rescuing Freya, but I guess that was just too damned bad.

Freya looked me up and down for a moment, regarding me just as frankly as I had her a moment ago. "You're from Earth, aren't you?"

"Born and bred. You can tell, huh?"

She nodded. "I'm from Mars. At least I can stand up straight back on Earth, but most lifers out here couldn't."

She glanced over her shoulder again at the irritable trio, and I got the feeling she preferred to be in the company of a more capable man.

"What did you want to ask me about, Devin?"

"Uh... about this crazy elevator. Why did it turn upside down?"

Freya didn't laugh, but I got the feeling she wanted to. "Because we'd all be pasted against the ceiling otherwise. You see, you can only fall at a rate of around forty miles per hour on Mars without being weightless. In order for this elevator to travel all the way down to the surface—about eighty miles, by the way—that would take hours. So, they engineered this contraption to go faster and allow us to stand on the roof."

I nodded, having figured out by now it was something like that. Space was full of strange things such as this, sometimes up was down and down was up.

"That's very helpful," I said, embellishing the truth. "Would you like to hang out with me and my friend over there for the rest of the ride down?"

Freya glanced in the direction I'd indicated. Private Ledbetter stood near the windows, staring down in rapture.

"No," she said, and I felt a pang of disappointment. "I'd prefer to spend the time just with you."

This uplifted my spirits all over again. In fact, they'd done a U-turn. I led her to the bar at the center of the flying contraption, and she accepted a drink from me. Hers was low-alcohol and non-narcotic. I was impressed by her forbearance.

"How fast are we going?" I asked her.

"About a hundred miles per hour."

"Huh… I hope nothing goes wrong. We'll end up as paste at the bottom. At least the view is fantastic."

She gave me a funny look, then. "Wait a minute… I know who you are!"

My mouth fell open, and my heart sank. It would be just my luck if she realized I was a lowly rock-rat dressed up in a marine's uniform.

"You were on the bridge during the crisis—right? When those pirates fired missiles at us?"

"Oh… oh yeah. I did serve on the bridge that day."

Freya squinted at me. "Why did Captain Hansen ask for you two to come play watchdog? Was she worried about a mutiny?"

I shrugged. "I don't know. I just follow orders when the captain calls."

She nodded. "I do the same."

We talked about nothing important for the rest of the way down, but I did manage to score an ID handle from her. A private one. That made me feel pretty good. Not everyone got into the social circle of a girl like Freya. I had the feeling, in fact, that the suits on the far side of this flying disk had tried and failed.

Suddenly, the floor began to become mushy under my feet. I spread out my boots and lifted my hands for balance. That's when I noticed Freya's dark hair was doing this fly-away thing.

We backed away a few shuffling steps from the monstrous bay windows and watched the planet's surface come rapidly up to greet us. We were moving faster than I'd realized.

"Finish your drink, fast!" Freya said.

I gulped mine, and she held out her hand. I took it without thinking.

While I watched slack-jawed, she did a spin in the air. We were floating now, toward the roof. I kind of wanted to spit up the booze I'd just gulped, but I controlled the urge.

We were both standing on the roof again—well, the original deck—within a minute. Freya had enjoyed my efforts and just about giggled during this transition. I'd been clumsy and off-balance, which made her laugh. It was an age-old story, everyone but me was a ballerina out here in space.

When the damned space elevator finally stopped moving, I walked off in relief. Then I looked up and around myself, gawking like a tourist.

The elevator had landed in the center of the dome. From here, the only colony city on Mars was a sight to behold. The city's structures stretched up toward the ceiling of the dome, which replicated a blue sky with fluffy clouds. It was as if I was standing in the center of a small Earth-like city, with tall buildings, paved roads, and lush green parks. The buildings were mostly made of metal and glass, reflecting the sunlight in dazzling beams. The roads were wide, and small autonomous vehicles were zipping past, carrying goods and people from one end of the city to the other.

The parks were covered in green grass, and various shrubs and trees adorned the walkways. I could see people strolling in the parks, enjoying the artificial breeze that blew in the dome. As I looked further toward the edge of the dome, the buildings started to get shorter, and the greenery gave way to reddish-brown Martian soil. I could see the distant mountains of Mars, their tops covered in a reddish hue.

Overall, the city under the dome was impressive, and it was hard to believe that I was standing on a different planet. The people of Mars had created a self-sustaining colony with all the amenities of Earth. The air inside the dome was breathable, and there was even a small lake, where people were swimming and enjoying the water. It was like a small slice of Earth had been transported to the surface of Mars.

"Say..." Freya said, "are you going to let go of my hand?"

I looked down in shock. Sure enough, I'd been holding onto her ever since she'd asked me to do so. Fortunately, I was holding on loosely, not crushing her light fingers like some kind of demented ape.

My initial thought was to let go, but I didn't—not right away. I smiled at her instead. "Would you like to show me around?" I asked.

Freya smiled back, and she gave my hand a squeeze. That was a signal, so I let go of her.

We just stood there for a second, smiling at each other. The three guys with twisted-up faces went walking by behind her at that moment. One of them flipped me off behind her back, but my expression didn't change.

"I'd love to," she said, as if she'd come to a big decision. Perhaps she had.

After that, we headed off into the domed city. As we spent more time together, I couldn't help but become smitten with her. Her infectious laughter and playful banter made me feel alive and carefree, and all thoughts of the dangers we'd faced on our mission faded away. I knew that I wanted to get to know her better, and perhaps even explore the red planet together outside the confines of the space station and *Borag*.

But then, before I could ask her to dinner, my comm lit up and started squawking at me.

"Private Starn?"

It was the unpleasant voice of Commander Kaine. I winced when I heard it and put my hand to cup my ear.

"Yes sir?"

"Where the hell are you?"

"Um... I'm in the city, sir. Under the dome... you know?"

"Of course, I know. I thought you would be up on the space station still. You learn fast, don't you boy?"

"I like to think so."

"Well, I've got a mission for you."

I clenched my teeth and closed my eyes while Freya looked on in concern. "What mission is that, Commander?"

"You're needed at the elevator station—right where you're at now. Don't move."

"Why not, sir?"

There was a moment of silence, then Commander Kaine became angry. "Didn't you just go through training? Didn't Cox teach you to hop-to and not ask questions?"

"He sure did, sir, but… this is my shore-leave."

"Oh. Right. Too bad, but this shouldn't take too long. You're going to escort Captain Hansen from the elevator to the government buildings. We'll do a charge-back on your shore-leave. Don't worry, you won't be paying for this."

"Okay, Commander. I'll do it."

I had a lot of questions, but I knew there weren't going to be any satisfactory answers. I thought about cashing out what meager pay I had and bailing out of Red Company right then and there—but of course, I didn't. I didn't even have enough money to get back to my home in the slums of Earth.

Staying on Mars was out of the question as well. It was expensive to live here, and I didn't know anyone who would help me out. I'd just met Freya, and as great as she was, she didn't seem to be rich, either.

"What's wrong?" she asked me, and I explained.

Freya crossed her arms in frustration. "We only just got down here. Can't the captain walk herself to midtown? I mean, this is weird."

"Yeah…" I agreed. "I don't know why she wants me to play watchdog for her."

"I bet I do," Freya said, giving my right bicep a squeeze.

I smiled at her sheepishly. "Hey, maybe we can see something. It will be a good hour before that elevator goes all the way up and comes down again, right?"

We checked the schedule, and with the switchover time to let people on and off the contrivance, the round trip was over an hour.

"Okay," Freya said. "I know where to go."

She took me to a little place that was cheap and full of good food. The food was weird, mind you, but flavorful. Apparently, they'd transplanted some strange creatures from Earth to Mars. One horseshoe crab looking animal was called a "bug" by the locals. It looked like a manta ray in a shell but tasted more like a lobster. We ate some mosses and various honey-flavored beverages along with it.

As Mars was in a state of early terraforming, they were working hard to breed and grow organic things that helped foster an ecosystem. These items fit the bill, apparently.

The hour went by in a flash. When it was over, Freya stood up and gave me a peck on the cheek. "Go get the captain and walk her into town. If she lets you out early... call me."

I assured her I would do so, and I headed for the base of the strange, massive elevator. Hoping against hope I'd get out of this duty somehow, I watched it descend and come to a halt with loud hissing puffs of released gas.

Chapter 11: The Audit

    I waited for Captain Hansen and Blackwood to arrive at the elevator station. When the disk finally glided down and braked, I stood at attention at the doors. I'd kind of half-expected Ledbetter or someone else to come along and join me, but no one did.

    At last, the big doors opened and a rush of passengers from the spaceport walked off. They gave me a few strange looks, but I didn't even blink. It seemed like the last two that exited the disk were the captain and the accountant. I saluted and received a nod in return. I fell in behind them as they walked out of the station and onto the domed city streets.

    As we walked, Captain Hansen surveyed the surroundings with a critical eye, taking in the sights and sounds of the bustling city—or maybe she was looking for someone or something. I couldn't tell which it was, but she was definitely on alert.

    The city was impressive, with towering buildings that seemed to scrape the dome's ceiling and bustling streets filled with people from all walks of life. The air was thick with the scent of food and the sound of chatter, a cacophony of voices that somehow blended together into a symphony of life.

    As we approached the city's midtown center, the crowds began to thin out, giving way to a large open plaza. In the center of the plaza stood a towering statue of Mars, the god of war. His form loomed over the city like a watchful guardian.

I couldn't help but feel a sense of awe as I gawked up at the statue. My personal display generated all the history and legends that surrounded the god. Like the deity, Mars was a harsh and unforgiving planet. Living here demanded a fierce and unrelenting spirit from those who dared to call it home.

As we made our way through the plaza, I could feel the eyes of the colonists on us. Their gazes lingered on the captain and her entourage. I knew that the captain was regarded warily. All outsiders were eyed with suspicion here, and we were clearly off-worlders.

Finally, we arrived at our destination. The triangular structure built with laser-carved red bricks stood a dozen stories high. Inside, we rode an elevator to the top. I was starting to frown—who were we going to meet up here? Someone with a fat wallet, that was for sure.

"I'm sorry, Captain," said a well-manicured receptionist. "You'll have to leave your soldier outside."

This was what I'd been expecting. A guy like me was a dog that needed to be left out in the rain. I understood the sentiment, and I wasn't even upset about it—but Captain Hansen was.

"I'm allowed to have security with me, even here."

The receptionist frowned and flicked her eyes to me and then quickly away again. It was as if my image offended her somehow.

"He's not appropriately dressed, and no weapons are allowed into these chambers."

"Perhaps—" Blackwood began, but Captain Hansen stopped him cold with a raised hand.

She turned to me. "Are you armed, Marine?"

"No ma'am. Not a gun on me. We're under Mars rules, here."

She inclined her head and turned back to the receptionist, who had clasped her hands together tightly under her obviously enhanced breasts.

"You see?" the captain said. "He's wearing a regulation uniform, just as I am. He's not armed. His presence is allowed."

The receptionist's jaw jutted out stubbornly for a moment, but then her fake smile grew back into place. "Very well. Follow me."

We were ushered into a large conference room filled with other high-ranking officers and officials. There were some brief, cold pleasantries exchanged. The group of suits that met us smiled momentarily at Captain Hansen and Blackwood—but they apparently thought I stank. None of them said a word or did much more than stare for a few seconds in my direction.

That didn't matter to me. I played the part of the guard dog on patrol. No expression, no nods, or smiles. Standing at the doorway, I did my best to turn into a wall-decoration, and to be honest, I liked it that way.

Looking around the meeting chambers, I was impressed. The sleek rooms were filled with polished steel, tinted glass, and top-end furniture. None of this seemed to have any effect on Hansen's expression. Her face remained set in a grim mask.

The room was filled with assistants and lawyers from the mining corporation that financed *Borag*: Interplanetary Excavations, Inc. I visually checked them all for weapons and decided they were a pretty harmless-looking bunch. Even if I'd been on Earth, I could have probably beaten the lot of them in a fist fight.

The man in charge was a fat guy named Controller Malkin. He had thinning hair, and he was wrapped-up like a burrito in an expensive suit that seemed too tight for him.

He leaned back in his chair and gave Hansen a scowl. He had a hawkish nose that perched on his face like a vulture ready to swoop in for the kill, and his beady eyes darted around the room as he spoke.

"This is a disaster," Malkin said, tapping a pile of computer scrolls on the table. "*Borag's* debts and losses on this mining mission are off the charts. To top it off, you came back here with half your holds empty and a bunch of pirates on your tail."

Captain Hansen remained calm. "We did our best, but we were ambushed by the pirates. We had no choice but to defend ourselves and our ship."

Controller Malkin snorted. "Your best isn't good enough. We need to cut our losses and move on. We can't afford to keep pouring money into this operation." His voice was clipped and precise, every word measured and calculated to get the most out of his argument. There was no warmth in his tone, only cold, hard facts, and his words sliced through the air like a scalpel.

Blackwood spoke up, and his voice was laced with anger. "You don't get to make that call. *Borag* is a valuable asset to this corporation, and we're not going to abandon it because of one setback."

Malkin turned on *Borag's* accountant next. He smiled in a predatory fashion. He seemed to relish in his power, and the way his words could make or break the fate of those around him. His demeanor made it clear that he was a man who enjoyed wielding his influence, and that he took great pleasure in causing pain to those who crossed him.

"We'll see about that, Blackwood. In the meantime, you'll have to deal with the consequences of your failure. We'll be withholding all payments until we can assess the damages."

Hansen's eyes narrowed. "You do that, and we'll be forced to take legal action. You can't withhold payment without a valid reason."

Malkin leaned forward, a sneer on his face. "We have plenty of reasons. You put our investment in jeopardy, and now you expect us to foot the bill."

Hansen balled-up her fists. "We did everything we could to protect my ship and my crew. If you can't see that, then you have no business running a mining operation."

The controller sneered at her. "I know exactly what I'm doing. And if you can't handle the pressure, then maybe it's time to find a new line of work."

Hansen jaw set in anger. "I still hold title to *Borag*," she said, her voice cold. "If you want to recoup your losses, you'll have to give us something new to do."

This raised the controller's eyebrows for the first time. "Are you volunteering for something more… hazardous?"

"More hazardous? No… but maybe something more lucrative."

The controller's expression flickered at the corners. It wasn't a smile, but it was an improvement. He crossed his arms and rubbed at his chin in thought. "All right. We'll come up with something. In the meantime, train your crew, recruit new people—I see you lost thirteen, and another nine are requesting transfer."

"They are? The disloyal bastards…"

Malkin smirked. "What did you expect? You blew their shares out of your aft hold."

The argument was about to start all over again, but Blackwood raised his hand for peace. "Controller, good sir, could you possibly see fit to advancing us some credits for recruitment, repairs, and training?"

"Absolutely not. Take those funds from the officers' payroll, if you have to."

Blackwood looked stricken. "Sir, if we are denied funds to operate the company is doomed to bankruptcy. If that is your final decision, I must tender my resignation—effective immediately."

For once, Malkin seemed to be impressed. He huddled with a few of the other suits. Blackwood and Captain Hansen kept up their poker faces, as did I.

Finally, the controller turned back around. "All right. We'll put up with this sinking ship for a bit longer. I must warn you, however, we're one step from foreclosure and liquidation."

"To be clear… We will be provided operating expenses?" Blackwood asked.

"Yes, damn you. That's what I said. But it will all go on your debt, Accountant. Don't forget that."

"I won't, sir. None of us will."

"Now, get out of here. We'll let you know what your new mission is when you're ready to fly again."

"What if we don't like it?" Hansen asked him.

The controller scoffed. "Then you can get a new job somewhere else—as a contract. We'll foreclose and sell everything and everyone."

As she had no answer to that, Captain Hansen turned around and marched out of the place.

We left the conference room, which was a relief, but I couldn't help but feel a sense of unease. The company's attitude toward *Borag* and her crew was callous and dismissive.

As the debt and losses piled up, keeping the ship independent and in operation was becoming more complicated by the day.

Outside, I felt a small sense of relief. Not everyone in the streets hated us. The city was full of the hum of electricity and lights that glimmered in the darkness. The air between the three of us was intense, but Captain Hansen silenced Blackwood with a gesture until we were far from the corporate building.

At last, she paused with a gleam in her eye. "Blackwood, you played a mean hand of poker back there," she said, grinning.

"I learned from the best, Captain," Blackwood replied with a nod.

Hansen laughed, the sound echoing through the business district. As it was after-hours, the streets were almost deserted. We walked in silence for a few minutes, the sound of their footsteps the only thing that broke the quiet.

The two of them continued their walk through the city, and I trailed behind. The stars shone bright in the sky, a reminder of the vastness of space beyond the dome.

"We'll take whatever shit-mission they throw back at us," Hansen said, "and we'll show them we're not a dismal financial loss."

"I have no doubt we will, Captain," Blackwood murmured in a tone that sounded like he'd said this many times before.

Chapter 12: Ambush

Before we reached the elevator station, Blackwood excused himself. He claimed he had plans to visit a friend—and that left me alone with Captain Hansen. I figured Blackwood wanted a drink after putting his job on the line, so I couldn't blame him. I could have used a drink myself.

The meeting had been important and interesting, but I'd rather have spent more time with Freya. I was distracted, to be honest.

The hour was quite late by local time. To humanity's great fortune, days here on Mars were twenty-four hours and thirty-nine minutes long. It was therefore relatively easy to get used to the day-night cycle, here. It felt almost natural.

Up ahead, we could see the space elevator when it was still a mile distant. It was a mesmerizing sight. The shaft itself was a towering tube of polymers that rose high into the sky, the transparent walls gleaming in the glow of the city's lights.

As I watched, I could see the faint outline of the disk moving down the shaft. The metal underside of this large dinner-plate shaped disk caught the city lights and cast back a soft reddish glow. The disk was like a tiny speck compared to the towering height of the shaft, but it moved with an impressive speed and grace.

We walked through the dark and narrow streets of the city, wandering into a zone that had probably been used to stack up empty containers since the colony was first established. Some of the barrels and bins looked like they hadn't been touched in years. It was eerily quiet, but I could feel the eyes of the locals on us as we walked by.

Then, we heard footsteps behind us. I turned around to see a group of rough-looking rock-rat miners were following us. Their eyes gleamed with malice. They were armed with pipes and chains, and I knew they meant to cause us harm.

Hansen and I exchanged a glance, and without a word, we prepared for the attack. I took a step forward and reached for my laser carbine—but of course, it wasn't there. I wasn't allowed to carry an automatic weapon around on the colony streets. So instead, I raised my fists, ready to defend against the onslaught. I was wishing I'd brought along at least a shock-rod, like a Green Company man might have.

The first miner swung his pipe at me, but I ducked and delivered a powerful uppercut to his jaw. He went down like a sack of dirt, and I turned my attention to the others.

The fight was intense, but my earth-hardened muscles gave me the edge I needed to take down the attackers. I punched, kicked, and dodged their blows, sending them crashing into the containers around us or face-first to the deck at my feet.

Finally, the last miner lay groaning on the ground. Hansen had handled one man on her own. She truly must have had some power in her arms that your average Mars man didn't expect. We were victorious.

We trotted away, not bothering to contact any authorities or wait around for more thugs. As I followed in her wake, I looked her over for injuries. She was limping slightly, but she seemed to be hale and whole.

When we got out into a well-lit street near the elevator station, we paused to catch our breath.

"You're quite the fighter, Starn," she said, a hint of admiration in her voice.

I just smiled, feeling the adrenaline still pumping through my veins. "You did a number on that one guy yourself."

We continued on our way, both of us feeling more confident and capable after the encounter. The rock-rat miners might think twice before attacking us or anyone else in the future.

When we made it to the elevator station, I felt a sense of relief. The elevator itself whirred as it moved, a deep and steady vibration that could be felt through the ground now that we were close. It was a constant reminder of the bustling activity happening high above in space, the constant comings and goings of ships and cargo. As the elevator reached the top of the shaft, I could see the bright stars above and the distant flicker of ships moving through the darkness.

Seeing we had a few minutes to wait for the next arrival, I dared to speak to the Captain Hansen directly. "Ma'am? May I ask you a question?"

She hesitated, but then nodded. "All right—but don't make a habit of it."

"I wouldn't think of it, Captain. My question is in regards to why you've been requesting me, specifically, for this kind of duty? There are other marines who are more experienced and could certainly do this job."

Hansen nodded. "That's true. You are green—but you've got physical power the others don't have. That's rare up here in the colonies. I'm from Earth, too, originally. I know the advantage we have over low-grav types."

"Okay…" I said. "But still…"

"Let me explain it to you another way. Who do you feel the most loyalty toward on my ship?"

"Um… probably you, sir. You helped me get out of the miners' barracks. You even paid my contract off."

She nodded. "Think about the rest of Red Company. Do you think they feel the same way?"

I scratched at a bruise on my shoulder. "I don't know…"

"Well, they don't. They have loyalty to me and my ship, I'm sure of that. But they probably care more about each other than they do their beloved captain. Even more importantly, they're more likely to be swayed by a bribe than you are."

"You think so?" I asked, grinning. "Maybe you don't know my history."

"I looked into it. I know about your parents—about their misunderstanding with the law. They had principles. Such traits are often hereditary. Unfortunately, they also had big mouths. Did you inherit that trait as well?"

I blinked at her, confused by her comments for a moment, but at last, I thought I got it. "No, ma'am. I'm not going to talk to anyone about any of this."

She smiled and nodded. "The perfect guardian. Big, strong, loyal—and *quiet*."

The elevator disk arrived at last then, and the captain stepped aboard. I followed her, wondering about a lot of things that had been said tonight. We were carried up into the heavens again, and soon I was back aboard *Borag*. It felt like going home again, and I headed for my bunk in the berthing areas.

Before I could go to bed, however, I was greeted with an unexpected outburst from Commander Kaine. The Commander was furious and began to berate me for letting Captain Hansen get into trouble. He went on and on, telling me that my job was to protect her, and I had failed. I stood at attention, silent, taking the verbal lashing. I'd already figured out by this time that arguing with him would only make things worse.

Finally, Commander Kaine ordered me to visit his office the first thing in the morning and left.

When I was alone with Sergeant Cox, the older man put a hand on my shoulder. "Don't worry about him, Starn. He's just worried about getting paid. You did a good job out there, protecting the captain from those miners. You showed them they shouldn't fuck with the marines from *Borag*."

I sighed, relieved to hear his words of support. "I didn't know who they were. I was just trying to do my job."

The sergeant chuckled, and he slammed a palm onto my back. "That's what makes you a good marine, Starn. You don't question, you just act. I think that's why the captain keeps asking for you to play escort."

I nodded, grateful for his reassurance. As I walked away, I couldn't help but wonder what other joys lay ahead of me in this job.

Chapter 13: The Wilds of Mars

The next morning, I stood at attention in front of Commander Kaine's desk. I tried not to hold my breath. I'd just completed my report, detailing the events of my recent escort mission on Mars.

"You know what I'm putting down on this report, Starn?"

"What's that, sir?"

"Shit for brains," he said, leaning back in his chair. "That's my final verdict. You walked Captain Hansen into an unknown area in the middle of the night. You protected the captain, sure—but it shouldn't have come down to that. You know, if Red Company was moron-free, you wouldn't have been around to put her into that dangerous position in the first place."

I opened my mouth to stammer out an excuse, but then I slammed it shut again.

Kaine nodded, watching me. "At least you're owning up to it," he said. "I don't want to hear any excuses. What I want to hear is fewer disasters with your name on them, Starn. Now, get out of my sight."

I hesitated, lingering at the doorway to his office.

"What is it now, you fool?"

"Sir... about my shore-leave. I—"

Commander Kaine bared his teeth at me. "I'll do you one better. Three days, no pay! You're on leave as of right now, Starn, but I'm calling it a 'suspension'. Are you happy now?"

I wasn't, but I knew when I should quit. I hiked it out of his office and headed for the docks. A few of my comrades laughed at me, and they speculated as to whether I'd pissed off the commander on purpose to get off the ship.

When I reached the domed city again, I was glum but also thoughtful. At least this would give me a chance to explore the Mars Colony and maybe even catch up with Freya.

After sending her a few notes, she was able to get some hours off from her duties as well. The ship's crew was rotating duties, after all, as we were rarely in any port and able to walk on firm ground.

It was late afternoon before I could get my second date with Freya started. She had asked me to meet her at a new place, and I couldn't wait to see what she had in store for me.

To my surprise, she asked to meet me at the far edge of the city. I walked through parks and neighborhoods, all of which looked better than the midtown district where I'd met up with some of Mars' finest the night before.

As I approached the soaring curved wall of the dome, I saw Freya standing at one of the airlocks. She was dressed in a black suit that was tight in all the right places, and her dark hair was pulled back in a sleek ponytail. She greeted me with a smile, and I went in for a kiss.

Something bumped me in the belly, holding me off. It was a space helmet.

"Hey, you," she said. "Are you ready for an adventure?"

I grinned. "Always."

Freya led me inside the airlock that was cut into the dome itself, and it began to cycle. The sound of air being pumped out filled the small space, and I felt the pressure in my ears change.

The pressure in my helmet started to equalize as Freya opened the airlock door. She was wearing that sleek, black spacesuit, and it hugged her curves nicely. I couldn't help but feel a little amazed at her ability to make a spacesuit look good. I, on the other hand, felt like a walking tin can.

After a few minutes, the outer door opened, and we stepped out onto the surface of Mars. I was struck by the vast expanse of reddish-orange landscape stretching out before me. We were standing on the edge of the dome, looking out over the Martian desert. The skies were red, and the sun was dropping to the west. Eventually, it would set and cast an orange glow across the sky.

Gawking and walking around in circles, I gasped at the sights. The alien world stretched out as far as the eye could see. The red rock formations contrasted sharply against the sky, which was speckled with two small moons.

Freya led me on a hike, pointing out different landmarks and sharing interesting facts about the planet. As we walked, we came across a small hill that overlooked the dome. Freya gestured toward it.

"Let's climb up there," she said.

Following her up the hill, I reached the top without being out of breath. The view was worth the climb. We could see the entire dome city, and it was even more beautiful from above.

Beyond the city itself a massive mountain loomed. I pointed at this hulking monster, gawking. "What the hell is that thing?"

"That's Olympus Mons, the biggest volcano in the Solar System."

I blinked in alarm. "It seems like a dumb idea to build a city near that monster!"

She laughed. "Yes… but it's been dormant for millions of years. We should be safe."

Squinting, I eyed the massive volcano doubtfully. It was both tall and wide—and it filled the horizon. "How big are we talking, exactly?"

"It's about thirteen miles tall, more than twice as high as Mount Everest back on Earth. The base of it is over three hundred and fifty miles wide, making it bigger than Arizona. But don't worry, it's farther away than it looks."

Staring, I studied the monster. I found I was fascinated by the massive volcano—but I didn't like it. Sure, it was over a hundred miles away, but if that thing ever went off, I had the feeling it wouldn't matter.

We were really going to terraform a planet that had a super-volcano squatting in the middle of it? Really? I had my questions, but I wasn't an engineer.

After I was done gaping at the view, I turned to Freya and took her hand. "This is amazing."

Freya smiled at me. "I'm glad you like it. I thought it would be a nice change from the usual dinner and a movie."

"Definitely. You know, you're not like any other girl I've met."

Freya raised an eyebrow. "Is that a good thing?"

I grinned. "It's a great thing."

"Good. I've got something else to show you."

She could have led me to the gates of Hell—but she didn't. she led me into a very strange field instead. Here, the land had been artificially plowed and the rocks had been removed. In an instant, I knew what I had to be looking at.

"Is this some kind of a farmer's field?"

"Sort of. We're growing lichen out here."

"What the hell is lichen?"

"A primitive kind of moss that doesn't need much warmth or air to survive. Eventually, we'll be able to grow more complex plants like Antarctic hairgrass. Someday, we'll even have trees."

We started walking, our boots crunching on the thin layer of red dust that covered the ground. We passed by rows of terraforming equipment, each piece whirring and humming as it worked to change the Martian atmosphere. The lichen that was beginning to grow on its own was a hopeful sign that they were making progress.

There were pathways between the rows of lichen so tenders could walk without damaging the fragile plants. We kept on those walkways, and I was alarmed to spot tiny crawling things on the moss. "Are those bugs?"

"Yes. Our first animal life, genetically designed to take these kinds of extremes. We're trying to build an ecosystem, thickening the atmosphere and raising the temperature levels."

We stood atop a mossy hill and looked out over the terraformed landscape.

Freya turned to me. "I'm glad we came out here tonight. It's beautiful, isn't it?"

I nodded, unable to take my eyes off of her. I felt a strong desire to lean in and kiss her, but I knew it was impossible with our helmets in the way.

"Yeah, it's amazing," I said, my voice muffled by the helmet.

Freya smiled. "You know, Devin, I've been wanting to do something all night."

"What's that?"

"This," she said, and she pressed her faceplate against mine.

I felt a jolt of yearning for her as our faceplates met. I know that's weird, I mean, we were still about six inches apart. But when you really want a girl, just getting close to her can turn a guy on. That's how it works. I closed my eyes and savored that moment. I really wished I could feel the warmth of her breath on my face.

I couldn't help but feel a little disappointed as she pulled away. I wanted to feel her lips on mine for reals. Right then and there I decided I'd manage it somehow. This girl was getting to me.

Freya smiled at me through our faceplates, sensing my disappointment. "We call that a Martian kiss. I know, it's not quite the same," she said, her voice muffled by the suit's speaker. "But it's better than nothing, right?"

"No... it kind of sucks, actually."

She laughed. "But good enough for now?"

I nodded, trying to shake off the feeling of a letdown. I couldn't deny that I was thrilled to be with Freya, even in the harsh environment of Mars.

Freya pointed to a distant ridge, and I followed her gaze. "Want to go see what's over there?" she asked.

"Lead the way."

We started walking again, making our way across the rocky, mossy terrain. As we walked, Freya chatted about her work. She talked about the terraforming project, her excitement about the progress they were making, and her hopes for the future of Mars.

I listened, fascinated by her passion and intelligence. I'd skipped or slept through most of my education as a kid, and I couldn't help but feel a little intimidated by her, but I also found myself incredibly attracted at the same time.

As we crested the ridge, the sun began to dip below the horizon, casting the Martian landscape in a reddish-orange glow. Freya turned to me, her face serious.

"I know it's a little weird, dating in spacesuits and all," she said. "But I really like you, Devin. I think you're different."

"You've got my attention too, that's for sure."

We stood there for a moment, just looking at each other through our helmets. Then, without a word, we leaned in for another half-assed Martian kiss, savoring the limited closeness that our suits allowed us.

We continued on—exploring humanity's new frontiers on Mars. As the sun set, we turned back toward the dome, our helmets reflecting the last rays of light.

Chapter 14: The Training Grounds

"Where have you been, Starn?" a voice roared inside my helmet the moment the airlock had cycled through.

It was Corporal Tench, and he seemed very upset about something. I glanced at Freya. She wasn't able to hear my conversation, but she knew something was wrong. She took off her helmet as we stepped back inside the dome. She looked worried.

"What's wrong, Corporal?" I asked Tench.

"What's wrong is I've just run a trace on your ass. Did you actually exit the Mars dome? That's a violation, marine. You're a non-citizen—on both on Earth and Mars. You can't just go off the grid and wander around."

"But... Commander Kaine put me on suspension. I'm on an unpaid vacation."

Tench laughed. It was an evil sound. "That's not how it works. It's supposed to be a punishment. You're confined to quarters when on report and suspended. Don't you know anything? You're a walking, talking wad of failure, Starn!"

"Sorry, Corporal. I'll head back up to the ship right away."

"Next time, we'll just lock you in the brig, so you don't wander off like some kind of stray cat. I'm putting that into your files... hold on, what's this? I see a note from Commander Kaine..." He laughed uproariously. "Did you know he renamed your file 'shit-brains'? That's really funny. Accurate, too..."

He was gone, and I gritted my teeth. After explaining things to Freya, she was full of apologies. I tried to shrug it off, but the moment between us was gone.

We raced back to the elevator station and, about ninety minutes later, I reported to my quarters.

There was a lot of shouting and laughter at my expense after that. I tried not to let it get me down. I'd gotten pretty far with Freya, and it was hard to think about anything else.

The next day, Red Company received the orders to attend a training camp on Mars. I'd been hoping to figure out a way to get a few more days of time with Freya, but orders were orders.

Commander Kaine cancelled my last day of suspension, so I could be part of the training exercises. As he put it, I could use all the help I could get. I met up with the rest of Red Company, who were also preparing for the event. To my surprise, there were a lot of new people present.

"Fresh recruits," Private Ledbetter clued me in. "The bosses are hiring up more troops than we've ever had. It kind of worries me, to be honest. We've got thirty people assembled here today."

I did a little quiet counting, and I found he was right. Counting the officers like Commander Kaine, there were thirty-five helmets in sight.

Sergeant Cox called us all into a huddle. He handed out carbines, to my surprise. "Won't these punch a hole in this here dome, Sarge?" asked a concerned private.

"Not if you keep the governor turned on. They're in training mode. Don't switch that off, or it's your ass!"

"No way, Sarge. I wouldn't do it!"

"Even if you did, these things only have about a three percent charge. Plenty to play laser-tag, but not enough to do any damage."

I was relieved. I didn't relish the idea of practicing with our service rifles. Some of these boys had questionable safety instincts.

We were inspected by our officers, and our noncoms. Everyone was kicked in the ass and thumped on the helmet for something. Lining up and jogging smartly, we made good time toward the airlocks. I thought about telling someone I'd been outside the dome just yesterday, but I didn't have the guts. I'd already gotten into trouble over that.

To my surprise, we jogged right past the public airlocks, which were built for foot traffic. Instead, we mounted up on two balloon-tired carryalls. These machines were rovers of a sort, very tough and built to last on the harsh exterior of Mars.

Each vehicle had a wide, low-slung body with a series of large, round wheels equipped with air-filled tires. The body was covered in a durable, heat-resistant material to protect against the extreme conditions of the planet. The interior was spacious and open, with bench seating.

But naturally, there wasn't enough room for all of us and our gear, so some had to ride on the hood, the running boards—even the roof. It was kind of fun until we went through the big vehicles-only airlock and found ourselves bouncing all over the place out on the open Martian landscape. I was on a running board right behind the driver, and I found myself clinging to the oversized vehicle for dear life.

Dipping my head down, I checked out the driver—it was Commander Kaine. I swore I could see a grin on his face as he drove right for various rock piles. The balloon tires provided stability and buoyancy on the uneven, rocky Martian terrain. The carryalls were able to traverse even the roughest ground, but there were limits. We were flying six feet up with our balls in the air when he went over something big.

Once, a private lost his grip and almost got run over. Commander Kaine stopped and flew into a rage, kicking the man until he got to his feet. This only took two kicks, as in the low gravity the force of such blows tended to lift you right off the ground. The private staggered a little, but he was game. I hauled him back onto the running board behind me and told him to hold on.

"Thanks, man," he said.

I glanced down at him. He was a fresh-faced recruit. His features were a youthful mix of confusion and fear.

I have to admit, right then I felt the same urge all my more experienced comrades must have felt when they saw me screw up. I wanted to bash him one.

The trouble was, a fuck-up on your team was worse than an enemy when you were fighting in space. Anything and everything was out to kill you. The wrong mix on your oxygen gauge, a slow leak you couldn't find—all of it was deadly. You didn't even have to have an enemy shooting at you to die on Mars or some spinning rock in the belt.

Accordingly, I lifted my lip to snarl at him, but I controlled myself. "Hang on tighter," I said. That was it. The sum total of my helpful advice.

Still, the recruit seemed to appreciate it. At least I hadn't knocked his teeth down his throat. Not yet.

We rode aboard our two carryalls and went over a row of low hills. On the far side of that was a crater. We ran up and over the ridge of the crater—and nearly flipped over.

Commander Kaine had crossed the ramp-like crater's edge with too much speed. He'd nearly lost it. I had to wonder what the hurry was, but I could imagine. He was simulating a hard-charging ride into a combat zone. If we'd had anything firing on us—aircraft, for example—the carryall drivers would have been running for their lives.

It was all part of the training, I told myself. It had to be.

Once inside the crater, the two vehicles slowed down. Up ahead, I saw a jumble of buildings and lights.

"This is Camp Sulci. Those hills all around us are called Gigas Sulci, a bunch of winding valleys that stretch for a thousand miles or more. And that hulking monster, off to the North, that's called Olympus Mons."

"The biggest volcano in the Solar System," I said.

The recruit who was still clinging to the running board behind me, just in case the commander started rolling again, looked at me quizzically. "How did you know that?"

"It's a long story."

Commander Kaine pointed toward the middle region of the crater, which was surrounded by a twisted valley of sorts. "The camp is over there. It's going to be your new home for a few weeks. Start loving it right now, that's my advice."

Groans went up from some of the troops. Since they were men who'd been in Red Company longer than I had, I figured they knew what they were groaning about.

The training camp was a massive complex of buildings and fields, with all sorts of obstacles and challenges for us marines to overcome. Sergeant Cox barked orders at us as we went through rigorous physical and combat training exercises.

At first, I struggled to keep up, but I soon found my rhythm and began to excel. My muscles were sore, and my mind was exhausted, but I pushed through the pain and kept going. I knew that I needed to prove myself to the rest of the company and to Commander Kaine.

Days marched by. Each new day, we were given a fresh challenge. These missions grew more and more intense. We went through live-fire exercises, hand-to-hand combat drills, and even survival scenarios in the harsh Martian wilderness. It was frigging tough on me. I was in shape from riding herd on a drill-bot for years, sure, but these movements were more varied. We had to use every muscle we had, not just the few I'd built up as a miner. But through it all, I kept my head down and kept going. I never gave up. I pushed myself harder than I ever had before, driven by my desire to be the best.

Then, on the eighth day, we were sent into the rugged hills in squads to hunt each other. It was a combat mission, and we were in it to win it.

The rocky battleground was a desolate and barren landscape. Jagged rocks and boulders were scattered haphazardly across the terrain, creating an uneven and treacherous path for anyone trying to traverse it. The ground was red and dusty, with a fine layer of sand that coated everything in sight.

The air was thin and dry, with little to no moisture or vegetation to be found. The sky was a deep shade of red, with a faint haze that hung in the air, as if the planet was permanently shrouded in a thick layer of dust and smoke.

The rocks themselves were sharp and rugged, with sharp edges and rough surfaces that could easily cut through skin or fabric. The area was devoid of any vegetation or signs of life, and the only sounds were the occasional gusts of wind and the crunching of rocks underfoot.

The battlefield was an unforgiving place, a true test of endurance and survival for anyone brave enough to venture out into it. And yet, for the brave and skilled marines of Red Company, it was just another obstacle for us to overcome.

Sergeant Cox led 1st Squad of Red Company. A pack of marines followed him across the rocky Martian terrain. The other squad, led by Lt. Quinn, was already in position, crouched behind a large boulder. I could see their red laser beams firing in our direction, ricocheting off the rocks around us. The weapons had been configured to leave visible trails even in the thin air of Mars.

"The enemy have the high ground," Cox told us, "but they also have fewer men. Stay under cover and get closer before we engage."

We rushed from rock to rock, using overwatch techniques to cover one another—but it wasn't good enough. Ledbetter bought the farm right off.

"Dammit, Ledbetter," Cox shouted, cursing at him. "You moron! You took it right in the helmet!"

Ledbetter played dead, just like he was supposed to.

Cox streamed out foul language and gave Ledbetter a punch as he went by. "Stay low and keep moving," he yelled, gesturing for us to spread out. "We'll never win if we let them pick us off one by one."

I took cover behind a smaller rock. Aiming and firing methodically, I plinked away with my low wattage laser rifle in the direction of the other squad. I saw a flash of red light whiz past my head. I could only see it due to the photo-reactives they'd pumped into the local atmosphere. The effect was just there to scare us—and it frigging worked. I pulled back, breathing hard. This was going to be a tough fight.

The rocks around us provided plenty of cover, but they also made it hard to move quickly. We had to crawl and scramble over the rough terrain to avoid getting hit, while also firing back at the other squad.

We inched closer and closer, each side taking potshots at the other. I could hear the hum of the laser rifles, the thud of the rocks as they were struck by the beams, and the occasional shouted command from our sergeants.

"Private Starn, move to the left and try to flank them," Cox shouted.

I nodded and began to crawl along the ground, trying to keep my head down as I made my way to the side of the other squad's position. I could see them firing in our direction, their laser beams cutting through the dusty air.

I took a deep breath and fired off a series of shots, aiming for the enemy's feet to keep them on the move. It worked, and I saw them start to scatter, trying to avoid getting hit.

"Keep advancing, marines!" Cox yelled. "Move around them and hit their flanks!"

We continued to exchange fire, moving and dodging as best we could. It was a tough fight, but in the end, our squad emerged victorious. We'd gotten too close with more troops than they could handle. The other squad surrendered, and we all came together to congratulate each other on a job well done.

As we made our way back to Camp Sulci, I felt a sense of pride and camaraderie with my fellow marines. I figured we were going to kick some ass out there in space. No pirate could stand against us. Seriously, that's how I felt.

At the time, there was no way for me to know how wrong that feeling was.

Chapter 15: Olympus Mons

Red Company had just received orders to start a new mission on Mars. Our objective was to learn low-gravity repelling techniques on Olympus Mons, the tallest mountain in the known universe. We were excited, but we knew the training would be intense.

As we prepared to leave, we loaded up our gear onto the carryalls. They were large balloon-tired vehicles designed to transport troops on the rugged Martian terrain. They were our only way to get to the site, and we knew we would be spending a lot of time in them over the next few days.

I climbed aboard one of the carryalls and took a seat next to Sergeant Cox. I'd wangled a seat inside the vehicle this time. I'd done so by jumping in first, which was usually a successful strategy. Cox threw me a frown, but at least he didn't throw me out. I studiously avoided looking back, and soon his attention shifted elsewhere as the engines buzzed with electrical life.

The rest of Red Company piled in around us, strapping themselves into the seats as the big vehicle lurched into gear. The ride was bumpy and uncomfortable, but we were used to it by now.

We made our way across the Martian landscape, and we could see the towering peak of Olympus Mons looming in the distance. It was a breathtaking sight, but it looked like a ballbuster of a mountain to climb.

Climbing a relatively gentle slope took all day. After camping for the night and finding a cache of fresh oxygen and batteries that someone had left for us, we finally arrived at the training site.

The Martian sky above was a deep, rusty red hue. The sun appeared as a small, distant ball of light, casting a weak, orange glow over the surrounding terrain. The edge of a cliff was nearby, and it was alarmingly easy to fall off it. Nudging myself up to the cliff, I found it was the rim of what amounted to a sub-crater.

Down below I could see an almost endless desolate landscape stretching out to the limits of my vision. The reddish-brown Martian soil was barren and dotted with the occasional large rock formations, with hints of dust blowing in the thin air.

The sheer drop-off of the cliff itself was intimidating, but we knew we had to conquer our fears and learn the techniques necessary to survive in this harsh environment. Over the next few days, we practiced repelling down the mountainside, using our low-gravity training to our advantage. We were only given so many minutes to reach the bottom and scale our way back up to the top. It was tough going, but we all managed to pull through and meet our required timing. In the end, we emerged stronger and more confident—but that's when the real trials began.

"All right, losers," Sergeant Cox boomed in our helmets. "Now, we're racing against each other. All you privates, line up on the rim. We're employing the buddy-system, and your team will be competing. The first team to make it down and back to the top wins an early stripe."

That got our attention. We'd been offered jack-squat in the way of promotions so far in Red Company, as the current recruits weren't considered to be eligible for a second stripe until we were fully trained and certified as marines. Up until this camp had begun, I'd never received any of the ground-based training required. Many of the physical skills could only be demonstrated under the gravitational pull of a real planet.

"Hey, Sarge?" Private Ledbetter asked. "Does that mean I might become a corporal? Is that even legal?"

"That's what I said. This isn't your granddaddy's Earth-Gov service, Ledbetter. We're under corporate rules here. The conglomerate approves ranks on the basis of performance, not just time served."

Ledbetter came to me, his eyes big with excitement. "You and me, man," he said. "Let's make a team and win this thing."

"Deal," I said without argument or concern. I knew Ledbetter was one of the best out here.

"Hold on, hold on," Sergeant Cox said, walking among us. He pointed at me and Ledbetter. "You two ringers are planning to team up, aren't you? Well, I'm changing the rules. Each of you boys has to pick a date from that pile of sad-sacks over there." He pointed at the newest recruits, the losers we'd just picked up from Mars City.

There was a general groan and a lot of grumbling from guys like Ledbetter and me, but we obeyed him. Walking along the line, I picked the recruit who had fallen off the carryall back when we'd just started out. His name was Desai, and he looked as happy as a stray dog with a new owner when I lifted a finger in his direction.

"Come on, Desai," I said. "Let's earn another stripe."

Ledbetter's attitude had changed dramatically now that I was the competition. He moved away and chose a female recruit who'd shown promise. He sneered at my choice.

"You took Desai, huh?" he laughed. "That loser would fall off a toilet seat."

He seemed to think this comment was uproariously funny, but I ignored him. "All right, Desai," I said. "No fuck-ups today, okay?"

"I'm on it! I'm on it! We're going to win this!"

"Okay, okay. Settle down. Let's do an equipment check, and—"

A loud whistle sounded, blasting my ears and making me wince.

"Everyone is teamed up!" Sergeant Cox boomed. "This thing is on. First team to make it to the bottom and back up again wins the prize—and yes, suiting up and getting organized—that's all part of the drill. Do you think you're going to have all day to do your hair when you're on deployment and performing a real mission? Go, go, go!"

I had to grab onto Desai just to keep him from throwing himself off the cliff, he was so eager. I had to wonder what kind of sewer-dwelling life he'd left behind under the Mars dome to be so motivated. "Hold on a frigging second, Desai. Anchor this bolt!"

He followed my instructions and soon we were ready for the descent. I sent him down first—I could barely hold him back.

We were supposed to stay together, but he was taking wild jumps downward. Swiveling my helmeted head, I took stock of the competition. We were already in third place, by my estimates, which put us in the middle of the pack.

"Steady, steady," I told Desai, but he didn't really listen to me. "Even jumps, don't try to hot-dog it a hundred yards down with one leap. If you slip, you'll crack your faceplate."

"We're going to win this, Starn," he told me, grunting with effort. "I was born on Mars. This gravity feels perfect to me. I know how far I can jump."

Shaking my head, I followed him steadily, but he kept getting farther ahead. We were supposed to stay more or less together, but he took it to the limits of our anchored lines with every bound.

He was, I had to admit, encouraging me to take greater risks and longer jumps. Each time I threw myself away from the cliff face, aiming my boots toward yet another distant jutting spur of rock below, I felt an exhilarating thrill.

Back on Earth, these jumps would have been deadly. The lower gravity was giving us super-powers—but it felt strange to me all the same.

In the end, Desai made it to the bottom in second place—just moments behind Ledbetter.

"That's a good touch," Sergeant Cox said. He was monitoring our progress through the eyes of a drone that was buzzing around watching us. Naturally, he wasn't hopping up and down these cliffs like a demented jackrabbit, he was standing up on top of the rock formation relaxing and no doubt enjoying our efforts.

Desai reversed directions and began climbing again the instant his landing was accepted. "Come on, Starn!" he laughed. "You're slowing me down!"

Muttering a few choice words, I reached the bottom and touched base, then began the climb back up to the top.

Climbing wasn't anywhere near as much fun. Instead of jumping with a safety-line paying out, we had to use that same line and good old-fashioned muscles to force our bodies upward.

But again, it wasn't about sheer strength. If it had been, I would have won this contest easily. The cables we'd left behind, anchored by bolts shot into the rock, were being sucked back into our climbing harnesses. Motors in each harness whirred, spooling up the line as we climbed. At each point where we'd anchored ourselves on the way down, we had to disconnect and then climb up to the next spot.

Of course, there were obstacles in our path along the way. Desai was sending crumbling showers of pebbles and dirt into my face as I caught up to him.

Grunting and straining, he reached the seventh bolt and paused to catch his breath. "You're doing good, man," I called out to him. "Don't give up on me now. We're winning this thing."

And it was true, we were winning. Looking off to either side, I saw struggling forms—but they were all farther down the cliff than we were. Desai's mad dash to the bottom had put us in the lead.

But now, things were different. Desai was running out of steam. He'd exerted himself so much, like a sprinter in a marathon, that he was puffing and probably hyperventilating.

"Just catch your breath," I said, climbing after him at a slower but much more maintainable rate. "We'll get there."

"We're going to be first," he said. His voice was raspy.

Then, he did something that wasn't in the playbook. Instead of pulling his way up with his arms, he threw himself outward, into open space. Then he hit the rewind button on his harness, and he held it down.

Swinging out there in the open, a good five yards away from the rock wall, he was drawn up quickly without using his arms at all.

"What the fuck—?" I began, but before I could finish the words, Desai was already crashing into the cliff.

He didn't stop there, however. He kicked off again, throwing himself far from the rock wall and let his harness do all the work, whirring as it spooled the line back into itself and pulling him upward at a surprising rate.

This wasn't how we'd been trained to do this exercise, but I had to admit—it was working. I followed along, using my old-fashioned technique. Desai was shooting up the cliff, leading me now by a hundred yards or so.

I was lagging, but I knew it didn't matter much. If he reached the summit first, he could haul me up to his position with relative ease.

Beginning to think I'd bet on a dark horse that was going to pay off big, I began to grin inside my helmet.

Right about then, though—I heard it. There was a snap, and shout—then I looked up, and something was falling—something big.

The dark shape of Desai was tumbling down the cliff face, directly at me. His arms pinwheeled, and he tumbled, out of control and flailing.

When I first realized Desai was falling, I couldn't believe it. But then, that moment passed, and I tried to save him.

I reached out an arm that was one of the strongest on the red planet. I reached out, and I tried to grab onto his flailing, spinning body.

I couldn't do it. Even though we were on Mars, where the terminal velocity of a falling body was quite a bit lower than it was on Earth, I couldn't stop his fall. All I managed to do was slap him as he went by.

My gloved hand touched his foot, then his hand—but I couldn't get a grip on either. A tangle of cord came down after that, and I managed to get my glove hooked onto that.

My arm was wrenched terribly. Desai, who had been spinning out of control, slammed into the cliff. He was limp now, but I didn't have time to worry about that.

Instead, I grunted with effort as I called in the accident and requested help. I was dragged upward by Sergeant Cox himself. The man never seemed to stop cursing the entirety of the following seven minutes that it took to get me and Desai to the top.

He glowered at me as I levered myself onto the edge of the drop and lay there, panting. Desai lay beside me, but I didn't have anything left in me to worry about him. I was utterly exhausted.

"Corpsman!" Cox shouted. "Check on that idiot over there." Then, he loomed over me, his eyes staring into mine. "What kind of a fool stunt was that, Starn?" he demanded.

"Desai... he wanted to win..."

"I know that, you idiot! Every man here wants to win! That doesn't mean you ignore all the—"

"Sarge!"

It was Corporal Tench, and he looked worried. "This man isn't responding, sir! We need real medical help, pronto!"

Sergeant Cox left me struggling to rise. I walked over to Desai, checking on him in concern.

I think I was the first one to see it. There was a crack in his helmet. He'd lost air pressure—and heat.

The average daytime temperature on Mars was still subzero, even with all our efforts to change that. Worse, far worse, were the oxygen levels. When we'd started our terraforming efforts, there had been less than one percent oxygen on Mars. Now, we'd gotten it up to two percent—but that wasn't much.

All the rejuvenation efforts on this planet had been to raise the carbon dioxide levels first. Plants breathe CO_2, just as humans and animals do oxygen. Oxygen was a byproduct of normal plant life. The essential terraforming plan, as I understood it, was to get the CO_2 level up, then grow plants, which would in turn produce the oxygen we needed.

All that hadn't happened yet. It was a bit warmer, sure, and there was more air pressure than there had been—but it wasn't enough for anything as big and needy as a human to survive. The air was so thin, it would have been infinitely easier to breathe on top of Mt. Everest. That fact, combined with the cold and the lack of oxygen in the atmosphere meant we had to have spacesuits to survive for more than few minutes.

Desai had been exposed to the harsh clime of Mars, the planet of his birth. It was killing him—or maybe it already had.

"I got him up here as fast as I could," I said, stooping over Desai and trying to help.

"Get away, you've done enough!" Corporal Tench growled, shoving at my groping gloves.

He worked on Desai for several minutes. He didn't give up, I had to give him that. He patched the recruit's suit and pumped in fresh air and heat—but Desai didn't respond.

An emergency team showed up ten minutes later. They shocked the body and used special gear to force oxygen into the lungs—but it was all for nothing.

Private Desai was dead.

In the end, no one got the stripe we'd been competing for. Private Ledbetter dared to ask about it, since his team was the first to reach the top intact—but he was rebuffed.

We returned to base camp in a glum mood. Commander Kaine himself came out from the spaceport that night, but he didn't come to console us.

Instead, he walked in front of our ragged line of weary trainees, fuming and reviewing vids of the action.

"This is entirely unacceptable... Sergeant Cox?"

"Yessir!"

"When did you give these soldiers permission to let go of the cliff face and use their harnesses on an emergency basis?" The flopping computer scroll Commander Kaine held in his hands was shaking. On the display side of the scroll, you could see Desai jumping around like a maniac.

"I didn't give anyone any such permission, sir," Cox responded.

Kaine set his jawline firmly. He turned on one heel to face the squad again. "Who was Desai's partner?"

With a heavy heart, I raised my hand.

"Starn...?" he said, nodding to himself. "I might have known. I hope you're happy, Starn. You've killed one of our greenest recruits."

"I didn't tell him to do it, sir," I protested. "I—"

He walked toward me with aggressive, angry steps. He shook the computer scroll in my face. "I didn't hear you telling him to stop either, did I?"

I shook my head. "No, sir. We have the same rank. I could give him some advice, but I couldn't give him an order if I tried."

Commander Kaine squinted at me. "You're a cold one, aren't you, Starn? I can't believe you'd try to suggest you deserve a promotion on a dark day like this one."

"No, sir! I didn't mean—"

"Next time a junior man breaks with safety regulations during an exercise, try harder to stop him. Dismissed. You're all dismissed!"

The meeting broke up. Afterward, Private Ledbetter came to talk to me personally. "It wasn't your fault, man," he said. "You did say something. Desai was crazy to win, that's all."

I nodded, happy that at least some of the squad saw things my way. But the truth was, it didn't matter what any of the enlisted men thought. The officers were blaming me. It was bullshit, of course, but there wasn't anything I could do. I'd just have to keep my head down and try harder.

We held a ceremony and shipped the remains back to Mars Colony. Corporal Tench personally stripped Desai's spacesuit off and brought it to me.

"Here. You clean out this suit for the next guy. This is all your fault, anyway."

The words stung, and I felt my face flush with anger. I knew Tench was wrong, and I wasn't about to let him get away with it.

"It's not my fault," I said, my voice hard-edged. "I did what I could to save him, and you did what you could to bring him back. Desai pushed things too hard, and he paid the price."

Tench's face was ugly and full of lines. He stepped closer to me. "That's not good enough," he said. "We're all responsible for the safety of our comrades, and that includes you. If you can't handle that, then you should get out now."

My fists were clenching and unclenching. I wanted to hit him, to make him understand what I was feeling. But I knew I couldn't. Maybe that was what he wanted. Maybe he *wanted* a chance to get me thrown into the stockade.

I just stood there, my anger slowly fading away as I looked out at the red Martian desert. I knew that Desai had given his life for a chance at proving himself to Red Company. I figured I could take a ration of shit for the same goal.

Corporal Tench straightened. "No response, huh?" he said in a more normal tone. "That's good… This whole cocked-up show today was a learning exercise for everyone, in the end. We must stick to regs—but some of us will probably die anyway. The company suits have big plans for this outfit, Starn. I'm glad to see one training death wasn't enough to get you to quit."

Tench walked away then, and I gazed after him in some confusion. Had he been testing me? Had he been trying to get me to throw a punch the entire time? I wasn't sure.

But I was sure Tench was right about one thing: the suits were cooking up something awful for Red Company. I'd been there while the captain had evaded her fate of being liquidated. From long experience, I knew it was going to take more than that to keep our masters happy. They wanted profit, and they were willing to risk all our lives to get it.

Chapter 16: A New Mission

You would have thought that after the death of one of our fellow soldiers during the training mission, they would give us a day off—but you would have thought wrong. In fact, if anything, I think they were working us harder after the accident than they had before.

The day after Desai's death, we were sent out into the red desert for a live-fire exercise. Fortunately, we weren't shooting at each other, but rather at moving targets. These turned out to be drones, robots that could walk and act like humans.

They fired back at us, but their shots were low powered. They were just enough to score hits. Our mission as Red Company was to destroy all the robots without losing too many of our own men. This proved harder than it would seem.

"Starn, what are you doing hiding behind that rock? Damn you, boy!" It was Corporal Tench. He still had it in for me. He still seemed to blame me, to some degree, for the death of Desai.

Was that because his own efforts had failed to bring him back to life? I didn't know. I hadn't even known that Tench possessed a reasonable amount of basic medical training, enough to call himself a corpsman in our group.

As full of surprises as ever, Corporal Tench appeared behind me and kicked me one in the rump. With Mars and its low gravity, this was a bigger deal than it might sound like. In fact, my butt was lifted up higher than my helmet for nearly a full second.

Uproarious laughter sounded all along the line of men who were, like me, hiding behind boulders and firing at the robots.

I got the last laugh, however. Corporal Tench had to stand tall in order to kick me—and that was a mistake. The robots, seeing a target that was higher than the level of the boulders themselves, lined him up and fired.

He was lit up redder than a baboon's ass, and a second wave of laughter ran through my comrades. I grinned a bit, pretending I'd planned the whole thing—but then all levity vanished.

"They're charging us!"

I think it was the fact that we'd been distracted, and therefore we'd paused in our counter-fire. That had kept the robots ducking. Now, their software had sensed an opportunity.

A crowd of spindly forms, things that looked like assemblages of towel racks and coat hangers, came rushing toward us. None of them had heads, which I thought was rather disturbing. Instead, they had cameras all around their trunks. I wouldn't call them torsos, not exactly, because they were round and cylindrical, like a trashcan or a fire hydrant. Each of these trunks boasted an array of cameras aimed in every direction. Their positioning was static and the cameras didn't swivel independently. Instead, they provided the robots with a 360-degree view of everything around them, like the eyes of a spider.

These robots, with their strange alien eyes, all charged us as a group. They were coming to finish us off.

"Don't just sit there, shoot them down!" Sergeant Cox boomed, his voice resounding in our helmets.

One advantage the noncoms had was the ability to increase the volume that they projected to all the men under their command at will. Both Sergeant Cox and Corporal Tench tended to overuse this feature, in my opinion.

Despite my complaints and misgivings, their techniques certainly worked. Everyone's attention turned back to the charging robots. We fired at them, and as they drew closer, our carbines became more effective.

I held down the trigger and sprayed at three of them that approached my boulder, taking hits to my shoulder and helmet.

I kept firing, and in the end, I killed all three of the robots. Two more of our men in the squad succumbed to the robots' efforts, but all the robots were marked as dead.

Sergeant Cox checked our scores, stopping in front of me and frowning. He informed me that I hadn't been killed in the exercise, but I had been hit, and I'd kept fighting as if I wasn't touched. He said we would have to change things up for me next time, and an injury-simulator software should have been turned on.

Corporal Tench, who had been pretending to be dead, got a kick in the ribs from Sergeant Cox for causing the earlier distraction that had caused the robots to charge in the first place. Seeing that did my heart some good. It was usually Tench who was doing the kicking.

Cox then called an end to the exercise and ordered Tench to load the robots into the carryalls. "We've got new orders. We're moving out in ten. You're riding on the back bumper on the way home, Tench."

The corporal scowled as he asked the question that was on everyone's mind: "New orders, Sarge? What new orders?"

Sergeant Cox looked at us, his face unreadable. "We're supposed to return to Mars City immediately," he said, his voice firm. "These exercises are at an end."

A wave of relief washed over the group. We'd been running around in spacesuits in the Martian desert for weeks, and we were all eager to get back to civilization.

As we climbed into the transport vehicle, Sarge frowned at me.

"Why do I always see you in here, Starn? There are better men like Ledbetter out there holding onto the running board."

"I climbed into the cab first," I replied, grinning.

Sarge nodded his head in approval. "All right, that's a good enough reason."

"Can I ask a question, Sarge?"

"What do you want?"

I hesitated for a moment before speaking. "I want to know if my basic training will be considered complete after this exercise. If even though we didn't finish out the entire three weeks we were supposed to."

Sarge frowned as he considered the request. He checked his computer scrolls and then made a few signatures. "I'll pass this on up to the lieutenant and then the commander," he said. "I think I can get a waiver for everyone."

As we rode back to Mars City Dome, I reflected on what I'd learned during the training exercises. I'd gained a newfound respect for my fellow Marines and learned a lot about teamwork and survival in extreme conditions.

Feeling emboldened, he decided to ask Sarge another question. "About those robots that we fought. They were pretty good at their job. Why doesn't *Borag* just buy a pack of those things instead of hiring guys like us and training us?"

Sergeant Cox grinned. "I'll tell you why. It's because of that prick, Blackwood. He did all the math and figured out one simple thing—we're cheaper. That's why you're here, boy, and you should be glad of it."

I sat back and thought about that for nearly an hour. Was I really cheaper than a decent combat robot? That was grim tidings indeed. I hoped against hope that I would never have to face a real robot enemy unit armed with full-powered weapons. Expensive or not, they did a pretty good job of killing Marines. What was worse was they had very little fear and would do anything necessary to achieve their mission goals, even if it meant essentially committing suicide to win a battle.

These disturbing thoughts weighed heavily on my mind as I passed out and took a nap, bouncing around on those big balloon tires all the way back to the Mars City Dome.

As it turned out, we weren't just called back to the Mars dome. We were hustled directly to the elevator station, which we promptly rode up to the spaceport. By the time we got there, it was after midnight, but no one was allowed to go to any bars or take any R&R. Instead, we were all hustled directly to *Borag's* docking station. There, one at a time, we wriggled through a tube onto our hulking ship.

The mining rig was quiet, and homey. I was grumbling, yawning, and heartsick. We were told we would get a briefing in the morning and ordered to our bunks.

Morning came all too soon. At approximately 0500 hours, we were awakened by klaxons and bells. We pulled ourselves together within a few minutes, mercifully allowed to piss and spit, but we weren't given food or showers. Instead, we were hustled to the meeting room, where the rest of Red Company was waiting.

Then more people showed up. Green Company piled up at the back of the room. All the foremen and shore patrolmen were there. Pretty much everybody who toted a shock rod and possibly a laser pistol, rather than an automatic laser carbine that was truly meant to kill.

When everyone was assembled, Commander Kaine appeared at the front of the room and turned the entire wall behind him into a display.

"Marines and security personnel," he said, "This is a special emergency briefing to bring you up to speed on what we're about to undertake. Everybody shut up and listen tight. Captain Hansen is coming on-screen in a moment."

Sure enough, there she was, standing larger than life on the back wall. The background behind her included the bridge and her numerous officers. She tilted her head, acknowledging Commander Kaine and then turned toward us.

Borag's top officer had always possessed a commanding presence. She stood tall and proud. Her hair was pulled back in a tight bun, and her piercing eyes seemed to gaze out into the infinite depths of space. She wore a sharp, black uniform with gleaming brass buttons and a matching black cap. Her stance was firm, with her legs slightly apart and her hands clasped behind her back, giving her an air of confidence and authority.

"Loyal fighting men of *Borag*," she began, "I'm calling this special briefing because all of you are directly involved. Our ship will be leaving port in approximately one hour's time to embark on a special mission."

These words created a murmuring among the troops. The noncoms cuffed men of the ranks, but still, they whispered among themselves.

It was quite a surprise. We'd been scheduled to complete our training and then be given some R&R. Was everything canceled? For my own part, I was particularly disappointed by a new, sick realization. I was going to have zero time to get more acquainted with Freya.

Sure, we might run into each other now and then on the decks of *Borag*, but that just wasn't the same. Oftentimes, people were assigned to opposite shifts, even sleeping while the other one was awake. The romance of Mars colony was going to be left behind, and there was nothing aboard this ship to replace the charming spaceport.

By comparison, *Borag* was cramped, and every inch of the decks tended to be full of hustling crewmen. There were a few taverns and social spots for people to gather during their off time, but they were lackluster at best. I sighed audibly.

Private Ledbetter gave me an elbow in the ribs. "Thinking about that hot little fluff from upstairs?" he asked, speaking in a whisper. "When are you *not* dreaming of romance?"

Unfortunately, his voice wasn't quiet enough. Corporal Tench had been walking nearby, and he kicked the back of one of Ledbetter's knees.

It was naturally the knee that had been supporting all his weight, so he almost went down. Cursing, Ledbetter straightened up and stood at attention again. Corporal Tench didn't even bother to say anything. He just moved on.

Damn, what a tool that guy was.

"And so, you might be wondering," Captain Hansen continued, "just where we're going. The exact location is a secret. How we got the coordinates is also a secret. However, what I can tell you is we're going into space, this time seeking revenge. We lost a number of good Marines and even more Green Company security men when certain disgusting rock-rat pirates attacked our ship. They also cost us a large percentage of our payload. Fortunately, our benefactors, the executives of Interplanetary Excavations, have located these criminals."

That caused a stir. This time, there were even a few cheers and some clapping. For once Sergeant Cox and Corporal Tench didn't react with fury to these outbursts.

Captain Hansen kept on going. "We know where they are, and we're going out to get them."

People cheered even louder.

"You may have noticed that Red Company is now much bigger," Hansen went on.

I looked around, and I saw that she was correct. Before, we'd numbered less than thirty souls. Now, we were close to double that, plus officers and noncoms. It was a significant group, rather than a couple of squads.

Hansen displayed words and images concerning the ship, too. While *Borag* had been in port, she'd been armed with new weaponry. We now had a greater ship-to-ship capacity for self-protection and force extension, as well as a larger troop complement.

"Altogether," the captain summarized, "we are a much more significant force now."

While she was saying all this, I couldn't help but wonder why the hell Earth's actual military wasn't getting involved. Earth possessed some pure military warships. These were rarely seen, especially beyond Mars, but there were always a few cruisers on station in orbit over Earth.

That was one of the reasons the pirates never ventured closer to the Sun than the orbit of Mars. I'd always kind of wondered about that. Why did the larger military units only patrol around our home world? The rest of humanity out at the fringes of the Solar System had to more or less fend for themselves.

I suspected that again, it had to do with cost. Supporting a deep-space warship was extremely expensive—especially if it did nothing else.

A mining ship like *Borag*, on the other hand, served a dual function. Such ships were generally able to turn a small profit. They paid for themselves while simultaneously handling chores such as fighting pirates.

A true cruiser from Earth could never do that. It generated no income, it was purely an expense. Just like in the case of robot troops, the corporations preferred running rigs like *Borag*. They were a cheaper—even self-supporting—method of policing the fringes of the Solar System.

I'd never really thought about such things before. But as the years had gone by, I had had increased exposure to people like accountant Blackwood. I now understood better how humanity had worked out the extreme economic realities of exploring and colonizing deep space.

Captain Hansen continued her briefing, but she didn't really tell us much more of interest. Our exact target was still a secret.

She introduced the new members of Red Company and Green Company, none of whom I cared much about because they weren't the most likely men aboard to kick me in the ass if they didn't like what I was doing. That special distinction still resided with Sergeant Cox and Corporal Tench.

There was, however, one individual whom I took serious note of. His name was Quinn, and he was a lieutenant. He was now in charge of Red Company under Commander Kaine, who was in charge of ship's security overall.

Lt. Quinn was a seasoned space marine veteran with years of experience under his belt. He stood tall and proud, his broad shoulders and muscular build a testament to his rigorous training and combat deployments. His face was chiseled, with a strong jawline and piercing blue eyes that held a hint of bravery. He wore his uniform with pride, every crease and badge perfectly in place, reflecting his discipline and attention to detail. Despite his tough exterior, there was a hint of a smile always lurking at the corners of his mouth. Overall, Quinn exuded confidence and competence.

We were told by the captain that we were to break up into our separate smaller units and continue the briefing. We shuffled out of the ready room and made our way to what turned out to be a converted mess deck. In fact, it wasn't all that converted. The kitchen-patrol, along with a few robots, were just cleaning up from the last meal.

"Marines," Lt. Quinn said, "I'm reorganizing this group into two new squads, one commanded by Sergeant Cox, here. The other will be commanded by me personally. Overall, I would say we're still somewhat understrength, but it will have to do."

Understrength? Red Company had just doubled in size with all this recruitment. What the hell were they expecting us to do?

"In regard to our new mission," Quinn said, "I will say that Sergeant Cox and myself are both experienced and capable men. *Borag* has, in fact, hired many people from other ships, along with buying a few new recruit contracts at the bottom. Now as for the nature of our mission, let me explain the role of ground forces in space. In vacuum, it's relatively easy to blow things up. In general, the easiest thing to do with any enemy target is simply stand off in space and blast it to pieces."

The group chuckled politely, and Lt. Quinn continued when we settled down. "In this case, several things prevent that from being an optimal strategy." Here, he displayed a map behind him, which again was an entire wall converted into a screen. In the center of that screen appeared to be a large asteroid.

"As some of you may have already recognized," he continued. "This asteroid is Vesta."

This caused quite a stir. All asteroids, especially the big round ones, tended to look quite a bit alike. But Vesta was a very significant asteroid among the thousands that swung around the Solar System. It wasn't just a rock, it was a *giant* rock.

The largest of all asteroids in the Solar System was known as Ceres. The second largest was Vesta. In fact, Vesta alone accounted for close to ten percent of the total mass of all the asteroids put together. Only Ceres was bigger, being really a dwarf planet.

Vesta was about 350 miles in diameter, bigger than many of the nations on Earth, while Ceres was approximately 600 miles in diameter.

Lt. Quinn continued to rattle off a lot of facts and figures about Vesta. In the end, what really mattered was that it was a big rock, not just something you could trot across in a few hours. It might take a running man a week to circumnavigate the entire thing.

"There's an enemy base on Vesta," he continued. "This is the home port of the criminals who attacked *Borag* just a couple of months ago, and who have been attacking other mining rigs in the area. Earth-Gov has therefore decided these criminals are a significant and outstanding threat to all commerce in the region. They've grown too big for their britches."

Everyone in the audience was nodding. We all hated pirates, and the idea there was a massive nest of them right out in the open—that was almost intolerable.

"In order to encourage ships like *Borag* to end this threat," Quinn continued, "Earth has seen fit to put a very large bounty on the capture or destruction of every pirate, every ship—and most importantly, their home base itself."

Here he used the laser pointer to tap and waggle on the surface of Vesta. There, in the middle of it all, right where the pointer was aiming, I saw a dark stain on the surface.

As if knowing when my eyes would be drawn, Quinn caused the image to expand. It zoomed in, increasing in resolution until just that one dark splotch filled the entire screen.

"Here we have the enemy base," he said. "Inside this crater, which is ringed with gun turrets and missile batteries, we have a significant pirate's den."

The level of noise in the briefing room was beginning to rise. After seeing the pirate defenses, all of us were questioning the sanity of this "mission" that we'd been given. This was a job for a squadron of cruisers, not for one lone mining rig with a single company of Marines.

"Don't panic, don't panic," Quinn said, lifting his arms high. "No, it's not our job to go out there and kill every pirate in that nest—although I wish we could. Instead, bounties have been placed not just on ships or pirates, not just on the base itself, but on *subsystems* supporting the base, such as this solar energy producing grid over here."

He moved the view so we could see the glinting blue and silver gridwork of the solar panels he was discussing. "Also, there's a water processing plant leeching ice from what is probably an ancient comet strike. That's over here," again he swiveled our point of view sickeningly, sweeping across the rocky surface of Vesta to spot another location.

He went on like that, spotting many supporting locations that were outside the crater itself, but which supplied food, oxygen, water, energy—everything that the pirate base needed to survive.

"Should we be able to destroy just one of these, all of *Borag's* debts shall be wiped out—and that goes for you crewmen as well."

"Whoa!"

We were stunned by this. All of a sudden, we lost our poor attitudes. Shock and dismay transformed into hopeful smiles. Everyone had debts, and no one liked them.

"And that concludes the briefing," Quinn said. "Now, who here is interested in dishing out a little revenge upon these snotty rock-rats, these pirates who dared attack and ruin our financial future just two months ago?"

A cheer went up in the room as we shook our fists in the air and shouted, "Hoorah!"

Lt. Quinn, whatever else you might say about him, was probably the best officer I'd seen aboard *Borag* when it came to the fine art of ginning up troops into a fevered pitch.

Chapter 17: Vesta

As *Borag* jetted across the Solar System toward Vesta, I spent my time training, gaming, goofing off, and trying to figure out a way to have a private moment with Freya.

In this last regard, I was fantastically unsuccessful until one fortunate day when I heard some ship alarms going off and saw her twenty paces down the passageway, headed in my direction.

"Freya?" I called to her. "Hey, what's going on?"

She turned around, bewildered, almost as if she didn't recognize me for a moment. But then her expression softened, and she smiled.

"Oh, hey, Devin," she said. "I'm sorry, I can't talk right now. The captain has called all-hands on the upper decks. I work on the bridge, remember?"

"Yeah, how can I forget? Listen, I haven't seen you for a month…"

"I know, I know. But as soon as this crisis is over, we can..."

"What's the crisis?" I asked.

She stood hesitantly, looking up and down the passageway to see if anyone might be listening. Then she leaned in close, and I could feel her warm breath on my ear as she whispered. "We spotted another ship, Devin."

"You mean a pirate ship?" I shrugged. "I guess it's only to be expected. We're in their territory, after all."

"No, no," she said. "That wouldn't be surprising at all. The unexpected thing is the other ship's sensor signature. It's another mining rig that's shaped just like *Borag*—and that's not even the bad part."

"Tell me," I said.

"It's heading for Vesta, just like we are!"

For a few seconds, we looked at each other. Then what she was telling me began to sink in.

"Are you serious?" I asked, instantly growing angry. "That sounds exactly like Interplanetary Excavations. Let me guess, they put out a general call, they set bounties on the pirates, and now every mining rig in the system is jetting over to Vesta to try to get a piece of the action. Is that what you're telling me?"

She nodded. "We think that's what's going on, yes."

I shook my head. "Great... What's the captain doing about it?"

"Well, right now she's calling me up to the bridge. But in general, we're going to try to beat the competition. We're going to put on the gas. We have to get to Vesta first." With that, she ran off.

Sure enough, acceleration warnings rang out around the ship ten minutes later. The big vessel began to rumble and shake. Normally, once you got up to cruising speed, ships like *Borag* tended not to burn their engines much. This was especially true when approaching an enemy target. The more thrust you applied, the more visible you were, and in space, it was quite easy to spot a spaceship, which looked pretty much like a comet. *Borag* was easy to spot, firing out plume of plasma and exhaust, not to mention creating a large heat signature. While cruising, our ship was pretty much invisible. But when we burned our engines, we were a beacon in space.

Captain Hansen was risking a lot to make it to Vesta first. This seemed alarming and somewhat worrying to me. After all, it was one thing to sneak up on a pirate den on an asteroid and attempt to do some damage. It was quite another to announce your presence. By applying thrust we were giving the pirates a warning—and we were doing it just to beat out another ship that was racing against us for the same prize.

I gave myself a shake, settled into my acceleration couch, and hoped against hope that all would turn out for the best.

Two more days passed. During this time, we were under acceleration for the majority of our waking hours. In fact, there was only a brief break as we felt *Borag* turn around and begin to decelerate when I had a chance to talk to Freya again. The first thing I asked her was what the hell was happening.

She grimaced and told me they'd detected even more ships.

"What?" I said, aghast.

"That's right. Several more mining rigs from all over the Solar System are descending on Vesta. It's like some kind of feeding frenzy."

"Are we going to get there first?"

Freya shook her head. "I don't know, but the captain is no longer worried about stealthing in. She figures that with all these ships coming at them, the pirates must know what's in store."

"That's great," I said. "That's just great. We're going to be marching into a ready enemy armed to the teeth. I'd hoped we were able to sneak up on them."

"Everyone did," she said. "I don't think that's how it's going to happen, now."

Later I passed on this information to Sergeant Cox. He eyed me and nodded. "I've heard things about this. I talked to Lt. Quinn and Commander Kaine. They say the same thing: this is turning into a Charlie-Foxtrot." He slammed a hand down on my shoulder. "One good thing though, at least we aren't the only target out here. The pirates have gotta be running scared."

He walked away, laughing hard. I hoped he was right.

A few days later, our engines cut out, as we had slowed down enough. We slid into orbit behind Vesta. The captain's goal had been to avoid their base with its ring of defensive guns and missiles batteries. If the pirates couldn't get a bead on us, they couldn't strike us and knock out our ship.

As *Borag* approached Vesta, the massive rock came into view, filling every viewscreen aboard the ship. The surface was rough and covered in craters, with large mountains and valleys visible. Streaks of different minerals could be seen on the surface, glinting in the light of the sun. The asteroid's rusty exterior was dotted with light from small deposits of metal. Despite its rugged appearance, there was an undeniable beauty to Vesta as it spun slowly in the emptiness of space.

Borag didn't land, not exactly, but we did get close to the surface of Vesta and skim along for quite a distance.

Corporal Tench fumed about every move the captain made—but he never had the balls to complain to her directly. Instead, he bitched at us about it.

"You, Starn," he said. "You're always up on the upper decks trying to snake your way into every skirt who goes near that bridge."

Hearing this, I frowned at him. He gave me a nasty smile in return.

"Come on, come on," he said. "I know you have a source. What do you think Hansen is doing? Is she as shit-off crazy as it looks?"

I shrugged. "Seems like the captain brought us in close to Vesta, right down to where we're blowing dust around on the surface. Now, she's gliding along, right on the deck, trying to get us closer before she sends Red Company out to go hopping across the asteroid toward our final target, the power plant."

Corporal Tench sneered. "I know all that, you idiot. Anyone with eyes can look out a porthole and see that. But what about loot, huh? Are we going to get a chance to recover any of our lost investment?"

I blinked at him and shook my head. "You mean, all our cargo? I don't know…"

"Useless," he said. "Frigging useless. Hansen won't tell us—did you know that? Not until we've completed our mission, she says. I just want to know if I can get something out of this—something of real value. These bastards owe us, after all. I don't want to run a hundred miles in low gravity for nothing."

When Tench found he couldn't get any more answers out of me, he called me useless again and wandered off. I was annoyed that everyone seemed to know I'd been talking to Freya whenever I could. I didn't want to get her into trouble somehow.

At last, the big ship slowed down and came to a halt, settling on the dusty surface of Vesta. As one might expect, Red Company was already armed, armored, and waiting for our deployment order. We had full oxygen tanks, full batteries, and fully charged laser carbines in our grips.

At last, the big bay doors opened, and we were allowed to rush down the ramps and out onto the bright surface of Vesta. It was kind of a relief.

"Go, go, go!" Lt. Quinn shouted. "Spread out, spread out! We're not expecting sniper fire, but you never know!"

We raced out of *Borag's* lowest passages and bounced away in random directions. We looked like fleas all racing away from a dog in a bathtub.

A few minutes later, we were all deployed and had found cover. There was plenty of shattered rocks, craggy outcroppings, and various scars in the landscape. These included craters and gashes from meteor strikes and close encounters with other asteroids. Vesta was an old world, millions of years old. She'd been pretty badly battered over the eons, and it showed.

Once we were all on foot and at a safe distance, *Borag* lifted off again and soared back the way she had come, leaving us behind.

"We're totally screwed," Ledbetter said.

"Belay that shit, Private!" Sergeant Cox shouted. "*Borag's* not abandoning us, they're helping us out. If they sat here with their hot jets idling, there's certain to be drone spy or another pirate ship out here looking for us. You want them to spot us right off? Believe me, it's best that *Borag* doesn't pinpoint the exact spot where we were inserted into this combat zone. You *never* want that, boys. Don't forget it."

I supposed Cox was right, even if it did sound like happy horseshit. We'd been dumped on a sunbaked, airless rock, sure—but it had been done with the best of intentions. That's what really mattered, wasn't it?

My squad moved out, and I got to my feet and bounced away. We moved in a loose formation across the landscape. According to my helmet's geo-mapping, we were making a beeline directly toward the crater where the pirate base was located.

We weren't even going to attempt to break into that crater. Instead, we were here on an advanced mission to soften up this enemy fortress. We were going to knock out their power—or die trying.

Our communications were set to stealth mode, meaning only weakest and shortest-range of radio signals were in use. Our helmets only worked in line of sight and only within a very limited radius. In addition, the signals were scrambled, so that anyone else listening in on our channel would hear nothing but background static. The kind of signals that sound like cosmic rays from a distance, or maybe the weird noises that a quasar made if you aimed the radar dish in that direction. We were, in fact, as quiet and secretive as we could be, moving in squads separated by a good distance, just in case one of us was taken out.

Several long, difficult hours passed as we crossed a few canyons, a few mountain ridges, and more than our share of blast craters. All these locations marked where, perhaps millions of years ago, Vesta had been struck by another rock like her and had survived.

After approximately three hours of marching, we reached the terminator line for Vesta, which was moving at a visible pace. At this point, the sunlight from Earth's primary star, Old Sol, ceased hitting Vesta, and we continued trotting into sudden darkness.

It was pitch black except for the distant, frozen points of stars above us. We avoided using our suit lights as much as possible, only giving off the slightest glow to see what our boots would be stepping on next. We didn't want to accidentally walk into a ravine or a jagged rock formation.

As stealthily and quickly as possible, we crept up on the pirate base under the cover of night. We were almost there, about three miles from the solar-powered station, when the quiet night was suddenly illuminated with blazing streaks of energy.

Screams soon followed. We had been ambushed.

Chapter 18: Battle in Darkness

Red Company had walked right into an ambush. Fire was coming from seemingly every direction.

"Take cover!" I heard Sergeant Cox call over our radios. "Turn on your night vision gear and return fire!"

We had been equipped with light-gathering optics, but as they cost quite a bit of suit power over time, we hadn't been running them until now.

The rocky, airless, moon-like surface of Vesta appeared before me. I could see the flashing heat rays being fired in our direction, explosions flared white off to my right—so I dodged left.

I dashed into a scar on the surface of the asteroid, then tumbled and crawled my way behind a boulder. A stuttering spray of beams seemed to follow me, but it didn't quite catch my fleeing ankles and knees as I pulled them back behind the rock and under cover.

Other soldiers were not so lucky. I could tell by their howls of pain and anguish.

"My suit's ripped. I'm losing air!" Padgett shouted.

Sergeant Cox responded, but soon Padgett's line was squelched. I could tell that the sergeant had tuned him out for all of us. None of us could hear him dying and pleading for help.

It seemed like a grim fate to suffer after all this marching across barren rock—to have your comrades tune you out when you had fallen to the ground, but I knew Cox had done it for a reason. If we were all hearing one man howl and complain about his injuries, we certainly couldn't think or coordinate our plan of attack.

"Okay everybody, on my mark. Up and return fire—now!" Cox ordered.

We did as we were ordered, and I saw that across the way, perhaps two hundred yards to our left 2nd Squad led by Lt. Quinn had done the same. It seemed like Quinn himself was directly commanding that squadron, and they were already hosing down our ambushers from an oblique angle.

Caught in a crossfire our attackers, who seemed to number fewer than we, melted back from the rocks. They stopped firing, then disappeared—and we dared to advance.

When we reached their position, we found it was empty. They'd left one man behind, already frozen in death on the unforgiving rocks, but the rest of them had retreated.

Sergeant Cox cursed for a long time. "They're falling back to set up another ambush position, I'd bet my left nut on it."

No one took his bet. We kept advancing, but much more cautiously, much more slowly. We were too paranoid to race ahead, taking flying leaps like kangaroos in the low gravity.

Over the next hour, we were ambushed twice more. Each time we killed one or two of the ambushers, and then as they fell back, we advanced.

By the time we got into sight of the solar panel array that we'd come all this way to destroy, we had lost nine good men. Not all of them were dead, but all of them were essentially out of the fight. Most were incapacitated, lying behind us somewhere in an alcove of rock, hoping against hope that rescue and medical aid would come eventually.

It was when we came within sight of the actual solar array, however, that our greatest shock and dismay occurred.

"It's wrecked already!" Sergeant Cox shouted. "I can't fucking believe this!"

It was true. The solar array was a smoldering mess. It looked like a vast sea of black panels, each one angled toward the sun to absorb as much energy as possible. The panels covered the surface in every direction as far as the eye could see, making it look like a massive, gleaming quilt.

The panels were mounted on tall, sturdy struts that rose up from the asteroid's surface, tilted toward the distant sky. In daylight, the sun's rays would have made the panels sparkle and shine, adding to the overall impression of a massive, well-oiled machine.

Now, however, the light we saw came from burning gases. The cooling systems were venting, having been shot full of holes. Many of the struts the panels had been mounted upon were broken as well. The whole installation had been wrecked and torn apart, no doubt by explosive charges like the ones we were carrying to do the job.

"Fuck…" Sergeant Cox repeated.

Lt. Quinn's voice crackled into our ears. "It appears someone beat us to the punch. The pirates that ambushed our forces must have slowed us down sufficiently for another group—probably from a different mining rig—to have reached this destination and destroyed it ahead of us."

"Take pictures, anyway," someone suggested. "Record it like we did it to file with Earth-Gov!"

"Sadly," Quinn responded, "that won't work. I'm sure the team that performed this demolition has already transmitted proof of their success into space and beamed it back to Earth. The perpetrators are no doubt celebrating right now on their way back to their own extraction zone… speaking of which, it's time for us to do an about-face and return to *Borag*."

Sergeant Cox took over from there. "All right, you heard the man. Make sure you pick up the wounded and the dead as we go. Leave no one behind on this shitty rock. The least we can do is make sure the pirates don't know who hit them."

We grumbled, cursed, raged and shook our fists at the glowing stars overhead. All of this had been for nothing. Nine men dead or seriously injured—and no profit at all.

I had to admit, my morale was pretty low when we dragged ourselves aboard the waiting ramps of *Borag* some hours later. At least Captain Hansen had returned to gather us up. She hadn't abandoned us here on this deadly rock.

After our mission failed, no one blamed it on me or any other member of Red Company. In fact, Captain Hansen came down personally and gave each of us a supportive lecture, something that amounted to a pat on the head, but it was better than nothing.

"Men, you did your part of this mission. If anyone failed us, it was me, not you."

We were shocked. This was not the kind of admission that we expected from our superiors.

Accountant Blackwood stood in Captain Hansen's wake, and he looked very distressed indeed. If we'd been worth a bounty, he would have blown us all up instead of that solar array that we'd failed to get to first.

But he said nothing. He only glowered in stony silence. His glaring eyes told us of his real feelings.

Finally, when the captain left, we turned to grumble to one another.

"I wonder if that big, tall freak sold us out," Sergeant Cox said.

"Sergeant? Belay that," Lt. Quinn bellowed. He'd overheard the sergeant's remark—and he clearly didn't like it.

"Sorry, sir," Cox mumbled. "Won't happen again, sir."

Although we all knew he didn't mean it, Quinn nodded. "No criticism of any officer on this ship is acceptable on my watch, Sergeant."

Quinn looked around the room and realized how low our spirits were. He decided to make a speech of sorts.

"Yes," he said, "the mission did ultimately fail, but only because we weren't the first to reach the target. We were ready and able—someone else simply beat us to it. That's the fault of no one here, except possibly dumb luck, because we ran into the ambushing defenders—and they didn't. I don't see how it was avoidable. If anyone's at fault, it was the company official who organized this Easter egg hunt, sending all of us for the same thing at the same time. They could have done a better job of coordinating our interaction."

I had to agree with Quinn on this one. If they'd simply given us all a different target with a different bounty—but never mind. They did what they did and operated the way they wanted to. They had little respect for independent mining rigs like *Borag*. To them, we were essentially mercenary companies. If they paid us or not, if we died or not—they didn't much care.

"But aboard this ship at least, we must hold together and not turn on one another when things go wrong," Quinn continued.

I glanced toward Corporal Tench, who was the worst offender when it came to blaming others. He tended to blame me in particular when anything went wrong.

This time was different, however. Tench was staring directly at Lt. Quinn, as if he thought it was all the officer's fault. Maybe he did.

After that, the return journey to Mars was a long one. I was somewhat surprised when we didn't go out and attempt to find a new mining spot. Why not at least drag home a few kilotons of titanium or something while we were out here?

Maybe it was too dangerous, or maybe Captain Hansen had bigger ideas in mind. Whatever the case, a month later, we returned to the spaceport orbiting above the Mars colony. We docked and waited, but no one released us from the ship.

Finally, a strange call came through. First Sergeant Cox got it, and he leaned forward to whisper to Corporal Tench, who shot a stare at me.

A moment later, there was a finger pointing in my direction.

"What's the matter, Sarge?" I said.

"You've been summoned," he said. "You're to report to the docking port. Get your ass in gear, Starn."

This evoked catcalls, and a few ankles snaked out to trip me. Having dealt with this sort of thing before, I made a point of slamming my foot into anyone's shin who dared to impede my progress. This action was met with howls of pain and dismay. Pretending to feel nothing, I continued on my way as their feet were withdrawn rapidly and rubbed in pain.

I grabbed my full kit and tried to move quickly through the passageways to the docking ports. There, to my surprise, I saw Captain Hansen, Blackwood, and a couple of other officers from the bridge.

"Private Starn," Hansen said. "Is there anyone else in Red Company that you trust—completely?"

"Sure, sir," I said. "Most of them are good boys. They'd die for you or me."

Blackwood snorted derisively. "There isn't time for anyone else to join us," he said. "The memo required an immediate response. We must go now, ma'am."

"All right, dammit." Twisting her lips, Captain Hansen banged a fist on the airlock doors until they opened.

We left the ship and walked through the spaceport, receiving numerous strange glances from the people who worked there. No one approached us or addressed us directly.

We marched to the space elevator station. The floating disk thankfully didn't take long to arrive and allowed us to board without difficulty. Soon, we performed the gravity-switch trick and were dropping rapidly toward the surface. Mars Colony was spread out below us, and grew slowly in size as we moved ever closer.

On the long ride down from orbit, the captain, Accountant Blackwood, and a couple of other henchmen stood together in a tight huddle. They whispered to one another and seemed to be in disagreement.

I ignored this as it was difficult to hear them anyway. I didn't really care what they were talking about. My job was to stand guard, so I took that seriously. After all, I'd been attacked the last time I was the sole guard for Captain Hansen.

Maybe she had good reasons to ask questions about whose loyalty levels were the highest. She wasn't taking bodyguards everywhere she went for nothing. I wasn't an experienced man when it came to corporate affairs, but it did seem to me that when you spent a lot of money and didn't make enough profit to repay that money—well, your life might be in jeopardy.

Looking back, I recalled that the first time we were docked at the Mars Colony, we'd been accosted by a pack of thugs carrying pipes in the middle of an otherwise quiet district. Had that been a matter of random chance?

My mind cast back to that day. I remembered that Blackwood himself, the ship's accountant, had made an excuse to disappear right before the attack had occurred.

Was that sheer coincidence? Quite possibly, but now that we had returned to Mars under similar circumstances, I felt myself growing increasingly paranoid.

We certainly had rivals—all those ships that had raced with us toward Vesta, for starters. They weren't fully on our side. Sure, they hadn't fired upon *Borag*, and none of our Marines had shot up their Marines—but we were definitely in direct competition.

That seemed odd to me, but I was still learning my way through the wild west of the outer Solar System. I wasn't yet an experienced hand.

Eventually, the space elevator came to a rest on Mars without further incident. We stepped out of the doors and made our way through the city to the same large building in midtown that we had visited before.

There, as I followed in their wake, Captain Hansen and Blackwood met with the execs. The company controller was there, along with his staff in their expensive nanofiber suits and fine, decorative electronics. Their faces were lit up by tiny holograms, displaying screens that only they could see, beamed directly to their retinas.

"She's all yours, Colonel," the controller said, and he walked out of the room, taking his whole entourage with him.

One man stayed behind. He was a tall, stern-looking fellow with a large mustache. He wore a uniform I recognized in an instant—he was from Earth-Gov.

Captain Hansen took a few steps forward, nodding to the colonel who nodded to her in return. Neither saluted the other, as they were essentially in different military organizations.

"Do you know who I am, Captain Hansen?" the colonel asked.

"No, sir," she replied. "I'm afraid I don't."

"I am from Earth-Gov, and I oversee the conglomerate that has the misfortune of owning your contract."

"My contract?"

The colonel made a dismissive gesture. "The *Borag* contract, the contract that guides the value of your ship and crew. Interplanetary Excavations has made a poor investment in your case—but I'm here seeking a way to turn things around."

Captain Hansen frowned. Blackwood looked positively white.

"What do you propose?" she asked.

The colonel sucked in a deep breath and let it out slowly. "There's no easy way to put this—our AI is recommending liquidation."

Blackwood made an odd sound, as if he'd swallowed a bug or something.

"Do you have a better proposition?" Hansen asked him.

He nodded.

"Well, let's hear it, man. We'd rather not be liquidated."

The colonel inclined his head. "No excuses? No accusations? This is good news. I like it when I find myself facing a competent person under these difficult circumstances. Yes, you've failed the conglomerate—but your attitude gives me hope."

Hansen blinked slowly, but she said nothing. Her face was more or less expressionless.

The colonel nodded again. "I was told that you are actually a competent officer. Your recent record does not reflect this, but we would like to give your outfit another opportunity—perhaps the fourth such in a row—to turn a profit."

"I'm all ears, sir," Hansen said. "*Borag* is at your disposal."

"Indeed, she is," the colonel said. "In fact, we've been considering disposing of your ship right before you got to this meeting."

Blackwood squirmed, but Hansen stayed cool. Neither of them spoke.

"Here's my proposal," the colonel said. "We will resupply your ship and replace the manpower you've lost. In addition, we'll pay each of you, every officer aboard your ship, a bonus in advance."

Hansen's jaw dropped open slightly. She hadn't expected anything like this level of generosity. "We… thank you, in the extreme," she said. "However, I'm forced to ask, what is the heinous nature of the mission you're asking us to perform?"

"Let me explain. You and your ship, *Borag*, are not the only failures on our balance sheets. There are, in fact, a number of others. Some of these," the Colonel continued, "we've already sent on the mission that you're about to embark upon, should you choose not to be liquidated."

He smiled at this point, as if the thought of us choosing to be liquidated was absurd—which in fact, it was. No one wanted to be sold off to recover a debt. I had already experienced that state before and getting out of it had taken a stroke of luck plus every ounce of internal fortitude I had. I had no intention of going back to that state again.

"I understand the generosity of your offer, sir," Captain Hansen said, "but this mission must indeed be deadly."

"Honestly, we're not really sure," the Colonel replied. "We're not sure what happened to those we sent into the dark in the past. They simply disappeared. Were they destroyed? Or did something stranger happen to them? That's a question we hope you may answer."

Captain Hansen tilted her head to one side and stared at the Colonel quizzically, waiting for him to continue. After a moment, he produced a display of stars in the air between us. I soon realized they weren't stars, but a presentation of the asteroid belt. By using his fingers to control the display, he brought in the inner planets and then, with a few more gestures, we went out further and further from the sun until the Oort cloud was displayed.

The Oort cloud was a large body of material which floated just outside the Solar System. Most of it consisted of chunks of old ice, mixed with chunks of rock, a grand mess that orbited out beyond Neptune. The region included many dwarf planets, the most famous of which was Pluto.

The Colonel pointed to a tiny dot far off in the distance. "Our target is a dwarf planet known as Eris," he said, flicking at the map to show its location, which was far from the sun and well past Neptune.

"You want us to fly all the way out there to explore Eris?" Captain Hansen asked.

"Yes," the Colonel replied. "You won't be the first to go on this mission—but you'll be the first to return—if you do."

"I don't understand," she said, stepping close to the holographic depiction and peering at it.

"We sent out probes to all the dwarf planets some years ago. As it takes quite a long time to get there, we've only recently received comprehensible results. When we did, we were impressed by certain structures of unknown origin that we found on Eris. Unlike all the other tiny planets, we sent another mission—and then a third. The final mission was piloted by humans—and it didn't return. We don't know what happened to them, and we're curious."

Captain Hansen stared at the tiny dots swirling on the display. They were so far away, so far from our sun.

"How long will it take to get there?" she asked.

"Something like six months. Call it a year, round-trip," the Colonel replied.

She winced at that. Blackwood, who had yet to dare speak a word, made a small gasping sound.

"A year?" Hansen asked. "You're asking us to go out there and spend an entire year inside the confines of *Borag*?"

The crew aboard our mining rig numbered several hundred, but not quite a thousand. I had to admit, even as I stood guard some distance away, my eyes were squinting in discomfort. The idea of spending such a long time—so many months in isolation—with this less-than-friendly group was difficult to contemplate.

"We'll need a bit of time to recruit," Captain Hansen said a few moments later, "and we'll want to see those balances you spoke of appear in our bank accounts before we depart."

"Done!" said the Colonel.

"In addition," Hansen continued, "I want one percent of what is given to the officers to be given to every crewmember aboard my ship."

At this, Blackwood made a strangled sound. She glanced at him questioningly.

"Sir," he said, "when negotiating, one generally requests for funds to go into the ship's general accounts, or possibly into the officers' trust. That way, later on, we can decide how to disperse—"

"No," Captain Hansen said. "It's not going to be that way. Not this time. We're going to see that money go straight into the hands of every crewman—even our D-class contracts."

"You don't mean...?"

"Yes. Even the rock-rats are going to share in this bonus. We're talking about a year-long assignment here, Blackwood. They're going to go crazy. They'll mutiny, and possibly murder us if we take them away from any safe ports for that length of time."

Blackwood frowned fiercely, but eventually he nodded. "I understand. You're attempting to buy their acquiescence. I can assure you, however, this can be done at a cheaper price if you would only allow me to—"

"No," Captain Hansen repeated. She turned back to the Colonel. "Direct funding will be injected into everyone's account. Nothing shall go into the ship's general fund. Is that understood?"

"That's all the same to me," he said, "I find your terms acceptable. Do I have your commitment to this mission, Captain?"

The colonel stepped forward, offering his hand. After a moment's hesitation, she reached out and shook it.

No one looked happy, not exactly. But there was a slight smile on the Colonel's face.

Blackwood, on the other hand, definitely looked chagrined. I could tell he wasn't too fond of all the arrangements.

For my part, I was conflicted—I liked Captain Hansen, and I understood why she'd taken this deal. We were in trouble and under threat of liquidation. No one wanted that, but at the same time, I didn't want to go on a year-long mission into the unknown.

What had happened to the ship and crew that had gone out there before us...? I didn't know, but I was fairly certain it hadn't been anything good. Quite possibly, this golden opportunity would result in our utter destruction.

Chapter 19: The Secret

When we'd returned to Mars from Vesta, morale had been low. We'd felt defeated after failing to achieve our goal of destroying the pirate solar array, and everyone aboard had been in a glum mood. The ship was in financial trouble. We'd had too many recent failures. We were all worried about what we'd have to face next.

Then, the captain had made her fateful pilgrimage to the corporate buildings and come back triumphant. When the crew was finally allowed to disembark at the spaceport and explore Mars City below, everyone was surprised and relieved. The fact we were allowed to exit *Borag* meant we were under no immediate threat of dissolution.

Then, the captain announced the good news: we'd been given a new mission, one with a startling upfront bonus attached! The worried crew immediately transformed into a happy-go-lucky crowd.

Everyone, including the Red Company marines, immediately sought ways to spend some of that newfound wealth in celebration. We spent a significant portion of that unexpected bonus money in Mars City. We ate real meat, danced with real women instead of robots, and generally partied in relief.

For my own part, I was somewhat more somber than the rest, as I was among the very few who knew the true nature of this new mission. The captain had only announced it was a very well-paid mission into deep space. She explained we would be completely outfitted, with every debt cleared before we set off.

While the ship was outfitted and new crewmen were recruited, a few days passed. I spent that time trying to get somewhat closer to Freya, but alas, the respite was all too brief. We were called back to the ship and ordered to cast off for parts unknown before a single week had passed.

I had to admire Captain Hansen's cunning. She had everyone aboard in a good mood, even while she kept us in the dark about the details. I reflected that she had the instincts of a salesman. She knew she should hide the ugly parts of this deal until the very end.

She'd only said we were on a secret mission to an unknown destination, and that for reasons of security, our goals couldn't be revealed until we were on our way and far out into space. Everyone accepted this, partly because of our general relief that we'd been granted a new mission at all—and also because we'd been paid a significant sum in advance.

Borag's massive frame rumbled as she began easing away from the spaceport. Her hull was a lumpy metallic gray, and her surface was covered in a patchwork of solar panels that glinted in the sunlight.

As she jetted away from the space station, her powerful engines roared to life, propelling her forward at incredible speeds. The ship's thrusters fired in short bursts, sending plumes of blue flame shooting out from behind her as she gathered speed. Soon, she was hurtling through the black void of space.

Inside the ship, the crew of experienced miners and engineers worked tirelessly to ensure that *Borag's* equipment was functioning at optimal levels. They monitored the ship's various sensors and navigational systems, scanning for obstacles. These days, with all the increased space traffic around Mars, chunks of debris were everywhere.

Borag's longest voyage began normally enough. The ship soon got up to cruising speed and the engines eased down to half-power. Stars twinkled in the distance, and the red glow of Mars loomed large in the ship's rearview cameras.

Everyone aboard seemed cheerful, even the officers—but there was one exception: accountant Blackwood. Every time I saw him lurking in the passageways of the upper decks, he looked glum.

As for Captain Hansen, I rarely saw her at all. She was either holed up in her personal quarters or busy on the bridge. Whatever her reasons were for remaining secluded, I was left to stew in my own thoughts.

Freya, of course, asked probing questions of me whenever we had a chance to talk. We even shared a brief kiss in a quiet passageway, but our privacy was short-lived. A couple of officers soon came marching along, laughing at us. Privacy was a rare commodity on *Borag* when the big ship was underway.

Freya was a smart girl, and she knew something was up. She was associated with the bridge staff, and they'd already done the math plotting our course. It was clear to anyone with a tiny modicum of navigational skills that we weren't heading for the asteroid belt. We were going into deep space, and there didn't seem to be any planets directly in our path.

That meant we were heading for an object that was alone in the cosmos. Either a wild asteroid, a comet—or something much stranger and farther out.

Rumors soon began running wild on the ship. Some said we were going to rendezvous with another ship carrying valuable cargo. Others claimed there was a pirate base located at a distant Lagrange point that no one had previously explored or suspected.

When Freya asked me about it, all I could do was shake my head and tell her I had been sworn to secrecy like everyone else. I didn't want to lie to her, but I couldn't tell her the truth, either. She knew I was hiding something. The look on my face gave that away.

"But I told you what was going on before," she protested. "When we were heading for Vesta, I acted as your private conduit for information from the bridge. And now you're not telling me anything?"

"I can't, Freya," I said, feeling frustrated. "You have to trust me on this. Even if you knew, there's nothing you could do about it."

She sighed, looking hurt. "I do trust you, Devin. It's just hard not knowing what's going on. We're in this together, you know."

I nodded, feeling guilty. "I know, Freya. I'm sorry. As soon as I can tell you more, I will. I promise."

She frowned, put her hands on her hips, and looked suspicious. I reached for her, hoping for another kiss, but she backed away.

"I think I've got some work to do," she said, and she skittered off.

I cursed under my breath and trudged back down to the lower decks. I wandered the ship in a glum and dismal mood.

"Hey, Starn!" someone called out behind me. I turned, wondering who it was. I didn't even recognize the voice. "Hey man, it's me. Charlie."

I stared at Charlie, blinked, and then smiled. "My favorite rock-rat," I said.

"That's me." He came forward and offered me a handshake.

I knew a regular marine would never be caught dead shaking hands with an indentured contract-D, but I grabbed his hand and shook it firmly.

Charlie smiled. "We're still brothers, man," he said.

I nodded. "I guess we always will be."

Charlie stepped closer and lowered his voice.

"Hey," he said. "You gotta do me one last favor. I'm in a bit of trouble."

I shook my head slowly. Maybe this chance meeting wasn't so random. "What is it now, Charlie?"

"Well, you know… I might have overspent," he said.

I raised my eyebrows. "Overspent?"

"Yeah, yeah… look, you know we all got a bit of money, right?" Charlie began.

"Oh no," I said. "Don't tell me you didn't put that against your contract—or save it for a better day."

He hung his head. "I should have. I know that—don't you think I know that? But... I got some ideas. If I'd banked it all, I would have paid half of my contract down right then and there and been on my way to being a free man again. But I got a little greedy."

"What do you mean, greedy?"

He shrugged. "Mars City got to me, you know? I haven't been off-ship on my own in over a year. I could never afford it. So... I just had to do something besides squat in the hold with the drill-bots."

I nodded, understanding.

"So, I rented one of the bracelets, you know, and I went out on the streets and had a great time."

I grimaced. I'd forgotten about the strict rules people like Charlie lived under, even though it had been my life just months ago. Everything cost money, or more time in service, when you were one of the D-class contracts. If you wanted to walk off-ship and go into a port of call, you were charged for the service. Additionally, you were marked with a tracking device. These tiny tags made it nearly impossible to escape into the populace and disappear. Not only did such a device track you and make sure you couldn't evade your financial obligations, it also cost money just to rent it.

"So," Charlie continued, "I had a few drinks. That's when an idea hit me."

"An idea? What kind of idea?"

He rolled his eyes and winced. "A stupid idea. But you've got to realize, when a man has a couple of heavy, narcotic-laced beverages... Well, it was the first time I'd been hit with that kind of thing in a couple of years. You got to understand, man, those drinks slam a man harder when you've got no resistance."

"Okay, okay. So, what happened?" I asked.

"I went into this casino, see—"

"Oh no. Come on, Charlie. Seriously?"

"Yeah... seriously. I went to the casino and there were a lot of pretty women there. I haven't seen such beautiful women in a long time. Anyway, I went in there, Devin, and it suddenly hit me like a bolt of lightning. If I put my money down and played smart, I could take that bonus money and double it, right-quick. Then, I'd be able to pay off my contract right then and there. There would be no more waiting, no more paying it down some and then watching it build back up again. Freedom was staring me right in the face, Devin. I just felt the luck was there. I felt certain of it. I felt like I could do anything."

I knew that Charlie was talking about the intoxicating effects of narco-laced beverages. In the old days, people drank alcohol and sometimes did drugs. These days, they did both at the same time in a legally prescribed fashion. But for the uninitiated, it was a very powerful and mind-altering experience.

"How much did you lose?" I asked.

Charlie shook his head. "Everything that I got from the bonus—and more. Then when it came time to walk aboard *Borag* again, I had to pay enough to get the bracelet off me. That put me into debt... I'm redlining, Devin."

I made an unhappy hissing sound on his behalf. Redlining meant that Charlie wasn't just a D-contract. He was now so far in the red, owing *Borag's* accounting software such a large amount, that the computer had automatically calculated that he would never be able to repay it.

Charlie had become a man who was such a debtor, such a lost cause, that he was literally costing *Borag* more than he was worth just by breathing.

That was a very dangerous place for any man to be. Crews, especially those who were under financial stress, tended to take matters into their own hands. They weren't supposed to, mind you. People had rights, even non-citizens, even those who were nothing but D-class contracts. They had rights on *paper*, at least.

But then again, there was always a hose full of oxygen feeding the deadbeat individual. If that hose were to become mysteriously cut, somehow... well, the ship's problem would be solved.

I tilted my head back and looked at the ceiling. "Seriously, Charlie, are you trying to ask me for money? Is that what this is about?" I asked. "Man, I don't have much money. I'm a marine, sure, but I'm just a private. I just got my second stripe, dude."

"No, no, no," Charlie said, putting his hands up. He covered his face with his laced fingers. "No, man. No, don't even think that. I'm not asking you for money. I would *never* hit you up for money. First of all, I know you don't really have any—and secondly, it just wouldn't be right."

"Okay. Okay. So what's this about?"

Charlie didn't answer right away. First, he looked over his shoulder, then craned his neck to look over the other shoulder. Next, he made a show of glancing over my shoulders as well.

He saw no one. We were in a quiet spot in the passageways, a place where there was no one listening and no one wandering. At this point, I was beginning to think he'd planned out this entire thing.

"Just tell me the truth, Devin," he said. "That's all I'm asking. Tell me the truth, and I'll leave you alone. I promise."

"What truth?"

"Where the hell are we going?"

I blinked, and my jaw sagged. "What?"

"You heard me. Just tell me where we're going. Doesn't a man have the right to know, Starn?"

"Look, man... I can't tell you. I'd be toast if they even suspected—"

"But they won't suspect anything," Charlie said urgently. "If you tell me, they might come and find out I was the source. I'll never tell anyone where I got the information. I'll let them beat it out of me, then I'll make up a dozen good names. I'll tell them Accountant Blackwood himself told me."

By this time, I was shaking my head and walking away.

"Hey, Devin? Where the hell are you going, man?"

"I don't see how this is going to help anything," I replied.

He reached out one skinny hand with even skinnier fingers, and he clutched at my bicep. He could barely get his fingers around it.

"Listen, listen, Devin," he pleaded, "we're talking about my life, here. I'm not going to last long. There are people who've asked me to help them out. If I don't help them out, then I don't keep breathing. Understand?"

I stopped, and I sighed. Charlie seemed encouraged. He whispered in my ear like Satan's sidekick.

"Just tell me this one thing, Devin," he said. "No one has to know where I got the information, or who leaked it. The truth is going to get out eventually anyway. We've been traveling for a couple of months. Anybody with half a brain and a calculator can figure out we're shooting right out of the Solar System."

I looked at him, thinking hard. Charlie smiled at me hopefully. A few of his teeth were missing.

"What is it?" he asked in a whisper. "Some kind of weird black rock full of metal? A dead abandoned ship with a lost cargo? Maybe there's a rich load somewhere that needs to be scooped up?"

Slowly, I shook my head. It was a sad shake because the news was nowhere near as good as everyone was hoping. As far as I knew, there was no pot of gold at the end of this black rainbow.

"All right, Charlie," I told him. "I'm going to tell you one word—just one word. And the only reason why I'm going to tell you that one word is because it's the only word I know—but maybe it'll help."

And then, I whispered the word to him: "Eris."

Chapter 20: Mutiny!

The hint I'd let leak out of my lips about our true destination was only one word long—but it was enough to make me regret it.

I didn't see Charlie again after that one single time, not for quite a while. But when I bothered to check the rosters, I noticed that he was still alive. He didn't seem to be under any special punishment or duress, nor was he incarcerated or confined to one of the tiny cells down near the radioactive piles. As far as I could tell, he wasn't mutilated, dead, asphyxiated, or otherwise abused.

That left me with a shrug of the shoulders. I guess I'd done my good deed for the day by helping him out.

Three days passed by after that, and I began to breathe easily again. This wasn't because my circumstances had appreciably improved, but rather because I was feeling less stressed about helping Charlie. With every passing day, the odds that the leak would be traced back to me diminished.

Sure, I'd released a secret that I had sworn not to—but the information wasn't sweeping across the ship. If it didn't turn into an ugly rumor, how could it be traced back to me?

Maybe Charlie had passed on information to just one party who'd been interested, but then that fellow had decided to do nothing with it. Or, maybe that single word "Eris" had meant nothing to them. After all, it pretty much meant nothing to me.

Whatever the case, as each day went by, I began to believe that my fateful meeting with Charlie in the passages of the lowest decks hadn't resulted in anything dramatic or unpleasant.

Unfortunately, my growing sense of optimism was wrong. Very, very wrong.

On the morning of the fifth day, I woke up to the sound of klaxons hammering and clanging away.

"Green Company to the lower decks!" a voice rang out. "Red Company to the upper decks, full kit! This is not a drill. Muster and move to your battle stations."

No set of words could spur Red Company into greater action. Being a marine aboard a starship like *Borag* was like being a fireman in a big city. Most of the time, you spent your days responding to occasional heart attacks, brush fires, that sort of thing. But once in a while, one of those big-ass skyscrapers lit up—and that's when you really earned your pay.

Red Company was like that. We were the final defense for the ship and her crew if everything went to hell in a big way. That was when our contribution really amounted to something. Most of the time, we trained, strutted around, and looked tough. We usually kept people from getting into trouble by looking mean and causing them to question their plans.

But now and then, that wasn't enough. Today was such a day. In fact, the simple detail that they'd called Green Company to the lower decks and Red to the upper was an obvious giveaway.

Corporal Tench prowled into the barracks, and we hit him up for information.

"What's happening, Corporal?" Ledbetter demanded.

Tench paused tensely, throwing a glance over his shoulder. I could tell by his sour expression that he didn't really know what was happening.

"There's a gangbang up on the bridge, Ledbetter," he told us. "Everybody says your momma is serving."

Ledbetter scowled at him. Tench laughed, and then continued marching into the passageways. We followed, muttering about what an asshole he was.

As we followed Corporal Tench, we realized he didn't know any more about what we were walking into than anybody else did. We met up with Sergeant Cox, and then 2nd Squad, which was led by Lt. Quinn.

Soon, the entire group had gathered and we deployed in force onto the upper decks. This time, we weren't posted at the doorway leading to the command deck. Instead, we were stationed outside the officers' quarters.

We lined up and checked our weapons twice. Quinn posted men in pairs at every intersection. We stood with our weapons ready, casting our eyes down long passageways that gave us good lines of fire and a little bit of cover by staying in alcoves and doorways.

"What the hell do you think is going on?" Ledbetter asked me once we'd been posted together at a quiet intersection.

We were outside the officers' mess, and some lovely smells were coming out of it. Whatever else you could say about being an officer, the officers aboard *Borag* ate pretty well.

The passageways were mysteriously empty, and just about the only people that you could see were lurking marines and an occasional crewman who was rushing to his station. Every time we spotted one of the crew, they soon ducked into the nearest passageway and locked a door behind them.

"The captain called for general quarters," I said, "I guess it's a lockdown."

Ledbetter rolled his eyes at me. "You think so, huh? But why? Nobody's telling us what's happening."

"Well, then I guess we don't need to know," I told him, trying to shut him up.

My stonewalling finally worked, and he stood across from me grumbling and glancing in every direction.

When Ledbetter was nervous and forced to stand around waiting for too long, he tended to take out a cloth and shine the muzzle of his laser carbine. He did this over and over again, polishing the glassy polymer tip until it gleamed.

This was supposedly because sometimes dirt could get onto the lens of the laser. Sergeant Cox had told us it didn't really matter when you fired a beam of such power at short range—but Ledbetter had never believed him. He wanted the emitter on his weapon to be as crystal clean and clear as possible. He wanted to deliver the hottest, hardest-hitting beam that it possibly could, when the time came. I couldn't really fault him for that.

My behavior during moments of waiting like this was somewhat different. Rather than working on my weapon, I kept my eyes moving and stayed in a high state of alertness, glancing everywhere at once. I checked all my instruments, all my communications channels, all my warning systems—everything. I wanted to know before anyone got close to us.

What might be the cause of this strange alert? I was clueless. If there had been incoming boarders, like there had been that one time with rock-rat pirates, we would have known about that quite a while ago. Normally, when you get boarded in space, it's pretty obvious where the ship is and who's coming up at you. You don't just sneak up on another spaceship out in the middle of nowhere. This was doubly true when you were in deep black space, nowhere near any gravity wells.

But out in the middle of nowhere like this, there was no planet, no moon to hide behind. No way to surprise anyone. If anything had been approaching us, we would have seen its jets, literally a million miles away.

As far as I knew, the ship had made no efforts at evasion, either. Therefore, my brain reasoned, the threat had to be from within.

I blinked twice, thinking that over. Green Company had been sent down to the lower decks. They were essentially our riot police, a form of shore patrol troops who were sent in first to deal with unruly individuals. But Red Company marines—we were the true fighters. We were meant to kill rather than beat someone down with shock rods. If there was a serious problem, we were the ones they'd send to deal with it.

But we hadn't been sent to the lower decks. We'd been sent to the upper decks. I puzzled over this for the next few minutes and finally came up with an answer.

"I really don't like the idea of a mutiny…" I said, talking to myself.

"What's that?" Ledbetter asked, casting his eyes my way. "Did you hear something?"

"No," I said.

"What did you say, then? Did you say mutiny? What the hell are you talking about? What do you know? Did that little chick Freya send you a private text, or something?"

I shook my head. "No, nothing. I'm just thinking things through. There's no ship coming up against *Borag's* hull. We would know about that."

"Yeah, yeah," Ledbetter said. "So what?"

"And they sent Green Company below. I haven't heard much from down there. I mean, if the rock-rats were throwing a party, trying to riot, we would know it by now."

Ledbetter frowned and looked at all his inputs. "I guess we would have heard something through the comms…"

"Right. They're all quiet down there."

He looked back at me. "Okay, so what the hell is going on?"

"The threat has to be coming from within the ship, and it has to be happening here—on the upper decks. That can only mean the crew has got ideas of their own."

"The crew?" Ledbetter said, incredulous.

"Yeah. Like… the officers."

Slowly, Ledbetter's head swiveled toward the door that led to the officer's mess. We were standing right outside a major meeting spot for the kind of men I was talking about.

"You think they're plotting in there? You think they somehow have decided that they've had enough of Captain Hansen?"

"I don't know," I replied, "but I can't think of any other reason why we've suddenly been called up here. Not unless this is some kind of crazy drill just to keep us on our toes."

Ledbetter shook his head slowly. "If it is, it's the first and only time I've ever heard of something big like this going down on this ship. I tend to agree with you. Something's gone very wrong, and it's gone wrong up here on the upper decks."

Suddenly, he looked at me as if gripped by a new idea. His eyes bulged. "What if the captain's already dead?" he hissed out.

Ledbetter's words shocked me, and my jaw dropped a bit. That thought hadn't even occurred to me, but it would fit the profile. If someone had found the captain dead in her quarters, that would be a good cause for a general ship lockdown, with no specific targets for us to shoot at.

"In a disaster like that... I think things will look exactly like they're looking right now. It would be total confusion. The XO would panic and order everybody aboard confined to quarters."

Ledbetter nodded. "Then, they'd put every man they had with a gun into the passageways to make sure nothing else went wrong until they figured out what to do next."

"Oh, hell," I said. "I sure hope that didn't happen. Hansen doesn't deserve it."

"You would know," Ledbetter said, tossing me a smirk.

I didn't take the bait. I evaded his glances and kept looking around, watching the environment.

Finally, after another ten minutes or so, the door to the officers' mess popped open. Four individuals strode out into the passageway.

Only one of them was known to me: the man in the lead, Accountant Blackwood himself. Behind him were three men—well, two men and one flopping, unconscious-looking officer that they dragged between them.

They were all officers, all crewmen in uniform. They looked to be ensigns, except for the unconscious victim they carried.

At first, it looked like Blackwood and his strange trio were going to walk right by us without even a glance. They all seemed intent on whatever they were doing.

Private Ledbetter and I both stood at attention and set our eyes front, not making eye contact with the officers or the angry accountant. This approach usually served us as a means of avoiding unwanted attention.

But this time, it didn't work. Blackwood frowned and halted. He pointed at me.

"I know this man," he said. "What are you doing here, Starn?" he asked, reading my name badge.

"I'm on guard duty, sir," I said.

Blackwood squinted at me. Then, he stepped to the rag-like man the two ensigns were dragging. He reached down and grabbed him by the hair. He wrenched his face up, holding his head aloft with skinny, white-knuckled fingers.

The man wasn't unconscious, not quite. He blinked at me in a daze. There was blood on his cheek and his teeth were red-rimmed.

I could tell the man wasn't quite unconscious, but rather in a groggy state, having probably been abused by numerous shocks and a few good punches along the way.

"Loman," Blackwood said, slapping him a couple of times to wake him up. "Lt. Loman! Look at this man, is he the one? Is this the rock-rat you mentioned?"

Loman gagged and drooled and stared. "That's a marine," he mumbled.

"I know that, you idiot. But he used to be a rock-rat. You said it was a rock-rat, didn't you?"

"That's a marine," the lieutenant said, clearly befuddled. "I don't know any marines."

"Dammit, you're worthless." Blackwood dropped the man's head by letting go of his hair and began walking again. The two ensigns grimly dragged their burden in his wake.

"You two," Blackwood said, "accompany us—just in case."

Shrugging, Ledbetter and I reported to Cox what had happened and then followed Blackwood. Technically, Blackwood was a ship's officer, although he had no role in a combat situation. He wasn't in the direct chain of command leading up to the captain herself, but there was no question that he outranked us. He had the authority to give us orders within reason. Since we were not immediately in any kind of action, I saw no reason to disobey.

Neither did Cox. In fact, he called together the rest of his squad, and they soon converged upon our position. Blackwood balked at this, but when he realized we weren't threatening him but rather moving to protect him, he waved us all back. "I don't want all of you. Stand at your posts. I'll take these two grunts, Cox. The rest of you, return to your stations. I don't know when the next rogue is going to pop out of his hole, and I want a laser rifle to be greeting his nose when he does."

Cox threw around supporting orders, backing up Blackwood's demands. Ledbetter and I found ourselves as the sole guardians of Blackwood.

The ensigns dragging the lieutenant down the passageway had pistols on their belts, but their weapons were nothing compared to our laser carbines and rifles. A pistol could stop an unarmed man, certainly, but it was no match for a serious threat like a drill-bot or a large armed crowd.

Blackwood led us up multiple flights of stairs, avoiding the elevators and taking us directly to the bridge itself. Once on the command deck, he diverted his path and walked into a conference room. He ordered the two ensigns to throw the body of their stricken comrade onto a large conference table in the middle of the chamber.

Ledbetter and I, not knowing what else to do, stood guard at the entrance. The half-dead lieutenant was hoisted up and tossed onto the battle table. He slid across the holographic imagery of the Solar System, which played above him in a ghostly nimbus. Planets and asteroids shimmered and flashed as his tangled limbs interfered with the projections. A long streak of blood was now smeared across the table as well, causing the projection of Jupiter and all of her swirling moons to turn a rusty red.

The captain entered the chamber next, and we all snapped to attention—except for Blackwood and the half-dead guy.

"What the hell is this, Blackwood?" she demanded.

"This man is the perpetrator, the source of the leak."

Hansen looked at the lieutenant. "How could he have found out anything?"

"I'm not sure, sir," Blackwood replied. "But I am sure that he is the one who has been spreading the rumor. I don't know where he heard it originally. It might have been from anyone. Remember, when we were first awarded the mission, we spent several days still on Mars. A lot of the men were roaming the colony spending their bonus money during that time... and by the way, I am still chagrined by that absurd waste of funds—"

Hansen lifted a hand to interrupt him. "No more about that, Blackwood. We've had that discussion many times before."

"Yes, ma'am. In any case, after our crewmen squandered the reward we gave them, I would guess that one of them managed to meet someone from Interplanetary Excavations."

Captain Hansen shook her head. "I doubt that. None of our people know the colonel. It's highly unlikely they would be talking to any of the suits from the company, either."

Blackwood shrugged. He spread his weird, spidery fingers wide. "Someone told the tale. This man heard it, and he's been spreading something infinitely worse than rumors—he's been telling the truth."

Captain Hansen checked the lieutenant's vitals, poking at the man sprawled on the table. She twisted up her face. "Did you have to beat him half to death? Then throw him dramatically across my conference table? I don't see how all this is helpful, Blackwood."

"I disagree," he said.

He had a floating camera drone out now, and he was taking a lot of still shots and video. "What we'll do," he said, "is post this evidence on *Borag's* social sites. The images will spread like wildfire—just like the rumor itself. Soon, people will learn not to have such loose lips and loud voices."

Hansen shook her head. "It won't do any good. The rumor is out. There's no putting it back, now."

"My software indicates that less than three percent of the people aboard this ship know the truth, and quite a few of them are in this room."

Captain Hansen continued to shake her head. "If your computer says three percent, it's thirty. A rumor will spread far and wide before it can be contained. This kind of overreaction will only increase that effect."

Blackwood straightened, and he stopped poking at the lieutenant and playing with his camera drone. "What do you suggest, then, for our next move? We could have a mutiny on our hands once everyone knows the truth."

Captain Hansen compressed her lips in a tight line. "It's my fault, in a way. They were going to find out eventually. I was only trying to delay the day of reckoning. Perhaps by doing so, I've made it worse. When the truth is revealed, it will now seem that much greater. We're going to have to come clean to fix things."

Blackwood nodded. "Understood, ma'am. I'll make sure this man is taken care of and charged accordingly." He turned to leave the conference room, motioning for the lieutenant to be taken away by the two ensigns.

As Blackwood left, Captain Hansen brought several of her officers in the room. They looked after the unconscious man, and the bloodstains he'd left behind, with a mixture of alarm and disgust.

"We have a difficult task ahead of us," she said. "We need to make sure that the crew understands the gravity of the situation, but we must also convince them they can trust us to lead them through it. We can't afford to have a mutiny on this ship."

An ensign named Lacroix spoke up. "What can we do to prevent a mutiny, ma'am?"

"We need to be honest with them," Captain Hansen said firmly. "We'll explain why we're going to Eris, and we'll make sure that they understand the dangers of the mission. We'll also give them reassurances that we're doing everything in our power to keep them safe."

"And what about the leak, ma'am?" Lacroix asked.

"We'll deal with that separately," Captain Hansen said. "For now, we need to focus on the mission and keeping the crew together."

The officers nodded in agreement, and Captain Hansen began to draft her announcement to the crew. It was going to be a difficult conversation, but it was one that needed to happen. The fate of *Borag* and her crew depended on it.

Chapter 21: The Riot

Here it was, about two months into a 12-month trip, and the men aboard *Borag* were just learning the truth: that we were going to be stuck aboard this cramped, uncomfortable ship right through summer, fall, Christmas, and well into the next year.

After that, we'd return to base at Mars next spring—but that was only if things went smoothly out at Eris.

One whole year—that was the best case that we could hope for.

After the Captain confessed the truth to everyone, there was plenty of griping. Plenty of people talked about how they'd been screwed, and tricked, and bought off cheap with a few credits before we left Mars.

A lot of that was true, but normally, such complaints would subside in time. This time, they didn't.

The third month passed, and then the fourth. I think the fourth was a pretty bad one, largely due to our astronomical position on the map.

Someone, in their great wisdom, had decided to equip big mining rigs like *Borag* with wall-based monitoring systems. You could pull up information such as navigational data anytime you wanted. This allowed interested parties to track our progress and our position in relation to the other heavenly bodies of our beloved Solar System.

And so, as we progressed outward, no one could help but notice as we passed Jupiter then Uranus. In the fourth month, we passed Neptune.

I think that was when people started to freak out a bit. Some calm prankster kept leaving those wall displays up, showing the navigational progress of the ship. It was impossible not to notice them as you walked around the passageways.

The arcs that marked the orbits of Neptune and Pluto were pretty close to one another out here at the rim—but they were now behind us. That brought a visceral fear to every spaceman who saw it. None of us had ever been out this far, not a single person aboard had even considered it. In fact, as far as I knew, precious few humans had ever bothered to venture all the way out into the Oort cloud.

This was the zone where comets were born. This was where the darkest objects slept, the kinds of things that lurked until, all of a sudden, they smashed into a planet like Earth. Once every hundred thousand years or so, they caused great destruction and even extinction. One incident had extinguished the dinosaurs forever.

Something about man's makeup causes us to forever fear the unknown. We all knew we were so far from home, there was no hope of rescue if things went badly. The region was unknown and virtually unexplored.

One day, four months and ten days into the journey, we received a fateful order. "Red Company, move to your stations."

I heard the alert come over the ship's public address system. "Green Company requests assistance. All Red Company is ordered to report for duty."

"That's our call," Sergeant Cox said, standing up. His gut knocked over a checkerboard in front of him as he stood. We'd been stuck within the confines of the ship for so long that he had grown a bit of a paunch.

The rest of us scrambled to the lockers, and we shrugged into our riot gear. Whatever was happening, it had to be pretty bad. Normally, Red Company was above problems like breaking up fights. We didn't often get out our batons and metal-studded gloves, but shipboard incidents had been increasing.

On this particular day, a riot had broken out upstairs, and it seemed Green Company was in over their heads.

We didn't bother with our laser carbines. We had pistols on our belts, but they were mostly for show. Our orders didn't allow us to shoot anyone unless we were shot first. Accordingly, we wore body armor, stern expressions, and held what amounted to good old-fashioned clubs.

Charging through the ship, I followed Cox, as only he seemed to know where the altercation had taken place. I hadn't bothered to check in and read the maps inside my helmet. What was the point? The ship wasn't all that big. We would be there soon enough.

My eyebrows raised just a little when I noticed we were marching upstairs rather than down. Most fights broke out on the lower decks, but not today.

We marched to the entertainment deck. The old salts called it the Lido Deck, harkening back to cruise ships of the past. Here, most of the officers consorted together, got loaded, played games, got into arguments—and once in a while, they threw a few fists at each other.

A full squad of ten men, led by Sergeant Cox, busted into the barroom. There, my eyes were met with the biggest brawl I'd seen since I'd left Earth slums years ago.

Two of Green Company's men were already on the floor. It looked like they were unconscious—maybe worse. The place was crowded with both officers and enlisted men—all involved in the fight. Somebody had set off the automated fire suppression system. It did smell like smoke, but I didn't see any flames.

Fire retardant foam, along with gasses like halon and INERGEN, were spraying wildly out of control. This added a lot of confusion to the scene and caused Sergeant Cox to order us to turn on our oxygen systems seal our helmets, just in case.

We waded into the melee, swinging batons at anyone who was swinging a fist. This settled down the crowd pretty fast. A squad of organized, sober marines in body armor and swinging batons was enough to convince most of the rowdies to flee just at the sight of us. Corporal Tench, in particular, took great pleasure in kicking the rumps of various ensigns and even one lieutenant who was scrambling to get away from him.

He laughed and declared his life to be a good one. "Where else are we allowed to kick officers in the ass?"

His attitude was uncharitable, but it brought a grin to all our faces.

"When these prigs are drunk and disorderly, we're in charge," he said. "If they don't like it, they can go talk to Commander Kaine and explain why they participated in this riot in the first place."

As the room was clearing out and the various foam-spraying devices were shut off, I spotted someone I knew. Yeoman Carter—my Freya.

She was at the back of the bar, and she was up close and personal with someone—a man in a fleet officer's uniform.

I breathed out a big sigh inside my helmet. A hand came down and slapped me on the shoulder. I saw Ledbetter's face—he'd spotted Freya, too.

"Sorry, man," he said. "Better luck next time." He walked away, trampling over fallen officers who were drunk and either crawling for the exit or simply sprawled on the floor.

The medical teams were arriving now, and the Green Company losers dared to show their faces. They'd been in over their heads to begin with, but now they were wandering back, raining blows upon the drunks they hated the most.

Soon, there would be nothing in here but broken glass and lost service caps on the deck, and I knew I should leave. If Freya had made her choice, so be it.

I knew I should walk out—but I couldn't quite do it. I kept nosing around, checking on the men, lifting a few of them, getting them to their feet and ushering them out of the place. All the while I was glancing toward that corner where Freya was making out with some dude whom I hated, even if I didn't know his name.

Finally, I couldn't help myself. I took a few steps closer. That was when I noticed she was moving a bit oddly. In fact, if I had to describe it, I would say she wasn't moving much at all.

Frowning, I marched over and laid a big, armored glove on the shoulder of the man who, as it turns out, was pinning her in the corner of a booth.

He turned around, his eyes wide, and right then I knew what was happening. There was a guilty look in those eyes. They were also wider than they should be, a certain sign that he'd consumed too much of the narco drinks.

"Let me help you up, sir," I said.

I picked the ensign up off his feet, lifting him by the armpits. He grunted and complained.

"Get your hands off me, Marine," he mumbled. "I'm Ensign Lacroix. Don't you know who I am? I'm Lacroix."

I remembered him. I had seen him a few times before. The first time he'd had been on the space elevator at Mars. He'd been the one leading the group that was encircling Yeoman Carter way back then.

The second time had been upstairs in the captain's quarters. We'd discussed the mutiny of various officers. He was only a junior officer, but he clearly thought he was a big deal—a bigger deal than he was.

I glanced back at Freya. Yes, as I thought, she was essentially in a stupor. He had been pawing at her when she was more or less passed out.

This made me angry. I didn't have the best upbringing back on Earth, and sometimes, my darker instincts from those early days came back to haunt me. Accordingly, my ankle somehow found its way in front of Lacroix, and he went crashing down on his face.

"Whoa, whoa," I said, reaching down and dragging him up to his feet again. Or at least, halfway to his feet.

He was cursing and mumbling, and when I got him up to a good height, I dropped him again. This time I made sure his face went into a hard, upright stool. He cut his cheek on that somehow, and the blood began to flow.

"Damn, sir, you're clumsy today," I told him.

"You fucker," he mumbled, turning around. I saw that he had a hand on his pistol, which was holstered at his belt. He hadn't managed to get the gun out yet, so I reached down and closed my hand over his.

There was a safety strap, which his half-numb fingers were fumbling over. I used my Earth-born strength to squeeze hard, crushing those fingers down onto the gun.

"Now, you don't want to go do that, sir," I told him.

"I'll have your badge," he told me, which brought a smile to my face for the first time since I had seen Corporal Tench kick another ensign in the ass. I was fairly certain at that moment that Ensign Lacroix barely knew where he was or who he was talking to.

"I've got my cameras on, boy," I told him. "Don't screw this up, or you'll get busted down into the ranks."

Ensign Lacroix gaped and gawked at me for a moment. "Cameras?" he said.

That single word seemed to strike through everything else. It caused him more concern and possibly pain than slamming his face into various chunks of metal had done so far.

"That's right," I said. "They're rolling right now. Everything you've been doing tonight is on camera."

He gave me a look like a fish. All of a sudden, he scrambled away on all fours and ran out of the bar.

I straightened up, laughed a little, and headed back to the corner of the bar to check on Freya. She was coming awake now, and I think she had witnessed a bit of what had just occurred.

"Devin?" she said. "Is that you?"

"It sure is, ma'am. Do you need some help?"

"I think I do. I'm really tired. I'm over-drunk. I don't know how much I had."

"Too much," I said, "that's my guess."

She shook her hair out of her eyes and massaged her face. "I guess I'm used to alcohol—but not these narco things. Maybe I blacked out. Did you see?"

"You were with that Lacroix guy. He was all over you when I came in."

Freya looked alarmed. "Really? We were just talking... That prick."

"Maybe he slipped you something extra. Maybe you want to get a blood test?"

She thought about it. She shook her head. "I'm okay. I've just got a headache. Can you help me get out of here?"

I put an arm around her waist, lifted her up, and helped her out of the bar in a much gentler fashion than I had anyone else this evening.

"Devin," she said.

"What is it?"

"I'm really sorry," she said.

"It's okay. It's a long voyage. Everybody's freaking out a little bit."

"Yeah, that's what it is. This mission. All those maps on the walls. We've got months to go, still. Back in the old days on Earth, naval ships could at least visit a friendly port now and then. We're in the middle of nowhere."

I thought about what she said. I had to agree, the maps on the walls were working on people's minds. They always showed the same thing, that we were heading farther and farther out into the dark.

"It's freaking me out," Freya said.

"I think it's freaking everybody out," I told her.

Once we were outside in the main passageway, the decks had pretty much emptied out. There were only a couple of Marines standing around, looking tough. One of them gave me the thumbs-up, probably thinking I scored myself a date for the evening.

I frowned back at him then turned my attention to Freya. With careful effort, I got her out of the place and back to her quarters.

There at the doorway, she lingered and put her hands on my gloves, examining them.

"There's blood on here," she said.

"Yeah, I suspect so," I told her.

"Were you in that fight, too?"

"Only at the end."

"Yeah, the crew started it, but you guys finished it," she laughed. "Devin, could you take off your helmet for a minute?"

I reached up and pried open the baseplate, unscrewing the whole thing. Then, Freya kissed me for a long time.

It was probably the first real, honest-to-God make out session we'd ever had. We'd had a kiss or two back on Mars, but this was different. It was real, and it was passionate. I didn't think it was all due to her state of mind, either.

"My lips are bleeding," she said, touching herself on the mouth. "Do you think that asshole bit me or something?"

"Could be," I said, and my mood darkened all over again.

She looked at me and read my expression carefully. "He's lucky you didn't kill him, isn't he?"

I shrugged. "I might have had an accident," I said. "It was a close thing."

She smiled. "Thanks for helping me out. I'm going to pull myself together. We all have to. We're only a third of the way through this trip. God, I can't imagine the six months on the way back."

"Yeah…"

"I bet we'll find nothing out there," she said, staring at the wall screens. One of them glowed nearby, showing how distant we were from any source of humanity. "There's going to be nothing out there at all. Then, we'll have to turn around and fly all the way home."

I nodded. I had to admit that she might be right.

Chapter 22: Accountant Blackwood

The fifth and sixth months went better. I think it was because someone had a flash of ingenuity. They'd put a big, round green circle on the map. That put a positive spin on our destination, which as everyone knew by now was the dwarf planet Eris.

Normally a dark, essentially invisible ball of frozen rock out in the farthest reaches of the Solar System, Eris definitely looked more friendly as a bright green circle. When you animated just about anything with a green blob of color, it made it seem like a much friendlier place. Instead of a deadly rock, it looked like we were flying toward the Garden of Eden.

Everyone's imagination ran wild as we came ever closer. The nearer we got to Eris, the more people felt the journey wasn't hopeless. Instead, we were going to be let loose on a new unexplored world.

Rumors ran rampant through *Borag*, describing vast secret treasures to be found. Palladium, radioactive platinum, and spikes of diamond that grew like hoarfrost. Of course, it was all hogwash. No one knew what we were going to find—if anything—but it gave us hope. In this dark time, we really needed hope.

As the grand flight came to an end, I thought about the kind of an ordeal it would be to fly to the stars. A voyage like that would take years—possibly centuries. It seemed like an impossible thing for humans to accomplish, at least not at the speeds our ships were capable of now.

Maybe we would never get to other star systems, or at least not ones that were worth colonizing. They were just so far away, so remote, and when humans were crammed together on a ship, I doubted they could hold it together that long. There would be a civil war long before we spent the decades it would take, flying in some hopelessly crowded Ark, to reach such a distant goal.

By the time we were in the final days of our long journey, Red Company had been assigned shifts to patrol the passages. There had been several serious incidents, like the bar fight that I'd helped break up. The officers up on the bridge had decided to make the marines more visible, to use us for the purposes of prevention rather than as a cure.

This approach worked to some extent, but it was annoying for my fellow soldiers. After all, we hadn't signed on with Red Company to be marching around, grim-faced, with our laser carbines held against our chests like ceremonial guards at some dead Emperor's tomb back on Earth.

But I did it because I was ordered to, and at the very least, it gave me a chance to wander around the ship and see what was what. One day, on the mid-decks, I came across a person whom I hadn't seen for months. He was looking at an astronomical chart that depicted *Borag* as she drew close to Eris. He was staring at it as if fascinated.

It was Accountant Blackwood. I glanced his way but took no special notice of him. I marched by with my gun held to my chest.

Blackwood, for his part, said nothing to me as I approached. But just as I was about to pass him, he spoke to me privately.

"Starn?" he said.

I paused, turned on my heel, and looked at him questioningly. "Can I do something for you, sir?"

He nodded, his head tipping forward, lowering his chin on that long, stick-like neck of his. "Indeed, you can," he said. "Did you know that I reviewed your performance on several different occasions? We have videos... and I took a special interest in your unusual case."

"I didn't know that, sir," I replied. "But I guess it makes sense."

He nodded again. "Yes," he said. "I found you've spent an inordinate amount of company time pestering women who are, quite honestly, above your station."

I knew then, he must be referring to Freya. I bristled a bit, but he took no notice.

"However," he continued, "when you are actually on point and on duty, you do a remarkable job. Do you know *why* I've been investigating you, Private Starn?"

"No, sir."

"Because I was curious as to what exactly it was Captain Hansen saw in you—not to mention that piece of fluff." He flapped his hand for a moment. "What was her name? The yeoman?"

"Her name is Freya Carter, sir," I replied evenly.

"Right, right. Whatever. I think I understand what these women find so fascinating. You come off like an ignoramus. An unimaginative thug—and you're all those things. *But*, you're also an obedient brute. When an order is given, you carry it out. So far, in every instance I can think of, you've been successful."

I did my best to maintain a stony expression. I didn't smile at him, I didn't nod to him, I didn't even acknowledge his backhanded compliment. Nor did I argue with it. I just gave him a flat stare. I didn't like the man. I never had, and I probably never would.

"The short version of this is that I believe I can use a man like you," he said. "We're coming into what might be a dangerous situation."

"That's true, sir," I admitted.

"We don't know what the hell's out there. You saw the smile on that colonel's face back on Mars. He was looking smug, even as he pretended to be ignorant of the fate of the previous ships he sent out here on this goose-chase."

I didn't answer. I just stared at him. Eventually, he continued.

"The colonel knew more than he was letting on. I don't believe the ships that came out here before us simply disappeared. I believe, perhaps, they were destroyed. Perhaps the colonel even heard their distress signals—and I would wager they were strange ones."

Finally, I nodded. Blackwood's suspicions matched my own. No company would forgive a stack of debts as tall as the one *Borag* had accumulated without having grim intentions.

"And so here we are," he continued in a bitter tone, "sent out into deep space to follow-up on the disasters of others. It seems like I'm always stuck with a crew of cleanup men. Space-going janitors, that's what we are. Men like you and me, Starn—we deserve better. It's disgusting."

I blinked a few times, not seeing any manner by which Blackwood and I could be found comparable. But I was smart enough to keep that opinion to myself.

"Anyway, I wanted to see if I can enlist your personal support. I'm talking about the kind of support you've given Captain Hansen upon occasion—or that girl Carter back at the bar. I need a good man to back me if things become… unpleasant."

I frowned at him and shook my head. "I don't understand, sir."

"That isn't the correct response. Rather, you should be asking: how much?"

"What? I'm still not getting your meaning—"

"Oh, I think you do, but I shall spell it out, regardless. Your sole concern should be the amount I'm willing to pay for your loyalty at some point in the not-so-distant future." Here he reached out a long, stick-like finger and tapped at the green dot, which was Eris. "According to my estimates, we're something less than ten days out from this dismal rock."

"I'm assigned to Red Company, sir," I told him. "I will defend this ship and everyone aboard her. That's my job—and I'm good at it, as you said."

"Yes, yes, that's all well and good. But maybe you'd like to become a corporal?"

I looked startled for the first time. It was only a Private Second Class, and to reach Private First Class normally took something like a year in the service. By the end of this journey out to Eris and back, I privately hoped to reach that rank. In fact, I figured I'd earned it by then.

But Corporal? That's not how things worked aboard this ship. Someone else had to pretty much quit in order for me to move up. Quite probably, after we returned to Mars and everyone on this crew disembarked. A few of Red Company's members might opt out of their contracts, deciding they'd had enough at that point. Promotions were possible, but at this time, it just didn't seem likely to happen.

"I doubt it, sir," I said. "Men like Sergeant Cox, Corporal Tench. They've got years of service on me."

Blackwood laughed. "Service isn't the only thing that gains rank. Or maybe you haven't figured that out yet? Remember when I was talking about prices?"

I knew what he was talking about. I'd dealt with bribes and corruption before—and I didn't want any part of it. But then again, it couldn't hurt to have this man, an important person aboard the ship, at least believing that I was on his side.

"I understand what you're saying, sir," I told him, which was true. "I will take your offer under consideration. If some terrible conditions were to arise, I will think of it."

Blackwood nodded. "No commitment...?"

"As you said, sir, there are recording devices everywhere aboard this ship."

"Ah, I see. Suddenly, you think I'm trying to entrap you. I get it. Good thinking. In my books, your estimated IQ has gone up three points just from this single interaction."

"Well, um, sir..." I started to say.

"All right, Devin Starn. I accept your statements for what I believe they are. Let's hope we land out there on this rock and all goes well."

"On that point, sir, we're in complete agreement," I said, and then I turned on my heel again to continue my patrol route.

By the next time I passed that same spot in the passages, Blackwood was gone.

This left me in a questioning frame of mind. Why had he been standing around idly, gazing at that map? He had to have known this was a very rare, lonely spot on the mid-decks.

Further, he had to have been aware I was going to pass by equally alone.

Everything had been staged, planned, and carefully worked out. This seemed like odd behavior to me. Blackwood had never done anything but sneer at me in the past. Maybe he really *was* worried about whatever we were about to run into out there on Eris.

On my third time around, I stopped and gazed at the astronomical chart. It seemed to me that *Borag* had moved a pixel closer to that round, green circle on the map.

What the hell was out there? After gazing at it and getting no answers, I moved on. I shrugged. I supposed that whatever it was, we would learn the truth soon enough.

Chapter 23: Arrival

After the strange encounter with Accountant Blackwood, I spent a lot of time thinking about it. I considered telling some of the other marines, like Sergeant Cox or Commander Kaine, but I realized that they all despised Blackwood. They were also somewhat afraid of him, in my judgement.

If I shared any private discussions I'd had with him, I would only become a source of suspicion to everyone. So, I abandoned the idea.

I also considered speaking to the captain herself, but I couldn't figure out how to approach her. She hadn't invited me for any bodyguard duties lately since she didn't need them. We'd been staying aboard *Borag* for months, and the riots and food fights in the bar had never escalated to anything serious.

The captain spent most of her time on the bridge, in her quarters, or on a few of the highest decks. I rarely saw her except when she passed by with an entourage in the top-level passages of the ship, and there was no time for a private conversation.

Who else could I turn to? Freya Carter? No, I decided against it. She didn't have the connections. I wasn't going to tell someone who couldn't do anything about it. That would only worry her and serve no purpose.

Naturally, I had no intention of following through with anything Blackwood had suggested. I wasn't going to be his private henchman. A few compliments were all he had given me, and that wasn't enough to buy Devin Starn.

Cash wouldn't have been enough, either. After all, Captain Hansen had supported me more than once, and I'd supported her a few times as well. None of those instances had been a cash transaction. I preferred that kind of arrangement. Sometimes, a private alliance between two individuals that was based on honor and honesty was better than making a purely money-based deal. It made you feel like you could trust the person more.

So, I did nothing about it, except to avoid Blackwood as much as possible. I thought about him every time I passed the lonely outpost where he had been standing, gazing at the astronomical maps that now showed we were almost merged with the green dot that was Eris. But I never saw him there again.

As the last week in the final month passed, we got closer and closer to Eris. We were now close enough to see it with the naked eye, and so I stopped worrying about Blackwood. I started wondering what we were going to encounter on this rock we were fast approaching.

We had been decelerating for weeks by now, using our jets to decrease our speed instead of increasing it. After all, we couldn't afford to slam into the rock or whip right past it, blazing deep off into the Oort Cloud.

Everyone aboard became fascinated with the new world. As *Borag* drew closer to Eris, the dwarf planet loomed larger and larger in our viewport. The planet's color was predominantly a deep, reddish-brown hue, with faint wisps of gas and dust emanating from fissures. The surface was covered by a patchwork of craters, ridges, and valleys, with massive boulders and rocky outcroppings jutting out here and there.

But what truly caught our attention was the planet's sheer size. Eris was larger than Pluto, and it showed. At one time, it had been considered the tenth planet in the Solar System. Then they'd decided to shrink Pluto down to a non-planet and call both of them dwarf planets. Its surface was a vast expanse of rugged terrain that stretched out as far as the eye could see. Mountains towered over the landscape, casting long shadows across the rocky ground below. Orbiting nearby, we could see the faint outline of Eris' single moon, Dasomia, hanging in the starry void.

Once *Borag* was close enough, we slid into orbit. We began scanning, but due to the dwarf planet's significant size, it took quite a while to learn everything there was to know about this planet from space. Periodically, the captain came on the public address system and made announcements about the progress of the scientific team conducting the survey.

"Looks like we have discovered some nice mineral deposits," she said.

The planet was composed largely of rocky materials and was denser than its sister dwarf planet, Pluto, which had a much higher content of things like ice and methane.

The captain paused for a moment while sweeping through various charts and deciding what was worth talking about. "We're getting significant internal heating measurements and radioactive decay, in addition to some venting... I'm thinking we could have an internal ocean of liquid water near the mantle. That's very interesting," she said. "One wouldn't think there'd be a lot of heat this far out from the sun. After all, we're now about twice as far from the sun as Neptune, about sixty times as far from the sun as Earth."

That was a sobering thought, talking about being deep in the middle of nowhere. If ever there was something called nowhere, *Borag* had found it.

Eventually, the bridge crew decided to land *Borag* near a fountaining vent that was releasing heat from the internal zone of the planet. This came in the form of steam, hot white geysers that blew off into space. It was a reasonable spot to look for mineral deposits since whatever we were seeing here had originally come from deep within the planet.

As we began our descent toward the planet's surface, we could make out the details of the terrain with greater clarity. The craters were deep and jagged, their edges etched in shadow. The ridges and valleys were sharp and dramatic, carving deep furrows into the rocky surface. All around us, we could see the swirling mists of gas and dust, lit up by the distant sun.

Despite its harsh and unforgiving appearance, there was a strange beauty to Eris that was hard to deny. It was a world of contrasts, where the rugged terrain and stark landscapes were tempered by the gentle glow of distant stars and the soft, swirling mists of gas and dust.

As our ship touched down on the planet's surface, I watched from the upper decks. Dozens of rock-rat miners wandered out onto the surface of Eris for the first time. They bounced around just as men walked on Earth's moon back home.

They hauled their drill-bots behind them, urged forward by eager foremen. The mining teams, after all, hadn't had many opportunities to make money. For many months, they'd been sealed up inside the ship, hoping for a big strike once they were let loose on Eris.

The drill-bots trundled, wobbled, and bounced over the surface. I was surprised to see that the various crewmen cheered them on. Everyone was watching them, and the crew seemed to view the D-Class contracts in a more favorable manner than I'd ever realized. We had always thought they hated us, but it didn't really seem that way. They watched us the way a group of farmers might watch oxen working a field, betting on one to be stronger than the rest.

I couldn't help but wonder if Charley was out there among them. I sincerely hoped that he wasn't. If anything went wrong, if one of those massive geyser puffs of steam shot up and hit him or anyone else, they were as good as boiled in their spacesuits.

The geysers erupted at random with tremendous force, heat, and pressure. They fired up great plumes of vapor from the bowels of the dwarf planet. If someone took a direct hit, they'd be blasted straight up into orbit.

The glow of the drill-bots cut through the darkness, illuminating the rocky terrain. Although the sun was up, it was dim and feeble, making the star look more like a huge, bright planet than a glowing ball of fire. It was depressing to think how far we were from home, with nothing but the vast expanse of space surrounding us.

Suddenly, gasps filled the air.

"Oh no!" one of the female officers exclaimed. My eyes darted downward, away from the distant sun, and I saw that something had gone wrong. One of the drill-bots had stopped moving, and its operator had vanished.

"What happened?" the woman asked in alarm.

One of the ensigns shrugged and pointed across the field. "You see that big geyser over there? When one of those things goes off, one of those big gushers like that, well... The planet has to inhale once in a while too, right? In order for that much pressure to go out?"

The female officer gasped in horror. "Are you saying that man was just sucked down into the guts of the planet?"

The ensign nodded solemnly. "Yeah, probably. It's a dangerous job."

As they stared out the window, I couldn't help but feel horrified. I hoped it wasn't Charley, or anyone else I knew.

I dared to hope that the miner had only fallen into one of these vents and would soon crawl back out, but it never happened. Eventually, a foreman wandered to the spot and wheeled the drill-bot away. I knew then that the miner was dead.

As the days passed, we gathered a significant amount of good ore and radioactives from the field. The mood aboard the ship lifted, and a lot of people were quite happy. Most of the surface-level veins of ore in the Solar System had already been mined out. But out here, at the very limits of our Solar System, the rules were different. No one had ever mined these spots before, and we were rewarded with the easiest, richest veins of ore we'd found in years.

Still, the knowledge of the dangers lurking beneath the surface of Eris weighed heavily on my mind. How many more miners might perish before we left this wild and unforgiving place?

While we were mining, Captain Hansen had wisely released a fleet of drones. They were busy searching, surveying, and scanning the rest of the strange little world. Some of them were tiny satellites in space, beeping and scanning every inch of the surface, while others were flying, buzzing, or even walking. Robots trotted over the surface from our landing location outward, seeking anything of value.

On the third day, reports came in that something had been found. I happened to be posted in the uppermost passageways on the command deck itself. I saw a pair of sensor ops rushing past me, almost crowding past me as if I wasn't there. I took no offense and let them pass, turning my shoulders, so they were able to go by on either side of me.

They were in the middle of an intense conversation. "What is it?" the first man demanded. "What could it be?"

"What do you think it is?"

"Well... it's metal. We know that much... and it's big. Really big."

I frowned at this and looked after them. What were they talking about?

"What kind of percentage of metal are we talking about?"

"We're talking about *pure*, man. We're talking about pure titanium."

Titanium, I thought to myself. That was a find. A large amount of pure titanium had real value... but it shouldn't be found naturally.

The second guy agreed with me. "Pure titanium? What kind of naturally occurring surface object is that?"

The first sensor op stopped and stared at the other. "What? Are you trying to be dumb? It's got to be a crashed ship or something. That's the whole damned point."

They hustled on, and they were soon out of earshot. They rushed through the doors onto the bridge itself and disappeared.

I stood there in the passageway, thinking about what I had just overheard. A big chunk of titanium had been discovered by one of the drones. They weren't clear on whether it was one of the flying ones on the satellites or one of those walking around on the surface, but it really didn't matter. They'd found something big and solid. They'd found a ship. There just wasn't any other explanation.

But *what* ship?

To me, there was only one answer that made sense. It was one of the ships that had come out here earlier to explore this place.

Maybe it had crashed. Or maybe the crew had gone mad, like ours nearly had during the long, long flight out from Mars.

Whatever the case, I knew in my heart that *Borag* now had a new goal, something important to investigate.

Chapter 24: The Ice Cave

The next day, *Borag* summoned all the miners back into the hold and lifted off. We drifted over the surface of the tiny world, heading west. Eventually, we went over the terminator line and kept going. Night closed over us, and the dark, frozen little world seemed even darker and colder than before.

After about an hour of slowly poking around, we crossed a small mountain range or two, then nestled in a rocky valley. I spent this time in the ready room, suited-up and prepared just in case we were needed for some emergency, although I didn't see why anyone would need a marine while landing on a dwarf planet in the middle of nowhere.

But the captain was thinking differently.

"Red Company," she said, coming over the PA system and speaking to us directly. "This landing is going to be different. I want you fully suited-up, fully geared, and armed. Make sure you have full charges in your carbines, and set your suit heaters to high. You're going out on the surface ahead of everyone else. Lt. Quinn will lead the first group, while the second will stay behind aboard ship. Hansen out."

Corporal Tench, Leadbetter, and I exchanged glances. Of course, we rushed to get our gear together, snapped down our helmets, checked our charges, and topped off our oxygen tanks. But we were also throwing odd glances toward Sergeant Cox.

He too, looked befuddled. "Why the hell was I left out of this?" he asked of no one, and no one answered. "Quinn..." he muttered to himself.

He said this as if we couldn't hear him, which we almost couldn't. None of us responded.

We gathered our gear and hustled down the ramps that led to the surface from the cargo hold. A few minutes later, Quinn led us out onto the surface of a brand new world.

I truly felt like an explorer at that moment. It was kind of exciting, actually. Sure, it was clear that I wasn't the first human to have walked on this planet, but I was probably one of the first to have walked in this particular location.

My footprints appeared in the crunchy, frozen methane snows as I walked. They were almost certainly originals.

"Spread out, men," Quinn ordered. "I don't think there's anybody out here to shoot at us, but we might as well make it hard on them if there is."

Right then, a realization hit me like a bolt of lightning. This was why Captain Hansen had sent Red Company first.

Before we'd taken a hundred steps, we could all see our destination. It was a vast hulk that started off as a shadow but became ever more clear as we approached in the dark. Soon, the outline was unmistakable. It was a ship—a big ship, at least as big as our mining rig. In fact, if I had to guess, I would say it was bigger.

The strangest thing about the ship was how quiet it was. As we got closer, we played lights over it. Swirling flecks of snow-like material, which were really made of frozen methane, frosted up our faceplates and occluded our vision. Every dozen steps or so, I had to reach up with my glove and smear some of it away from my visor so that I could see again.

The ship was big, really big.

"She's a miner," Lt. Quinn said. "A miner just like *Borag*—but see that flag painted on the tail? The one that looks like a computer with eyes? This ship is from Teklutions."

I glanced over at him in surprise and alarm. Teklutions was a rival conglomerate, a monstrous organization that was as big or possibly even bigger than Interplanetary Excavations.

"What's a Teklutions vessel doing all the way out here, sir?" Corporal Tench had the balls to ask.

"The same thing we are," Quinn said, marveling at the ship.

"Then why is she dead and lying on her side?"

Quinn glanced at the corporal. Tench had always been the mouthy kind of enlisted man, but Quinn didn't shout him down. He just looked at him and looked back at the big hulk that wallowed on its flank before us. "Obviously, she's in some kind of trouble. We'll render assistance if there's anyone left alive to help."

We broke up into squads and circled around the entire ship. We didn't find anything obvious. No gaping holes in the hull, nothing like that. There were, in fact, a variety of drill-bots encircling the area, especially up against one large hill that was a few hundred yards from the big ship's resting spot.

We found a variety of airlocks, but they were all sealed up. No one answered when we tapped the butt of a rifle on each door.

"Looks like there's nobody home," Corporal Tench said.

"Looks like it," Lt. Quinn agreed. "But we're going to have to go in there and check it out, anyway."

"Hold on, Lieutenant. Hold on," Ledbetter said. He'd been sweeping on his own recognizance, walking a path farther out from the perimeter. Instead of looking at the big ship that we'd just circled around, he was looking at the hill. "There's a lot of equipment over here, sir. A lot of machinery was going in and out of that hill. In fact, it looks like they've dug some kind of a mineshaft."

"A mine?" Immediately, Quinn's voice rose high. He, like everybody else aboard this miserable expedition, had been hoping against hope that there was some profit to be made out here. Perhaps an abandoned mine was just the thing *Borag* needed.

"All right," Quinn said. "I'm going to call this in, and then we're going to check out that mine before we do anything else."

He contacted Captain Hansen, telling her about the situation. She agreed to send out a team of scientists and engineers to cut their way into the derelict mining ship if she had to. In the meantime, she ordered Quinn and the rest of us to investigate the hole that Ledbetter had found in the nearby hill. More than one marine cursed Ledbetter's name during that long trudging walk, let me tell you.

A dozen steps and then a hundred more took us to the opening on the side of the hill. We were already on the darkest side of the darkest planet any of us could imagine, and now we were going to walk down into a hole drilled into the surface. I could hardly think of anything less appealing.

What if there was a sudden venting, as this planet experienced now and then? Maybe that's what had knocked out this ship and possibly killed the men who were running the various drill-bots and ore carts that we'd seen strewn over the area.

Lt. Quinn wasn't thinking like that. He was thinking with greed in the mind. He was thinking about making a big strike, not about what had caused the obvious disaster that was evident all around us.

Without hesitation, he snapped his suit lights to their brightest and then marched into the yawning cavern. We followed him with grunts of disappointment.

As we descended deeper into the rocky shaft, the temperature dropped sharply, and the frozen landscape became more prominent. Rock, metal, and a lot of methane-based frost was everywhere. It was a hazardous environment, and we had to be cautious with every step we took.

Lt. Quinn led the way, his suit lights illuminating the path ahead. We followed him, zigzagging and descending deeper into the unknown terrain. The walls of the rocky descent were covered with melted patches and gouges from laser drills. The risks were evident, but we had to continue. We had to find out what had caused the disaster and whether there were any survivors.

The ice-crusted walls of the cavern were jagged and irregular, with sharp edges and uneven surfaces everywhere. The temperature within the cavern was extremely cold, well below the freezing point of water, and the atmosphere was composed primarily of methane gas.

The weirdest thing was the ice itself. It wasn't water, but frozen methane, which was used to make propane gas back on Earth. One would think a planet made of such a highly flammable chemical would be dangerous, whether it was frozen or not, but fire takes more than fuel to burn—it takes oxygen as well.

One thing Eris didn't have was oxygen, which made it virtually impossible to light a fire of any kind. *Borag* had her own supply, of course, but since the thin atmosphere of Eris had none, at least there should be no chance of an explosion.

Quinn marched deeper into the mineshaft, and we all followed him. I could tell the rest of the men were getting a little nervous. Even Corporal Tench looked unhappy. Our communication systems were no longer able to reach the surface due to too much ice, rock, and debris above us. We were spiraling downward instead of going down in a straight line.

"What in the nine hells were they trying to find down here?" Quinn muttered to himself.

All of us glanced at each other, hoping against hope that the man would call a halt to this insane march straight down to Hell. We all wanted to turn around and head back up to the relative safety of the surface.

But no, Quinn straightened up his shoulders and kept going. We followed in his wake, hoping for the best.

When we were several hundred yards below the surface, the tunnel changed in nature, making one last turn before opening up into a giant cavernous zone.

"This has got to be it," Quinn announced. "There's got to be something valuable down here. Get out your sniffers, boys—metal detectors, everything."

Being crewmen from a mining ship, we actually had sensors built into our spacesuits to detect rich veins of ore. It was, after all, the main business of *Borag* to find such things.

Immediately, gasps went up from a half-dozen marines around me. I checked my own instruments and stared in disbelief.

"This place is *all* metal," I said. Being a miner, I knew the signs. I could read one of these sensors better than any marine.

Quinn whirled around and marched up to me. "You," he said, pointing a big finger at my chest. "You were a miner once, weren't you, boy?"

"That's right, sir."

"All right, you lead the way. You take us to this big treasure trove I'm seeing on my instruments right now."

Gritting my teeth, I nodded and followed the path laid out for me.

At first, I was confused. We walked up onto a large humping hill—all of it underground, mind you. The cavern was so large that it actually had room to have a rise in the flooring of the cavern. It was like climbing a hill, crunching on frozen chunks of ice.

When I reached the highest point in the cavern floor, I looked around and shined a beam around me. A huge pile of ice under our feet reflected the beam off of a thousand facets.

The critical moment came when I shone a bright light directly downward into a thin spot in the ice. There was something big down there—something dark that gleamed back at me.

It was metal—it had to be.

That's when I realized the whole bottom of the cave was metal. I stood straighter and looked around, my mouth gaping. I directed the light up high to see the jagged ceiling of ice above me and then flashed the light down low again, looking at that crusty coating of more ice that was hiding the smooth, rounded hull of a monstrous hunk of metal.

"This is what we've been detecting all along. That's why our sensors were going crazy…"

I knew in my heart that this was why the Teklution ship had come here and landed just outside this cave. They'd bored their way down here all the way to the bottom.

They'd somehow detected what we'd just found—a very large, frozen mass of manufactured metal.

Lt. Quinn had been on a treasure hunt, but he'd gotten more than he'd bargained for. When I carefully explained the situation to him, he stood there in the middle of that vast cavern and looked in every direction, gaping just as I'd done. He finally turned back to face me and asked the question that was burning everyone's mind as they all gathered around and stared.

"Are you kidding me?" he said. "This thing is huge. If you look at the parabolic curve, it's got to be way bigger than *Borag*—even bigger than the Teklution rig."

I nodded. "I'd have to agree, sir," I said. "This thing, whatever it is—it's friggin' huge."

Quinn stood quiet for a moment. Everyone else was gaping, gawking and standing around crunching on the ice. We were looking every which way and shining our lights at the ice.

Suddenly, Quinn's voice changed. Instead of greedy, he sounded somewhat fearful. "It's got to be dangerous," he said. "That's the only thing that makes sense. How did that other ship get to be a derelict? What happened to them? To the first crew who discovered this thing?"

I shrugged, and I decided right then and there to confess a little bit of what I knew from the meetings back on Mars. As far as I knew, no one else in Red Company had been privy to the details of our mission.

"Sir," I said. "I've got to tell you something."

"What now, Starn? Make it snappy. We've got to go back and report this."

"We will, sir. I'm sure we will. But sir, it's about the nature of this mission."

I confessed then to the fact that I'd been in the conference room with the Mars execs for Interplanetary Excavations when Captain Hansen had been given her fateful charge to fly out to Eris. I explained that there had been another ship, one they'd sent out earlier and lost contact with.

Quinn's jaw sagged lower to an improbable point. I didn't even think there was room inside of my helmet for my chin to sag so low. "Are you shitting me, Starn? You were there? You knew about this all this time, and you didn't say a goddamn thing?"

"No, sir. I was under orders not to—orders from the captain. The last time I looked, she's above your rank—or Commander Kaine's."

Quinn nodded at last. "Right… So, you're telling me now because it doesn't matter anymore? We might as well know, right?"

"That's right, sir. If Red Company is in danger, I'm not going to withhold information, even under orders."

Quinn reached out a hand and slammed it on my shoulder. A little puff of frozen ice and gas flew away as he did this.

"Good man," he said. "All right. I've got to think. I've got to think about what the hell are we going to do."

"I found something over here, sir!" it was Corporal Tench, and he was shouting and waving. "I've found something!"

We looked in his direction, and we saw his light flicker toward our eyes. Quinn hesitated for just a moment, and then he marched over there, mumbling curses.

Corporal Tench was standing right at the center of the arcing dome of ice. He'd apparently done a little searching while we were having our private discussions. He'd made it up to the summit, and he'd indeed found something to crow about.

You couldn't see it from any distance away, but once you got up close, there was a dark patch in the ice. A hole in the frost that revealed the metal below.

We all shined our lights down into that hole. We played lights over the smooth metal surface, the gleaming, twisted ice, and jagged crystalline growths that surrounded it.

"That, gentlemen," Lt. Quinn said, "is a hatch. Have you tried to open it, Corporal Tench?"

"Hell no," Tench said.

Quinn stared, and he thought about it. I could tell he was considering opening the hatch or trying to. Finally, he marched down into the hole, which was about three yards across and five long. The hatch—if that's indeed what it was—wasn't circular, but rather oblong with rounded edges.

Quinn looked for a wheel or something to spin, but he found nothing obvious. There was no clear way in.

"Whatever this thing is, it seems to be sealed tight," he said. "I can see the outline of the hatch, but I don't see any way to get it to open up…"

"They burned their way down here," Ledbetter was saying. "The guys from Teklution must have melted this open spot in the ice. Hey, Devin, you're the miner. You see this? See all these scars in the ice? That's laser drills, right?"

"Sure is," I told him.

"How the hell could they fire lasers with all this methane around and not blow up?"

I shook my head. "It won't burn. Not without oxygen. The atmosphere here is way too thin for that. Methane wouldn't burn on the moon either."

"I sure as hell hope you're right."

"I'd better be," I said, pointing. "They obviously burned and melted away the ice. They melted away the methane without lighting it"

"Yeah," Quinn said, "I guess you're right. You've got to be right. We need to get the miners down here. We got to deploy tech teams. They'll have to find a way in."

We all looked at Quinn. Our eyes were big and round already. He was talking about getting into this thing.

Did nothing impinge on this crazy officer's sense of self-preservation? Hadn't we just found a dead ship up above? Weren't we following in their footsteps even now?

I didn't know what to say, so I said nothing. A lot of the marines around me were stepping from foot to foot. They were looking in every direction at once. Everyone was feeling spooked.

"Where are the bodies?" Corporal Tench asked suddenly, asking the question out of nowhere. But when I thought about it, I realized he had a point.

"What bodies?" Quinn asked.

"The crew of the Teklution ship. Shouldn't we have found them dead somewhere?"

"Well…" Quinn said, "they aren't necessarily dead, and if they are, they're probably back on up on top. Inside their ship."

"But what would have killed them in there?" Tench pressed. "If they came down here and they opened that hatch, and they found their way inside… assuming something killed them, shouldn't there be some bodies?"

Quinn fell silent. All of us did. He looked down slowly toward the hatch. Finally, I think even he had had enough.

"Marines," he said, "we're doing a U-turn. We're marching back up to the surface. We're going to talk to Captain Hansen, and we're going to let her decide what to do next."

Chapter 25: The Dead Ship

We all breathed a big sigh of relief as we began the trek upward. As we marched up the spiraling rampway that had been cut by a Teklution team, who knew how long ago, we moved markedly faster than we had on the way down. Despite the fact that we were going uphill, it seemed as if our boots wanted to hustle us out of there.

By the time we came out of the mineshaft onto the open plains of Eris, we were bounding like giants. Lt. Quinn halted and called the troops to halt as soon as we were out in the open. He immediately reported in privately, and after a moment, he switched back to our channel.

"I've just had a talk with Captain Hansen," he said. "It looks like they've managed to break into the Teklutions ship. We're to report to the breach point—right now."

He bounded off, and we followed him, double-time. The amount of ground a trained man could cover on a low-gravity airless surface like Eris was shocking. Fortunately, there weren't too many boulders or other large obstacles on the landscape to trip us while we were bounding along.

Normally, it was difficult to make good time on a very dusty or icy surface. Running over loose dust was kind of like running on a beach, it always slowed you down. But our boots were built for this kind of thing. They automatically released cleats, especially in the toes, to give you a solid grip. And these smart cleats weren't just rubberized spikes. They were more advanced than that. They would adjust themselves to the ground as you ran, and they deployed just the right length of spike to give you the most grip. That allowed a man's musculature to be fully used to send him sailing across the landscape.

Quinn and the rest of 1st Squad raced to the aft side of the great Teklutions ship. There, right under one of those big painted emblems, was a blasted-open hatchway.

"Looks like a secondary airlock right next to the main cargo hold," Quinn said.

Two dockyard types stood there waiting for us. One on either side of the passageway they'd managed to cut open. They just looked at us and showed no inclination to go inside themselves. These men were often called yard-dogs because they typically worked in spaceship yards. Sometimes we shortened that down to just "dogs." Both of the dogs had naval ranks. One was a boatswain, and the other one was a boatswain's mate.

"Chief?" Quinn said, turning to the boatswain. "What can you tell us about the interior?"

The dog shook his head. "Absolutely nothing, sir. We haven't set foot in the place."

Quinn looked back and forth between the two of them and chuckled. "I guess that's our job then, isn't it?"

"That's right, sir. You're Red Company. We're paid to sling torches, not rifles."

Lt. Quinn turned back to the squad, and I knew by the way his eyes were traveling over the group of us, he was looking for a volunteer.

Nobody moved a muscle. Then he opened his mouth. I could see that through his faceplate, and he was about to pick a victim when we heard a new voice crackle into our headsets.

"Wait! Halt! Do not defile that ship. Not yet." It was a female voice, but kind of scratchy. "Lt. Quinn, are you listening to me?"

"Yes, doc," Quinn said. "We're standing by."

On our private tactical channel, a lot of chatter began. "Are we really just gonna stand here waiting after we raced all the way across the plain?"

"That's what I said, Tench," Quinn answered. "We're going to stand right here and wait."

There was a lot of complaining after that. Everyone seemed to need a nap or have to go to the bathroom. Quinn told everyone to shut up and take a shit in their suits. The complaints turned to muted grumblings after that. We wandered around, finding a place to sit down and rest.

If there's one thing a marine knows while on deployment, it's that whenever you can take a break, you take it. You never knew how long it would be until your next one.

We took a few sips of our precious body waters which the suits provided for us, checked our energy levels, and generally relaxed.

When the science team approached, we saw that there were two men and a woman. The woman, named Dr. Sharaf, was in charge.

"My marines have been given the charge of escorting you into this ship, Doc," Quinn said.

"So I've been informed, Lieutenant," Sharaf answered. She sounded a bit snippy to me.

Dr. Sharaf was *Borag's* science officer, serving in the labs down in the ship's bowels. She was a petite woman with short, curly hair which she kept pulled back into a tight bun. She had a sharp mind and an even sharper face, which could sometimes be intimidating to those around her.

"As I understand it," she said, "you uncovered something unexpected down in that cavern."

"Yes. A large metal surface—it has to be a ship."

Dr. Sharaf immediately threw up a hand. "Please, don't embarrass yourself by jumping to premature conclusions. I will determine the nature of this anomaly—if there truly is one."

"I know what I saw," Quinn said, sounding annoyed. "If you want us to take you to the spot—"

"All in good time, Lieutenant. For now, this unresponsive ship is mysterious enough. Let's proceed."

"All right, Doctor—but I would think this ship is of less importance. After all, it's not going anywhere."

Dr. Sharaf tossed him a cold stare. "Opinions," she said. "Everyone has one, don't they? Well fortunately, in this case, your opinion does not supersede mine."

Lt. Quinn began to argue, she cut him off again. "In the interests of clarity, I'll explain. You found something at the bottom of a mineshaft, something beyond your understanding. Presumably, the people in this ship, this derelict Teklutions vessel, found that same unknown entity below. It appears to have done them some damage, some kind of harm. I would rather search this ship and discover the nature of this harm before I expose myself—or anyone aboard *Borag* to any possible contamination."

"Contamination...?" Quinn said. His voice shifted from anger to concern. "Do you think they ran into a dose of radiation or maybe some kind of biotic thing—a virus or something?"

"We really don't know, now do we?" Dr. Sharaf said. "That's why we're here, to do some tests. Now, if you don't mind, I would like you to send in a few scouts before I walk in there myself, just in case there's something physically dangerous. I would severely doubt there is, but it's possible."

Quinn nodded thoughtfully as he turned back to the squad. His eyes ran over the group, and he pointed to me. That was probably because I'd lifted my hand.

"Are you crazy, man?" Ledbetter whispered, helmet-to-helmet.

I shrugged. "Maybe," I answered. "But somebody's got to go in there, and I'm kind of curious to see what's what."

Ledbetter shook his head. I could tell he figured he hadn't properly trained me in the ways of a Red Company private. One of the primary rules was that you never volunteered for anything. Never.

"Ledbetter," Quinn said, "you go with him."

There was a bit of cursing in my ear after that. Ledbetter and I had been paired together many times before, and it seemed like it was becoming a thing. I got the feeling Ledbetter did not always appreciate this bonding. But as he wasn't any more highly ranked than I was, it really didn't matter what he thought.

We marched together into the gaping open hole, which was essentially an airlock that had been opened with cutting torches. We stepped onto the slanted decks of the Teklution ship trying to look everywhere at once.

Walking into the ship, we immediately realized several things. One was that there was no power. In fact, there was nothing—no oxygen, heat, or emergency lighting. All of it had been shut down or had run out some time ago.

"I'm watching your helmet feed, Starn," Quinn said. "But I'd appreciate some commentary on what you're seeing along the way."

"So far, there's not a whole hell of a lot to report, sir," I said. "We're past the airlock. It seems like both ends of it have been ruptured. Did the dogs do this?"

"No, we sure didn't," the boatswain's mate answered. "All we did was crack the entrance. Don't blame me for anything else."

"All right, all right, keep going," Quinn said.

Ledbetter was fooling around with a side panel, and he managed to get some lights to flicker on. At least it was something.

Dust and ice particles drifted around. Eris was pretty much airless, but when you kicked up a cloud of dust or ice, it tended to swirl and float, taking a long time to adhere to the deck again.

This kind of dust had always been a severe problem on rocks like Eris. The Moon had permanent bases on its surface these days, and the personnel posted there had constant trouble with the dust. The problem was it was electrostatically charged and without any moisture, it adhered to almost everything. It got into base equipment, into your gear and it even made air hoses hard to plug together. Grit was always found in every connection, every joint.

Even as far back as the original moon missions of the 1960s, the dust had plagued the first astronauts, getting into everything and damaging all kinds of equipment. Over time, however, we had developed some sophisticated means of dampening the effects of this scourge.

Absently, I reached up and turned on my suit's electrostatic charge-producing system, and it helped somewhat to clear my vision. The device attracted the dust to key points and was designed for this exact purpose.

Ledbetter and I took cautious steps, shining lights into every crevice and keeping our guns unslung. The passageway was eerily motionless. There were no sounds other than the gentle hum and hiss of my life support systems in the background.

The lack of air pressure was immediately noticeable, with any small movements causing the grit to drift up into clouds. The only source of light came from the dim glow emanating from my chest lights, which cast jagged illumination across the metallic walls and floors.

As we moved deeper into the ship, the passageway had clearly seen recent action. There were signs of a fierce gun battle. Scorch marks and melted holes pockmarked the walls, and overturned debris littered the deck. However, there were no bodies to be seen, just the remnants of a brutal conflict. It was as if the occupants had vanished into thin air, leaving behind only the haunting evidence of their struggle.

The emptiness of the passageway seemed to magnify the sense of danger and foreboding, making it feel as if anything could be lurking in the darkness ahead.

"I don't know what happened in here, sir," I reported back to Lt. Quinn. "But it seems to me like there was a fight right here at the entrance."

"What's your evidence, Starn?" Quinn asked.

I turned and lowered my faceplate near the deck, and I showed where there were dried blood stains and gouges in the floor and the ceiling.

"Are you getting this, sir?" I asked.

"Yes, I am…" Quinn said. "Looks like laser bolts have been fired. Dr. Sharaf, when you go in, I want samples of all that."

"Of course, of course," Dr. Sharaf replied. "We'll do the samples. That's what we're here for, Lieutenant."

I had to grin inside my helmet. I could already tell there was no love lost between Dr. Sharaf and Lt. Quinn, nor would there be in the future. She was quite a self-important person.

We kept going, but there wasn't really all that much to see until I got to the second intersection. There, I discovered what could only be described as a makeshift barricade.

"Take a look at this, sir. Someone strung up crisscrossing wires and hung furniture on the web-like result. And look... are these spot-welds? They seem to have taken some benches, chairs, anything they could find, and stacked it all up right here and welded everything into place."

"Are you able to get through?" Quinn asked.

"Yes, sir, I think so. All I've got to do is reach up, pull, heave, and finally snap off one of the dangling cables," I replied.

It seemed to me that it was an odd type of barricade, more the sort of thing that would be expected to stop a dog than a thinking human. A human, after all, could just reach up and unhook some of these wires and shift aside these steel struts and benches—but an animal either wouldn't think of it or wouldn't have the hands to manipulate objects in such a fine manner. Overall, I found the whole thing baffling.

I unhooked some of the wire loops that were strung up with hooks on the walls and scooted past the barricade.

"Careful there's not a landmine in there or something," Ledbetter said following me.

"Boom," I said, laughing at him.

"Very funny," Dr. Sharaf complained, "extremely funny. Are your men comedians, Lt. Quinn, or are they soldiers?"

"It's honestly a little bit of both, I think, Doc. Are you ready to go in the ship now, or should I send my men all the way to the bridge first?" Quinn asked.

I heard a bit of muttering and grumbling. Apparently, the woman and her sidekicks were discussing the matter.

Finally, she released an angry puff of air. "We'll go in. Let's all go in."

"Starn, Ledbetter," Quinn said, "you two standdown. Hold your position and wait for us."

It was with some relief that we did as he ordered. The whole ship was giving me a creepy feeling, sort of a dark vibe. It was like walking through a funeral parlor, but one that was low-gravity, airless, freezing, and mysteriously unpowered. If you've ever been inside a derelict spacecraft, you'll know what I mean.

"Hey. Hey, Starn!" Ledbetter called. "Come over here, I found something."

He hadn't listened to Lt. Quinn and had wandered off down one of the side passages. He was standing in a doorway, gesturing wildly toward the deck. His laser carbine was unslung in his arms and pointing downward.

Frowning, I followed after him. "What have you got, Ledbetter?"

"Look, just take a look."

I walked up, and I did look. He'd found a frozen corpse.

"Is that a marine?" I asked.

"No, I think it's one of their Green Company types. A shore patrolman. See, he's got nothing but a pistol. And that armor is different than ours, different colored, a little bit bulkier, but essentially the same idea."

"Right, right," I said, bending down and checking on the man. Ledbetter hadn't gotten any closer to him and had done nothing but aim his gun at the body. The poor bastard seemed quite dead and harmless to me. So, I knelt, flipped him over, and took a look.

The moment that freaked me out a little came when I saw the man's face inside his helmet. There were two things wrong. First of all, the helmet's interior light inside was on. It was illuminating his face. But that wasn't the freaky part.

What I really didn't like was what I saw on that face. A look of sheer terror, a jaw that was open and twisted at such an angle that it seemed like the man's jawbone had been broken and slid to one side. On top of all that, he was frozen solid.

His eyes were open and staring, his lips were retracted, exposing his teeth. Even his popsicle-like tongue was extruded in that moment of terror and horror in which he had finally died.

"Whoa," I said, standing up and backing off. Ledbetter laughed and walked forward, giving the corpse a gentle nudge with his boot. "Never seen an asphyxiation case, have you? This is what happens to you when you get exposed to pure vacuum. Don't forget it, Starn. You don't die instantly, and it's far from painless."

I stared, not liking what I'd seen.

"First off," Ledbetter said, warming to the topic He seemed to enjoy my concern. "Did you know the temperature at which liquids boils is directly related to the air pressure and temperature you're exposed to?"

I didn't bother to answer. I was too fascinated by this frozen-faced dead man.

"Well, what happens when you're exposed to open space is your blood boils in your veins. Can you imagine how fun that feels? This guy can." Ledbetter laughed again and nudged the man with his boot.

This kind of pissed me off. It was disrespectful to the dead. I pushed his foot away.

"Knock it off," I said. "He's suffered enough already."

Ledbetter scowled and wandered off, but at least he left the dead man alone.

Chapter 26: The Missing Crew

The interior of the abandoned Teklution ship was a haunting sight. The passages were dark and silent, with only the occasional flicker of emergency lighting to break the oppressive gloom. According to our biohazard detectors, what little air the ship had left was contaminated by toxic vapors, mostly oxidized metal.

The ship's interior was littered with debris. Rusty tools, mining equipment, and scraps of metal were scattered haphazardly throughout the ship, giving the appearance of the vessel having been abandoned in a hurry. The walls and floors were streaked with dirt and grime, and the once-pristine insulation was now chipped and peeling.

As we made our way deeper into the ship, we discovered many of the rooms and compartments had been sealed shut or barricaded. Those that were accessible revealed signs of a chaotic struggle. Furniture was overturned, screens were smashed, and equipment lay scattered on the decks. It was as if the crew had been desperately searching for something before they disappeared.

In one of the ship's storage bays, we discovered a disturbing sight. Dozens of mining drones lay strewn about the room, their metallic bodies twisted and torn as if they had been attacked by some unknown force. The walls and ceiling were scored with deep gouges, and the air was thick with the acrid scent of burnt metal.

As we delved deeper into the ship, we encountered more signs of violence and destruction. Blood stains decorated the walls and floors. There were odd gouges in the doors, and ominous blinking displays spoke of emergencies. Everything hinted at a dark and terrifying past. It was evident that something had gone horribly wrong on the mining ship, and the crew had paid a terrible price for it.

Despite the oppressive sense of foreboding that lurked in every shadowy corner, we pressed on, driven by our mission. We'd been charged with the task of uncovering the truth about what had happened aboard the Teklution ship, and we weren't going to be scared away by a few bloodstains.

As we explored deeper, I felt a growing sense of dread. However, it wasn't until we reached the lower deck crew quarters that things went from grim to fantastic.

"Hey, Starn," Ledbetter called out. "Look over here, through this porthole."

Many of the doorways in the ship had small, thick-glassed windows. I floated over to where Ledbetter was waving. My boots barely touched the slanted deck as I moved. I crowded my helmet into the limited space and peered through to see what he was looking at.

Then, I spotted a figure. "Is that someone's back?" I asked. "Someone's standing over there against that wall?"

"Yeah, I think so," Ledbetter replied. "Either that, or the guy froze to death in a really weird place." He laughed.

I glanced at him in mild disgust. It seemed to me that many of the Red Company regular marines had a callous attitude toward death. Perhaps that just came with the territory, so I was going to have to get used to it.

"Hold on," I said. "I think I just saw him move."

As we watched, he moved again. One of his arms drifted up and then down again.

Ledbetter pushed me aside, crowding to look through. "Nah," he said. "That's just some kind of air current or something. I think that room is fully pressurized."

"Yeah," I said, checking the gauges. "I think it is. Good thing we didn't just pop this open on him. We might have killed him with the explosive decompression."

"He's not alive, man. He *can't* be."

"We'll see."

We reported back to Lt. Quinn, and soon the entire group rushed to our location. "We've got a possible survivor," Quinn said, talking into his headset. The message was relayed back to *Borag*.

"Get away from that door," Dr. Sharaf said. "Before you kill the poor man."

We backed off and let her examine the doorway. "We have to pressurize this passageway, so we can open the chamber. Let's close down either end of this area then pump air in. We're reading about a two percent oxygen levels in the ship's tanks—that's enough."

Ledbetter and I looked at one another in alarm. Two percent? That wasn't much. Most of the ship had to be uninhabitable.

"Gods," Dr. Sharaf said, peering through the glass. "I wonder how long he's been trapped in there."

Quinn shook his head. "Maybe he can tell us if we let him out, but he sure is acting weirdly."

Dr. Sharaf frowned at him. "You'd be acting strangely too if you'd been trapped for months in a ship like this."

"I can only imagine what he's been eating…" Corporal Tench added.

We all wrinkled our noses in disgust. We watched as Dr. Sharaf's team began to work. Say what you will about them being nerds, they knew how to operate virtually every control system on the ship.

They quickly sealed off either end of the passageway then raised the temperature and pressure. Eventually, it equalized enough so that Dr. Sharaf instructed us to open the door.

I couldn't help but notice that Sharaf and her team backed away significantly when she gave this order. What were they worried about? I couldn't fathom it. Whoever this guy was, I was pretty sure he wasn't dangerous. He was probably starved and raving mad.

While the repressurization process was going on, we tapped on the glass and the door, making various sounds in an attempt to gain his attention. We hoped maybe we could get him to turn around and face us at the very least.

None of our efforts worked. He continued to stare fixedly at the wall opposite us.

At last, the door opened.

Quinn frowned, looking at the strange man and the even stranger surroundings. "Are those bodies over there?"

Indeed, they were. We hadn't really been able to see them through the small round portal in the door, but there were a number of bodies strewn around the room. The only one standing was that single man...

Quinn waved for me and Ledbetter to move forward. "You guys found him," he said, "he's all yours."

We moved into the chamber reluctantly. At one time, this had probably been the crew quarters, or perhaps a meeting area for lower deck personnel—but now it was a garbage-strewn mess. There was only debris, a few dead men—and one weird guy standing with his nose in the corner as if he was punishing himself.

I turned on my external speakers and tried to talk to him. "Hey, buddy! Are you okay? We're here from *Borag*, another mining rig just like yours. You've been rescued, man."

"Yeah," Ledbetter said. "Try to act grateful." He seemed to think this was funny, but I shot him a glance of disapproval.

"Ah, jeez," Ledbetter said. "Let's just grab him." So saying, he marched forward and put a heavy glove on the man's shoulder.

This caused an unexpected and violent reaction. The man whirled around, facing us. For the first time, I saw his face. I was instantly sorry we'd made the effort to come in here and check up on him.

His face reminded me of the twisted pain we'd seen in the dead man's face a couple of passages back. Apparently, he wasn't frozen or dead—but that didn't make him any happier to meet us.

He whirled around and made a slashing motion with his hands. What was in his hand? What was he holding? At first, it seemed like it must have been a bundle of knives, but no, it wasn't that. It was a set of long, razor-sharp claws. The lunatic slashed at Ledbetter's armored chest and drew lines across it.

"What the hell?" Ledbetter said. "Back off, buddy. Stand down, stand down!"

Ledbetter had his gun out, and he was backing away in alarm. I had to admit, I was doing the same.

Lt. Quinn, back at the doorway, was shouting orders at us, but we could barely hear him.

That face. It wasn't quite human. It was the face of a man who'd already suffered death and was still thinking about it every waking second. It was a face of unrelenting pain.

The man was a rock-rat, that much was easy to see. He was powerfully built, and although he wore a bulky spacesuit, you could still see the muscles bulging and rippling underneath.

A strange, menacing sound was coming out of him as well. I wouldn't call it a growl, not quite. It was more of a rattling sound, but it sent a sudden chill down my spine in any case.

The man didn't heed our warnings. He went for Ledbetter again, thrusting this time, stabbing with those long claws. He caught Ledbetter's leg just above the knee.

To my surprise, that unarmored spot was punctured. Spacesuit fabric is quite tough and multi-layered. Those claws at the end of his fingers must have been extraordinarily sharp to have penetrated it—either that, or he was wielding them with unusual strength.

That was enough for Ledbetter. He unloaded probably ten percent of his battery's charge, blazing away with his carbine until his attacker was left in a tangled, smoking heap.

There were laser bolt holes, charred and deep, riddling the body. The crewman twitched a bit, but he didn't get back up again.

Quinn walked up then, putting his hands on his hips. "Outstanding," he said sarcastically. "Here we find our first survivor in this entire rig, and you go and blow him out of his boots. What have you got to say for yourself, Private?"

Ledbetter turned and displayed the cuts in his spacesuit's legging. Quinn looked shocked. Stepping forward, he nudged at the corpse and splayed out the curved claws at the fingertips.

"That's really weird," he said. "Where'd he even get those things?"

"Sir..." Corporal Tench said, "Sir, I think we've got a problem!"

Lt. Quinn turned and saw Corporal Tench standing over one of the other bodies. It seemed to be stirring, beginning to squirm on the deck.

"What the fuck?" Quinn said.

"Out, out!" Dr. Sharaf cried from the doorway. "You've got to get out of there. The heat of your bodies and the warmth of the air are waking them up." She gestured wildly, urging us to retreat.

"They're *waking up?*" Quinn backed away, noticing more men were beginning to stir and rise onto their hands and knees.

Shock and disbelief transformed into fear as we all realized we were in grave danger. Quinn gave the order to retreat. We quickly ran out into the passageway, not needing any further urging.

As we slammed the door behind us, several former rock-rats from the Teklution crew rushed after us, groping and tearing at the doorway.

Quinn spun around and marched over to Dr. Sharaf, looking as if he was going to grab her and give her a good shaking, but he controlled himself.

"What the hell's going on in here? What are these things? Zombies? Monsters? Some kind of experiment?"

"None of those things, Lieutenant," she said. "They are mutations."

"Teklution mutants? How did you know we'd find something like this? And why didn't you tell us about it?"

"They are only men," she said, "men who've been exposed to something we don't quite understand."

"This is what we flew all the way out here to investigate, isn't it?" he asked. "And somehow, you knew they'd be here, didn't you?"

Dr. Sharaf gave a dismissive shrug. "Something killed this ship," she said. "What did you think we'd discover when we came out here? This ship didn't malfunction or crash. It was overwhelmed by... something."

Growling and dissatisfied, Quinn turned back to Ledbetter and inspected his injuries. There was some blood seeping out, but it wasn't too bad. We patched up the skin and the suit and called him fit to serve.

Lt. Quinn made sure the door we'd found was sealed tightly. "I think we've seen enough," he said. "Something happened to this crew. I don't know what it was, and I don't want to know. I'm getting out of here. You can stay behind if you want, Dr. Sharaf."

She complained bitterly, but in the end, when we marched out of the ship, she followed in our wake. Not even Dr. Sharaf, with all her arrogance, was willing to stay alone and unarmed aboard this strange, haunted vessel.

As we were leaving, Quinn began his report, speaking directly to Captain Hansen herself. He didn't bother to encrypt the transmissions, so we were able to overhear. I guess that was probably because he was in a hurry to get back to *Borag*.

"Repeat that last statement, Lt. Quinn," Hansen ordered when he was midway through his explanation.

"Can you hear me, sir? We encountered something aboard this ship—something strange. Dr. Sharaf claims they're mutants. We got into an altercation with a few of them. We had to put one down because it attacked Private Ledbetter. But now that we're exiting the ship, I think that—"

"Let me understand this," Captain Hansen interrupted him, "and I want you to be perfectly clear, Lieutenant. Did any of your people come into physical contact with these survivors?"

"Yes, ma'am. One of them seemed to have claws of some kind. It slashed at Ledbetter, cutting through his suit. He's bleeding, but it's not really a serious injury. We've got the suit sealed up again. There's no oxygen loss, so—"

"Lt. Quinn," Hansen said, cutting him off again. "This changes everything. Unfortunately, there are protocols in place which I cannot alter, and which I must follow. I'm sure you understand."

"Protocols? What do you want us to do, sir?"

"Do not leave the vicinity of the Teklution ship. I'm sorry, Lieutenant, but certain precautions must be taken. Do not allow any of your men to leave the area where you broke into the ship. You are all to consider yourselves quarantined."

"Quarantined?" Quinn echoed. He sounded puzzled. "But sir, we haven't been exposed to any kind of—"

"Lieutenant, you have your orders. Hansen out."

"Holy shit," Ledbetter said. "We might have to stand around out here for a week. God damn it." He was still grumbling as we headed down the final passageway toward the exit.

Before we left the ship, however, he paused and looked into a side passage. He appeared to be puzzled.

"Hey Starn, come over here," Ledbetter called out to me.

I walked to where he was standing. "What is it?"

He pointed down at the deck. "Isn't this where that other guy was? You know, the one I was going to kick before you stopped me?"

Frowning, I eyed the spot. "I think it is…"

"Do you think he got up and ran off?" Ledbetter asked. He was only half-joking.

I shook my head. "I don't know."

Suddenly, there was a commotion at the exit. We raced down the passageway, expecting to see someone who had found the crewman we'd thought was dead. However, as we burst out onto the surface of Eris, we found Lt. Quinn had his arms wrapped around a violently thrashing Dr. Sharaf.

"Let go of me, Lieutenant! I'll have you up on charges!" she shouted.

"No, Doctor, I'm afraid I can't do that. We are officially quarantined."

Dr. Sharaf continued to put up a fight, calling Quinn a fool, but he held onto her. Her two minions looked on, baffled.

As I walked out onto the surface of Eris, I was confused by their reactions and those of Captain Hansen. However, I did note that the two yard dogs we'd left out here had disappeared. There were tracks leading away directly toward *Borag's* landing site. They guided my eyes in that direction.

Then, I noticed something important.

"Hey, Lieutenant? I think *Borag* is lighting up her engines."

It was true. All of us gawked. We couldn't believe it.

The big ship had arrived here just a few hours ago, but now she was glowing with new power. She'd redirected her engines downward, and they were gently thrusting. *Borag* rose vertically another foot or two every second.

A group of people were running toward the ship from the direction of the mine. There must have been another investigatory team out there. We all winced as a number of them were incinerated. Two were moving more slowly than the rest, however. Driven back by the clouds of dust and radiation, they turned away and came in our direction instead.

Spooked a bit by now, some of our marines raised their rifles. But Quinn walked among us, slapping down our weapons. "They're crewmen from *Borag*, stand down."

Two members of the mining crew had escaped the blasting exhaust of *Borag*. They came trotting toward us, and I recognized them. One was Charlie and the other was the same foreman who'd tried to shock me to death some months ago.

This surprised me until I noticed Charlie was on a leg-chain. Apparently, he'd gotten himself in some further trouble since the last time I'd seen him. He was working with an escort. That must have been what had saved these two, slowing them down when the others had raced to board *Borag* and were burned to death.

I had to smile, Charlie had the luck of fools and drunks.

"Lieutenant?" the foreman said, "*Borag* just bugged out on us. Do you know what the hell's going on, sir?"

Lt. Quinn raised his eyes up toward the spectacular sight of *Borag's* belly. Fortunately, we weren't close enough to be incinerated, but we were still closer than I felt was comfortable.

"I don't get it," Quinn said. "She's actually going to ditch us out here? We're going to be marooned on this rock forever."

"Yes, you fool," Dr. Sharaf said. She'd wriggled loose from his gripping gauntlets while we were distracted by the liftoff. "I should have stopped you from reporting the incident with Private Ledbetter. A direct injury is a classic opportunity for a blood-to-blood transfer. Once you admitted that a man's suit had been breached, this sequence of events was a foregone conclusion."

We gaped at her. "You mean to tell me this is all his fault?" Corporal Tench demanded, backhanding Ledbetter's shoulder.

"Captain Hansen had no choice," Dr. Sharaf said. "Any unknown pathogen must be isolated, no matter what the cost. She can't risk her ship—or Earth. There was no other possible outcome but this."

She pointed a gloved hand at the rising ship. *Borag* was mile up by now, maybe more. The sight of the great ship leaving us filled everyone with despair.

Chapter 27: The Thing in the Cave

We tried hailing *Borag,* but she was soon out of range of our suit radios. We didn't have powerful transmitters that could reach all the way up into space.

Those of us who had been left behind gathered in a dismal circle. We had ten marines, three techs and two rock-rats, one of whom was a shifty criminal. Everyone else was either dead, or riding in orbit right now aboard *Borag.*

"Charlie?" I said, gripping his shoulder. "Sorry you didn't make it back to the ship, man."

Charlie shook his head. Inside his faceplate, I could see him grinning. "Don't worry about it, Devin. I wouldn't have missed this for the world. But... uh... do you think Captain Hansen will come back for us? Like... someday?"

"I think we're on our own," I said.

Charlie was deflated, but he took the news stoically. He was a man who was accustomed to bad breaks.

I checked my oxygen meter. I had about seven hours left in my tanks, provided I didn't exert myself too much. I noticed just about everyone else was doing the same thing. We were all calculating how long we had to live.

Lt. Quinn took command as he was the highest-ranking officer there, except for possibly Dr. Sharaf. The good doctor was not in any state of mind to be organizing the rationing of the supplies we had. She was too busy delivering recriminations.

"That's the fool," she said, pointing a finger in Quinn's direction. "He's the one who brought all this upon us. Unless you count that idiot over there," here she pointed at Ledbetter, who was limping a bit. "He managed to get himself injured inside that ship. He's contaminated. His carelessness has killed us all."

"Dr. Sharaf," Quinn said in a tired voice, "I'd appreciate it if you'd shut up, or at least turn off your transmitter, so the rest of us don't have to listen to it. Now, as I'm the highest-ranking officer, I'm going to assume command," he said. "Let's take stock of what we've got. Oxygen, then water, then food, in that order."

We all began checking our supplies and reporting the information back to Quinn. This at least gave us something to do.

It turned out that we were going to run out of oxygen first, then power. Water and food would come later, but it really didn't matter whether we ate and drank or not. If you can't breathe and you're freezing to death, you're not too worried about starvation and thirst.

All told, we had about nine hours to live as a group. That was unless we adopted some of Dr. Sharaf's suggestions.

"A lottery," she said. "That's how they do these things in a civilized fashion. A simple lottery. I've got a randomizer app here on my tablet. It would be best if we chose immediately who will be first."

"The first to do what, Dr. Sharaf?" Quinn interrupted.

"Why, sacrifice themselves for the greater good, of course. That's what," she snapped. "Naturally, top-level officers, individuals of true merit, should be restricted from the initial lottery. Once most of the lower-deck types have been selected, if no one has returned to us with any sort of rescue package, we can move on to another round of sacrifice. If we begin the process promptly, without whining and arguments, the survivors will double their hours before succumbing."

"You're quite mad, aren't you?" Quinn asked. "No one here is going to kill themselves. If we run out of air and power, we might as well all die as a group."

"Insanity," Dr. Sharaf snapped. "Why should all of us perish? If half of us gave up their lives right now, the other half would survive for twice as long. This leaves a reasonable chance for some of us to escape this world."

"How exactly are we going to escape? We're approximately 60 AU from Earth. That's billions of miles."

"Yes, but I'm not suggesting we flap our arms and fly home," she said sarcastically. "We're going to have to avail ourselves of all our resources."

"What would you suggest?" he asked.

"Well, we have two additional sources of energy and air." Here, she pointed toward the Teklution ship. "One is the crashed vessel. The second is the anomaly below, the structure you discovered at the bottom of this mine." Here, she pointed toward the cave mouth.

I realized then that she was right. There was something down there. Could it possibly provide life and sustenance for the rest of us? That was unknown.

Lt. Quinn pondered these possibilities. "We've been chased out of the Teklution ship, and we've been ordered not to return. There are hostile individuals inside the ship. However, it's also true that those hostiles were alive. They were breathing. They were eating something—even if it was each other. In fact, they somehow survived for months aboard that ship..."

He stared at the Teklution ship for perhaps a full minute, thinking. During this time, Dr. Sharaf continued to prattle on about her recommended sacrifices. I couldn't help but notice that low-ranked marines were high on her list of expendables. Ledbetter topped the list, and he was scowling at her and fingering his carbine's trigger.

Finally, Quinn spun around and took a step toward her. She took a step back in concern. I couldn't blame her. She was probably used to people wanting to kill her after a rather short amount of time in her company.

"You're right," he said. "We've got to decide now. We've got to make our move—*right now*. Either we go inside the Teklution ship, or we go down into this cave."

"We could do both," Corporal Tench suggested. "Half of us go one way, half of us go the other."

Quinn thought about that, but he finally shook his head. "No, we're going to stay together. If we run into a fight like we did aboard that ship, we want to have all of our strength in one place."

"More foolishness," Dr. Sharaf said. "If we split in half, one group is more likely to survive."

"Yes, well, we don't know much about the thing in the ice cave, but we do know what we saw aboard the Teklution ship. There are hostiles there, and very little in the way of supplies. We might be able to survive for a few days, maybe a week, but there are a lot of us."

Dr. Sharaf brought up her lottery idea again, but Quinn wouldn't listen to it.

"Forget that. If we're going to have a chance to survive—possibly for months before rescue—we've got to have more than what I saw aboard that ship. Our only hope is to get lucky with the hatch below. At the very least, we'll get to see what's inside."

"A gambler," Dr. Sharaf said, "you're a madman gambling with all of our lives."

"You, Doctor," he told her, "are free to go where you wish. You can come with Red Company, or you can go on into that Teklution ship and make some new friends. It's all up to you."

With that, Quinn turned and began marching down the tunnel. We followed, and soon the dark ice cave swallowed every marine. There was a bit of grumbling and a lot of bemoaning of fate, but in the end, everyone followed us—even Dr. Sharaf and her minions.

I've got to say, I was sorry to see the dim sun disappear once again as we entered that tunnel. The jagged ice looked like white daggers overhead, or perhaps the teeth of a monster as we walked into its mouth.

We wound around and around, and it seemed this time that it took longer than ever to make the trip to the bottom. That was probably due to Dr. Sharaf and her team. They were inexperienced, stumbling, and slow. They were technical types, science nerds who rarely got out of their lab aboard *Borag*.

Every mining ship had a team such as this. They rarely did anything as adventurous as go outside and check out anomalies deep under the ice of an unknown dwarf planet. Normally, they simply worked on geological issues, like deciding the best way to dig into a big chunk of rock and extract its ore with maximum efficiency and speed. They were somewhat out of their league today, but they were game, I had to give them that.

Fifteen minutes later, we finally made our way to the top of that odd hill of ice deep underground and found the hatchway. It was still sealed as it had been before.

Lt. Quinn was jostled when Dr. Sharaf rushed over the ice to see the hatchway. "Amazing," she said. She'd been saying that the whole way down.

"Dr. Sharaf?" Quinn asked. "What exactly happened to the people aboard the Teklution ship?"

She glanced at him, but she didn't answer. Then, she began climbing down to the strange, sealed hatchway. She got down on her hands and knees in the end, crawling into the hole and running her fingers into every crack and cavity she could find.

At least, I thought to myself, she had some spirit. I knew quite a few of the marines right here in Red Company who wouldn't want to do what she was doing right now.

She spoke over her shoulder to us as she searched for a way in. "The ship is sealed tight," she said, "as if it's waiting for some kind of attack. My instruments indicate the metal is quite thick—I doubt we can burn our way inside."

We sent messages and tapped on the hatch, but we weren't able to communicate with anyone inside—if there was anybody in there.

"No transponder systems, no emergency code transmitters," Dr. Sharaf said, consulting with her team. They had a variety of instruments the rest of us didn't carry. "If there is someone inside, they're either staying quiet, or they died some time ago. If the hatch has lost power completely, we'll never be able to get in."

"Can't we just cut our way in?" Quinn asked.

She shrugged. "I just said your weapons and my tools aren't up to the task."

"Um… sirs?" Charlie said, daring to speak up for the first time.

The foreman, who still held onto his leash, shook the chain and glared at him.

"I have a suggestion," Charlie said.

"Let's hear it," Quinn replied, waving the foreman back.

"Maybe we could use one of the laser drill-bots. I bet I could burn a hole in that hatchway."

"If we do that, we risk depressurization," Quinn said. "We need that air."

"Yes, but if we can't get inside, we're dead anyway."

Lt. Quinn nodded, acknowledging the truth of Charlie's words. "We don't know who built this thing, or if they're still alive inside. If there are any survivors inside, we'll pretty much kill them on the spot. I'll consider that as a final drastic option."

Charlie and I exchanged glances. To our minds, it was high time to try something drastic. Whoever was inside there, after all, had obviously been in there for at least six months, the time that it took us to fly this far. More likely, they'd been there for closer to a year. They were probably dead by now.

But it wasn't my job as a simple grunt in a marine attachment to second-guess the ship's chief scientist, so I kept my mouth shut.

Eventually, Dr. Sharaf gave a little squall. While we were arguing, she'd spent her time working on the hatchway.

We rushed to the frosty rim of the opening, aiming our carbines and our flashlights into the hole after her. We illuminated her from a dozen directions at once.

"Turn off those damn lights," she complained. "I'm not hurt, but I found something."

"What?" Quinn said. "What'd you find, Doctor?"

"It's strange… but this edge, I don't think it's just an edge. I think there are tiny grooves in the metal. And I think that if I touched a series of these contacts in the right order, an electrical charge would…"

As she was saying this, she was fooling around. She had a number of instruments deployed. Some of these had logic probes, small needle-like tips of metal that were wired to something that looked like a voltmeter. I thought the instrument must be more complicated than that, because there were at least six probes and wires going back to the thing, not just two.

Whatever the case, while she was fooling around with the dials and the other instruments on her device, the outline of the hatchway lit up. Suddenly, it rose right under her feet, pushing her up at least a foot or so higher than the surrounding ice.

It began to slowly slide away, pushing ice aside. Dr. Sharaf made a squawking sound and bounced out of the hole. Due to the low gravity and her panic, she leapt a good five yards into the air and landed in a heap on the ice outside the hole. We caught her and stood her up.

To our utter surprise, the hatch began to open. As nothing came out immediately to attack us, we edged closer.

"Oh my God, it's opening up!" Sharaf exclaimed. "I got it to open!"

A puff of vapor rose up from a small revealed chamber.

"That's an airlock. It has to be!"

Encouraged by this welcome development, we began to crowd around. The hatchway continued to slide open, revealing a dark and ominous interior. Our team of marines and scientists hesitated for a moment, unsure of what they might find inside.

Charlie had no such qualms. He bounced inside and explored the interior. "I think it will hold all of us—if we squeeze."

Quinn stepped forward, shining his flashlight into the opening. "All right," he said, his voice firm and resolute. "There's no point standing around out here in the ice. Let's do this."

The group followed him into the ship, stepping cautiously over the threshold. The air was musty and stale, and the darkness seemed to press in around us.

We cycled through the airlock until all of us were in a mysterious passageway. It was not flat and even with the surface of Eris. It slanted down rather sharply instead. We followed it along, and I realized after a bit that we were hearing the clank and clatter of our boots on metal decks.

"Air..." I said. "We've got pressure, Lieutenant."

Sharaf and her sidekicks began testing the atmosphere. "The pressure is low. Give it minute. It appears to be cycling up."

"Do a chemical analysis," Quinn said. "Can we breathe this mix?"

"What do you think I'm doing, fool?" Sharaf grumbled. She worked her instruments and she slapped at her minions until they came back with a solid verdict.

"It's breathable," she said at last. "The argon, the nitrogen, the percentages are off a little from Earth normal, but it's nothing dangerous. The oxygen content is actually a little too high. Don't breathe too deeply, you might actually become hyperventilated."

"Great!" exclaimed Quinn.

"But," she warned, even as Lt. Quinn reached up to open his helmet, "be forewarned, there might be some kind of contaminant."

He looked at her. "Like what?"

"I don't know, something we can't measure. A toxin, a biotic pathogen. There are lots of tiny things that our instruments will not detect—things that could kill us all."

Quinn shrugged and took off his helmet anyway. He breathed deep and then snorted with his nose a few times. "It smells kind of lemony," he said. "Not bad, really…"

Then he sneezed. Everybody took a step back, and he laughed.

"It's just dust," he said. "At least, I think it is."

"Are you really going to leave your helmet off and breathe this stuff?" Corporal Tench asked.

"Yes, in fact, I'm going to order all of you to do the same. As long as we're breathing in our helmets, we're actually wasting oxygen that could be used out on the surface. We can't go out on the surface of Eris without oxygen in our tanks. We've got to save every puff of what we've got."

"He's right," Sharaf said, taking off her helmet next. "At this time, we don't have a way of recharging our tanks."

"But you were talking about possible contaminants," Corporal Tench complained.

Sharaf shrugged. "If this air is dangerous, we're all dead anyway. I judge it worth the risk."

Reluctantly, everyone opened their helmets. Soon, big plumes of steam poured from everyone's mouth as we breathed. The air was frigid. It had to be below zero. It burned the nostrils and throat with every breath.

To deal with the cold, we soon put our helmets back on and only cracked the face plates open to let in life-sustaining oxygen, but not to let out any more of our heat than we had to.

"Electricity," Tench said, almost talking to himself. "That's our next problem. Power, then water—if we last long enough."

"Come on," Quinn said, "let's find out what else we've got here."

He marched deeper into the ship, and the rest of us followed him. We didn't know where we were going or what we would find, but we had no choice.

Chapter 28: The Aliens

For once, Ledbetter and I weren't on point. That honor went to Corporal Tench and his team, and I was glad to see it.

We hadn't taken fifty steps into the tomb-like spacecraft before someone began shouting far up ahead of us. As we were curious, we did a little crowding and got up close enough to hear what was happening at the front of the group.

A human boot. That's what it was. The word traveled quickly back down the ranks.

"They found something."

"Someone's been in here—someone besides us."

Of course, it only made sense that *someone* had been here. The Teklution crew had gone somewhere, hadn't they? But when I caught sight of the boot, I saw that it had indeed been torn loose from the bottom of a spacesuit. There was plenty of bloodstains around the tear, which was about mid-shin.

I suddenly felt as if we were a little bit crazy to have come in here at all. Sure, there were strange mutants and not much power, water or food aboard the Teklution ship, but whatever had destroyed them had almost certainly originated from this place.

"Talk about walking from the frying pan into the fire…" I said.

"I think we're in the fire right now," Ledbetter agreed.

"This has got to be the weirdest spaceship I've ever seen," Lt. Quinn said as we trudged along. "Look at this strange, singular passageway. It seems to be running farther than what's reasonably possible. And who the hell builds a ship with slanting passages, anyway?"

"That's because it's not a spacecraft, Lieutenant," Dr. Sharaf said.

Quinn halted, and we all halted with him. He stared at her, and we joined in the staring contest. "If it's not a spacecraft, and what the hell is it? And who built it?"

Dr. Sharaf threw her hands high in defeat. "A base? A laboratory? An installation built by... someone..."

"Yeah, who?" Quinn asked, "and how do you know all this?"

"I don't *know* anything. I'm making logical deductions."

"I don't believe you."

She glared at him for a moment, but he didn't back down. At last, she bared her teeth and seemed to come to a decision.

"All right," she said. She paused and sighed, studying the strange deck under our boots. "I guess we might as well talk more clearly now, as we seem to be trapped, and we're probably going to meet our deaths within these metal walls."

"Yes, I think that's a good idea, Doctor. Clue us in. What's going to kill us, and why?"

"The caretakers of this place, most likely. This is an alien laboratory stationed here to monitor and perform experiments upon humanity. At least, I think that's what its original purpose was."

Quinn squinted at her. "I gather this isn't the first such installation we've discovered?"

"No, it isn't," Dr. Sharaf admitted. "When your captain took on this very special mission, the colonel informed me. I told him I was checking out—but he ordered me to continue serving aboard *Borag*. I didn't want to go on this expedition, any more than any of the rest of you wanted to come out here. But like all of us, I owe the banks."

Quinn grunted with amusement. "You owe the banks, huh? Even the great Dr. Sharaf?"

"Yes, scoff if you must. I've had a few mistakes in my career. There have been a few... blemishes. Some of the grant money I was given didn't return the results I'd promised. Anyway, it doesn't matter. Interplanetary Excavations owns me just like it owns the rest of you. That's all you need to know."

"All right, all right, Doctor. What are we facing? Violence? Starvation or possibly dehydration? You're not answering my questions."

"All in good time. During my tenure as a lab director working for Interplanetary, I've come into contact with places like this before—but I've never seen one this big, this complex—and most importantly, never one that's active and alive. But I've seen places like this long after their destruction."

"Destruction?"

"Yes, usually when we find an installation like this one, it has been gutted out, burned, and destroyed."

"But by whom?" Lt. Quinn asked.

Ledbetter and I exchanged frowns. Dr. Sharaf was giving us all fresh concerns.

"We don't know," she said. "All we know is we didn't do it."

"Huh…" Quinn said, thinking that over. His jaw worked in the air. All of us were trying to chew on the information that she was giving—and no one liked the flavor of it.

"So," Quinn said at last, "let me get this straight. There are some aliens around who built installations like this one around the Solar System. The government boys back on Earth are keeping that quiet. But these aliens must also have enemies of their own? We're talking about two sets of aliens? Maybe more?"

The doctor shrugged. "Whatever the case, in every installation we've located they've all been dead and their installations destroyed—until we discovered this one on Eris."

"Where are the others?" Corporal Tench interjected. He couldn't help himself, and I couldn't blame him for that. We all wanted to know more.

"In various hidden sites," she said. "One of them was discovered on Mars, in fact. We found it a long time ago, nearly thirty years back now. It was just a buried enclave like this one, full of passages inside an ovoid-shaped shell of metal. It's buried beneath the surface of the planet at the southern pole, the coldest place on all of Mars. They seem to like the cold, for some reason."

"Mars, huh?" Quinn asked. "Other places, too?"

She nodded. "Europa, Ganymede, a few other sites. They seem to favor lower gravity—lower than Earth-normal—and cold. Other than that, they're able to thrive in an atmosphere somewhat similar to ours. I believe their computers automatically filled these chambers with the gases we need to breathe because it sensed our presence."

"That's chilling," he said. "So... there's some kind of computer running this place right now?"

"Yes, definitely. Haven't you noticed the increasing temperature? You're no longer blowing steamy breath, are you? Why has the temperature risen so much? We didn't turn anything on, we didn't adjust any thermostat—in fact, we haven't found any controls at all. And yet, the environment here inside this lab is slowly transforming itself to meet our needs."

We all looked around the ceilings and walls, wondering what we were going to see next.

"Okay, so there are aliens," Quinn said. "What's their nature? You must have found some of them. Have you found any bodies? Have you dug any of them up?"

"No, not me personally," she said. "I've never seen anything that you would call a typical flesh and blood alien."

"That's pretty useless. We could have deduced all this from what we've seen here today."

Dr. Sharaf glared at him. "I don't know everything. I've only been involved in a few projects. What I *do* know is that every undamaged chamber we've found is operated robotically. There are... *guardians*, sometimes. They have advanced physical forms, both electromechanical and biochemical."

"Okay, okay, so we're dealing with some kind of alien robots? That's just wonderful. You think they're still here? They're still active? Are they running this place, or is it just some automated computer responding to our presence?"

"I suppose we'll find out in time."

Lt. Quinn turned again to examine the strange walls. He ran his gloved hands over the metallic surfaces, but nothing revealed any secrets to us.

"What's their purpose?" he asked. "These aliens... what are they doing here with these little weird labs buried underneath the ice?"

"We don't know. Whoever built these installations, whatever the original purpose was, is essentially dead or gone or destroyed. All we are seeing is the remnants. These labs are at least forty thousand years old, Lieutenant."

"What? How the hell do you know that?"

Dr. Sharaf looked furtive, as if she were about to release a grim secret. "I've heard rumors," she said. "They say we've found Neanderthals and Cro-Magnon in these places. The DNA of our distant human ancestors from long ago has been identified and confirmed."

"So... you're saying they were visiting Earth? Thousands of years ago?"

"That's what I'm saying, yes. That's the best of my knowledge."

"That is truly unsettling..."

She shrugged. "Perhaps, but at least we know their purpose was to study us, perhaps it was nothing more sinister than that. If they'd wished to destroy humanity, they certainly could have done so long ago when we were a primitive species."

Quinn squinted at her. "So, there were once some relatively peaceful aliens out here. But somewhere along the line, somebody else came along and wrecked their labs. And it couldn't have been us, not if we were a bunch of Neanderthals and Cro-Magnon..."

"Yes, the destruction we've witnessed in these places certainly wasn't delivered by anyone from Earth. Whoever destroyed their hidden bases around the Solar System was obviously more powerful and advanced than the people who built the labs in the first place."

Quinn was nodding and rubbing his chin. He'd opened up his faceplate, breathing in the air deeply, as it was now fresh and almost warm. He rubbed at his chin and his carpet of stubble, and he thought over all this shocking information.

Tench spoke up again. I don't think he could help it. "I bet I know why they're buried in remote locations underneath ice like this," he said.

Dr. Sharaf, for once, did not admonish him, and neither did Quinn. Everybody looked at him, hoping for an answer—hoping against hope, given the source.

"Well... just think about it," he said. "They built underground in hidden locations because they were under threat. This base is thickly armored with heavy hatchways to prevent intruders. But why?"

He looked around at our blank faces for a moment before continuing. "It's not like some guy from Earth with a spear was going to come out here and kill them. No, they knew they had an enemy. They knew they had someone to hide from way back when they first built these installations. Back then, we were running around grunting in caves."

We thought about that. None of us could find a flaw in his logic. There would be no reason to build a highly defensive hidden installation if you were simply examining earthlings. It didn't even matter what your purpose was.

"I get what you're saying," Quinn said. "Way, way back—around the time of the Ice Age—we were no threat to them at all. I think you're right, Tench."

Dr. Sharaf grumbled, but she was grudgingly willing to admit Tench was right. The logic was pretty much unassailable. She definitely didn't like the source, but she accepted the idea.

"But I don't see how this gets us anywhere," Quinn said. "We're still stuck inside this place. We've been deserted and marooned. Even if we figure out every secret this lab has in the way of technology, it wouldn't matter much because we'll probably all die long before anyone comes out here from Earth again."

"That might be true," Sharaf admitted, "but we might as well do it anyway. For the good of science."

Quinn snorted. "Maybe we can write it all down, throw it outside the hatch, and leave it there for the next guy that comes along—to give him a little leg up. Huh?"

"That's very altruistic of you, Lt. Quinn," Dr. Sharaf said in a sarcastic tone. "Anyway, let's keep looking around."

The passages wound deeper into the ground and sometimes split up. But there were no rooms, no chambers—only more passages. It was an irregular labyrinth. We soon found that every passageway we went down ended in a dead end. When we ran out of passages, we stopped searching, dumbfounded.

"There's got to be more to the place than this," Quinn said. "Spread out, tap at the walls, the deck—even the ceiling. If anyone detects a hollow sound, report in."

We did as we were ordered. Pretty quickly, we found what might be a hollow chamber at the end of every corridor. The wall there seemed to be completely seamless metal, but there was indeed a hollow sound when you tapped the butt of your gun on it.

Quinn allowed Dr. Sharaf to work on these spot looking for possible alien doorways for several minutes. When there were no results of any kind, he unslung his laser carbine, aimed it at a wall, and held the trigger down.

We all snapped our helmets closed, backed away, and watched as the laser bolts flashed and banged, scarring up the metal. He gouged the wall significantly, but he wasn't breaking through.

"Lieutenant," Dr. Sharaf said, "stop wasting power. The energy in your weapons can be used to keep us alive."

Lt. Quinn stopped firing and turned to look at her. "You know as well as I do, someone or something is heating up this place. Energy isn't going to be our problem. Food and water, that's our problem. If there is any, it's on the other side of this door. Have you got any more ideas about opening it?"

She shook her head reluctantly and walked away grumbling. Corporal Tench joined Quinn, and together they fired a very focused set of beams on a single spot. This soon began to make headway. We'd dug in several inches when all of a sudden there was a strange burning sound and a wild screeching hiss of gas.

"We've breached it!" Quinn shouted.

It was true. All the air and heat were rapidly depressurizing through the hole they'd punched through that wall. I had to wonder if he'd managed to kill all of us by exposing our pressurized chamber and opening it up to the cruel, unrelenting cold of Eris.

Dr. Sharaf raced forward with a patch in her hands, attempting to get it over the hole, but Quinn pushed her back.

"It's not hissing anymore. Look!"

It was true. After a brief escape of gas and, I'm sure, a thinning of the atmosphere in the passageway, the pressure seemed to have equalized with whatever was on the far side of that burnt wound in the metal wall.

As we gathered around, peering and shining flashlights into the wounded metal, we were met with a fresh shock. The hole began to move. It began to crawl upward, in fact, without a sound.

It glided up and seemed to merge with the ceiling, as if the metal had turned to liquid and flowed upward, retaining that burnt hole in it the whole while. Soon, a dark passage could be seen beyond.

We'd been keeping our suit lights dim since there was a bit of a glow of light inside the passageway, and we instinctively wanted to preserve our batteries for as long as we could. One never knew, especially when one was on a remote planetoid, just how long you would have to rely on your suit, your batteries, all the very minimal life support systems that we carried with us.

"There's something moving in there," Tench said. "Look out!"

We recoiled from the doorway. We'd been edging forward, probing with our lights.

Inside, we saw *things* moving, things in the darkness. As I got a better look at them, I realized they were artificial, that much was clear. They weren't flesh and blood.

I'd never seen anything like them. They were insectile, kind of like giant grasshoppers or praying mantises. They had manipulative arms which were covered in spikes and thorns. Their eyes were bulbous and multifaceted. All of them seemed to be made of the same strange metallic surface that the corridors and the passageways, even the hatch of this massive installation, were made from.

They whirred smoothly as they moved—and they moved wickedly fast.

Being Red Company Marines and seeing as we were surprised by an obvious threat that looked quite dangerous, we unlimbered our carbines, formed a line, and fired without even having been ordered to.

Only Dr. Sharaf was yelling "Wait, wait!" she cried—but it was too late. We weren't listening to her. In fact, I threw an arm out, blocking her from marching in front of our field of fire. Ledbetter, Corporal Tench, Lt. Quinn, and several others, we were all shooting.

Two alien monstrosities made it to us somehow, one of them falling just as it reached out with one of those strange, hooked, metallic claws to gouge at Quinn's foremost boot. It died there—if you could even use that word. It ceased functioning anyway, rasping, whirring, and churning its strange legs on the deck.

Its strange, multifaceted eyes had been punctured, but they didn't bleed. Instead, they released strange vapors and smoke, as if a fire had been lit within the machine by our laser bolts.

The second robot performed better. Private Mendoza had stepped aside to get a clear shot, and the second robot managed to reach him before we could bring it down. We had focused so much of our time and fire on the first robot that by the time we turned our attention to the second one, Mendoza was in trouble.

The robot seemed to know how to kill a human, slashing at him with its claws and thrusting deep. One of its claws aimed for Mendoza's heart, but his body armor protected him. The second thrust, however, came just under his helmet. It found its way into Mendoza's throat, where hooked spikes ripped his throat out. His esophagus was thrown from his body, and blood was everywhere. Less than a second later, the robot finally succumbed to our shower of bolts and collapsed like the first one.

Dr. Sharaf approached with her hands on her hips and pointed first at Lt. Quinn and then at the dead man. "This is what you get when you proceed without caution," she said. "You didn't give me enough time to work on that lock. You didn't give me enough—"

"Shut up, Doctor," Quinn said. "I'm in charge, and there's one thing we don't have much of here: time. We have a serious enemy aboard this vessel, and we must act decisively."

"It's not a vessel, you fool," Dr. Sharaf corrected. "It's a base, a laboratory. I already told you that." She seemed somewhat hysterical.

Lt. Quinn looked worse for the wear, as if he might shake Dr. Sharaf, but he forced himself to calm down and turned away from her, ignoring her hysterics. She'd clearly lost it, probably frightened by the alien machines.

She was obviously a person who would lash out in anger when she was afraid or confronted with something unexpected and unpleasant.

Once we confirmed that Private Mendoza was indeed dead, we quickly divided up his power cells and weapon. We gave the extra weapon to Charlie, who looked at it as if he didn't know which end had the trigger and which end had the emitter.

"Just carry it," I told him. "Only try to fire it if you really have to."

He nodded, his eyes wide. "We're all going to die here, aren't we Starn? I mean, that's what I'm feeling right now."

I shook my head and smiled, then I began lying. "Nah, Lt. Quinn will figure it out. We'll get out of here." I turned away before Charlie could realize I was lying, but he continued to stare at me and fondle the strange laser carbine in his hands.

We got a little bit of water, food, oxygen, and power from Mendoza's corpse, but we couldn't use his suit or helmet as they'd been torn up during the attack. Every time one of us died, it meant the others could live for perhaps another hour. It was a ghoulish way to survive, and I tried not to think about it.

"Ah-ha," Dr. Sharaf said, drawing our attention. "It's obvious! I'm such a fool." It was the first time I had ever heard her refer to herself as a fool, and I found the admission refreshing. She was usually our resident expert in detecting fools, but this time she was beating her fists against her own head.

"These doors," she explained. "We can tell where they are by tapping along the walls and listening for a hollow sound. That's a doorway. You can't see it, it's too perfectly made, almost seamless. If I had a microscope, I might be able to see the fine line where the door meets the wall, but it doesn't matter."

She looked around us with an expression of triumph, while we stared back in a bewildered fashion. Her face soured. "Try to turn on your primitive brains," she said. "Think about it. Would a door built for robots like these respond to the touch of a human hand? Or to warmth or moisture? No, it would respond to things a robot possesses: magnetism, electricity, a tiny static charge, perhaps pressure."

She was right, of course. We had spent a lot of time pressing, nudging, and feeling every crevice, hoping to find a pressure plate or button that would open the door we had blown our way through, but we'd never found anything like that.

"So, are we going to tear off one of those big claws and tap it against the wall?" Quinn asked.

"That's actually not a bad idea," Dr. Sharaf said. "But it may not have to be something like that. Maybe any metal item would work: a knife blade, or perhaps the barrel of one of your guns. Try it."

Quinn approached the wall where she'd identified another door, but she stopped him.

"Do we have a plan of action for this next room?" she asked.

Quinn looked around the room. His Marines had gathered, and we had our carbines ready. Essentially, our main plan of action as Marines was to shoot down anything that came at us.

"You're right," he said. "Let's set up a charge on the floor—right here. Maybe this time we won't have to lose a man if we get rushed again."

Specialist Edgars, who was the closest thing we had to a sapper, stepped forward. He carried a few explosive charges. These were usually meant for blowing holes in doorways or airlocks, but they could also be rigged as a mine.

"You have mines?" Dr. Sharaf complained. "Why didn't you use them on the first door?"

Lt. Quinn eyed her with displeasure. "Because I'd rather bore one small hole through a door into the unknown than blow a gaping hole in it. If it led to something even more dangerous, we couldn't have plugged it up if we'd blown a monstrous hole in it."

Dr. Sharaf thought about that and nodded, finally backing off and stopping her complaints.

Edgars placed a small, flat mine and set it up with a proximity fuse. "Don't put your foot close to that thing," he warned us.

Quinn and the rest of us stepped back.

"All right," Quinn said, "be careful with the mine. Ledbetter, tap around the outer edge of that doorway."

"Me, sir?" Ledbetter squawked. Quinn gestured furiously, and Ledbetter approached the wall, grumbling. He reached toward the invisible doorway at an oblique angle and began lightly tapping on the metal wall with his knife. As he got closer, you could hear a small difference in tone, indicating he was indeed tapping on a hollow spot.

Suddenly, the door seemed to melt. It shifted form and flashed upward, rolling away into the ceiling just like the previous one.

There was a gush of depressurization, but this time, we were prepared. Our visors were down, and our suits pressurized, so we weren't frozen or asphyxiated.

The interior of the chamber Ledbetter exposed was pitch-black, but the chamber we were in had adjusted to our presence. It was now filling with breathable air, heat, and a soft, warm glow of light. Whoever had built this place had designed it so that creatures like us could survive.

We raised our carbines and put our fingers on the trigger, tensing up and aiming into the dark hole.

Suddenly, I saw movement out of the corner of my eye. Another door had opened to my left, and as I wheeled to face this new threat, two more doors open as well. Apparently, activating this latest door also opened all the others.

There was no movement coming through the door that Ledbetter had opened. Nothing rushed through and activated the mine on the deck. But from the other two doors, there were sounds and signs of movement.

They were coming at us—from our flanks.

Chapter 29: The Laboratory

I shouted the alarm, but it was utter confusion. This time, the enemy got in the first blow instead of us.

Dr. Sharaf and her two minions had taken refuge at the back of the room. They had placed themselves as far away from the charge on the floor as possible. A moment ago, this had seemed like a good strategy, as they were far from the potential danger of the explosive and the opening doorway that was likely to contain a charging, vicious alien robot.

Unfortunately, this also placed them between two opening doors when the alien robots rushed in. Of the noncombatant group, only Charlie was armed. He let out a wild stream of curses and laser bolts. He swung the carbine wildly, sending a spray of bolts across the room, making everyone duck. He managed to hit the nearest robot with many bolts, but it wasn't enough to kill it.

The robot turned to face Charlie, but before it reached him, it reached one of Dr. Sharaf's minions. It's possible that the good doctor had pushed her assistant in front of the robot to save herself, but later I could never be fully sure of this. I couldn't be certain of what I saw in all the confusion. It did seem to me that her position had shifted, placing her hapless sidekick between her and the charging alien horror.

The enemy robot, being a machine, went for the closest item on its target list—which was Dr. Sharaf's minion. He was closer to it by perhaps a foot or two than Charlie was.

The robot turned on the unarmed man and tore him to ribbons. The scientist had no body armor, and every thrust of the robot's spikes and hooks easily punched through the spacesuit. Gouts of blood and organs flew everywhere.

Charlie was making a low wailing sound as he held down the trigger of his laser carbine and fired away. A few of the bolts may have hit the scientist, but it didn't matter, as the man was already dead. Meanwhile, the robot was busy attacking the man on the deck, allowing Charlie and a few of our Marines to finish it off with short bursts of fire.

Another robot had entered through the door closest to Lt. Quinn and myself. It was quickly defeated, as we were more prepared and faster to react. In the end, we killed both robots, but lost one scientist.

After the battle, we checked the newly exposed chambers but found no more robots. As far as we could tell with our probing lights, there were no more robots to be found. They'd all rushed us and died in the effort to destroy us.

We were licking our wounds and shaking our heads when Quinn looked around sternly. "Where's Tench?"

We counted heads and came up one short.

"Where's Tench, dammit?" Quinn demanded. "Did anyone see him leave? Starn, are you running your cameras?"

"I am, sir—but just the one on my helmet," I replied.

"Back it up, play it, and send it to my helmet," he instructed.

I did as he asked. I'd been more or less aiming in the direction of Corporal Tench, expecting to see a robot run out and activate the mine on the floor.

Looking at the video retrospectively, both Quinn and I saw the same thing: when the action had begun, Corporal Tench hadn't participated. He hadn't fired his weapon, but instead withdrew and went back through the door in the direction we'd originally come—the door that was now wrecked with a hole in it.

"Let's go find him," Lt. Quinn said.

Dr. Sharaf approached and put a small hand on his bulky elbow. "Lt. Quinn," she said, "one might expect a deserter under this kind of pressure."

"I don't expect anything of the kind," he replied. "This is Red Company. If he's deserted us without good reason, he'll face the consequences."

Dr. Sharaf dropped her hand and shrugged, and we all followed Lt. Quinn as he walked through the passageways. The path slanted upward toward the entrance. As we moved forward, searching through the corridors we had searched before, we reached the original hatch and found nothing—no sign of Corporal Tench.

"That is really strange," Quinn said. "Do you think he went through the hatch and outside? Why the hell would he do that?"

Dr. Sharaf chewed her lip, and her eyes moved around the group, but she made no comment. For once, she held her tongue.

Baffled by the corporal's disappearance, Quinn had us search every passageway in the complex, mainly by tapping on the walls to see if we discovered any hollow-sounding responses. We found five spots that sounded like doorways rather than solid walls.

He also instructed a small group, including myself, Ledbetter, and another man named Morrison, to go through the airlock and check outside. If Corporal Tench had gone that way, he wanted to know.

We went outside through the airlock, and we looked around out there on the jagged ice in a very paranoid fashion. We resembled gophers poking their noses out of a hole for the first time in a year. It was funny to think that we were more comfortable inside our air and warmth-filled passages now, even with robots lurking, than we were out here on the open, exposed surface of Eris.

We were unable to find any tracks that obviously belonged to Tench. Of course, they could have gotten mixed up with the countless other footprints that we saw etched in the ice. There was no sign of Tench, and transmitting radio calls resulted in nothing. We returned after about ten minutes of searching to report back to the Lieutenant.

"Damned strange," he said. "He's got to have gone through one of these five doors."

Charlie laughed. "Well, sir, if he did, he has bigger balls than I do. I think he's probably robot food by now."

That was the general consensus from the group. If Corporal Tench had lost his nerve or gotten a wild hair for whatever reason, he'd most likely met a grim fate. Wandering off in this complex by yourself would almost certainly be fatal.

I could tell that Lt. Quinn was more upset and baffled by this desertion than any of the rest of us were. None of us liked Corporal Tench much, and if he had gotten himself killed, it was going to be hard to cry too much at the funeral. Still, it was unsettling to note we'd lost another man. Red Company seemed to be shrinking by the hour.

While all this searching went on, Dr. Sharaf did many tests on the atmosphere, the decks, and the aliens. She declared these last to be a combination of biotic and artificial creatures. Essentially, they were cyborgs.

"Cyborgs?" Quinn asked her. "Are you sure? That sounds crazy."

"Yes, I'm sure. They're outer carapaces are metal, but there is some meat inside them. They have organic muscles and brains. Some of their organs are cellular in nature as well."

"That's really disgusting," Quinn said, twisting up his face. "We should drive them all out of this ship, or burn them, or something."

Dr. Sharaf made a choking sound and moved as if to protect her fallen robots. "That's insane," she said. "First of all, burning them would waste our precious oxygen. Secondly—"

"Never mind, Doctor, never mind," Quinn said. "I've got no intention of lighting a fire in here, don't worry. But if they are partially organic, they're going to start to stink after a while, aren't they? They already do, if you ask me."

He had his helmet open, as did most of us.

Sharaf eyed us all. "There is another matter…"

"What's that?" Quinn asked.

"Well, we have been exposed to organics that are most likely alien in nature. That's pretty much undeniable at this point."

"Yeah? So what?" Quinn asked.

"So, certain protocols must be observed."

"Like what?" Quinn asked, squinting at her.

"I have here a set of injections," Dr. Sharaf explained. "I've mixed them up from my medical kits. They should help prevent any kind of infection that these creatures might have already delivered into the air or into our bloodstreams directly. Some of us were injured," she looked around, eyeing Ledbetter pointedly, "and we've already seen what such injuries might cause."

"What?" Quinn asked. "Are you talking about those psycho half-dead people? The crew of the Teklution ship? You think we might end up like them?"

Dr. Sharaf shrugged. "How else would you explain their state? They obviously came into contact with these creatures. They probably fought a battle with them aboard their own ship. According to my observations, they clearly lost that fight.'

"Yeah..." Quinn admitted. "You've got a point there. Somehow the Teklution ship was overcome. It could have been disease, some kind of madness, some kind of parasite—or these weird robot aliens themselves."

"That's right, the cyborgs might have been the cause. We really don't know the truth."

"All right, all right," Quinn said. "So, what's in this compound of yours?"

"It's a tri-ox compound mixed with several other key ingredients. Antivirals, things like that."

"Hey," Ledbetter said. "That's the same stuff you said you injected into me. When that zombie-dude scratched me on the Teklution ship."

"Naturally," Dr. Sharaf said. "It's the same compound. Experimental Lot Six."

Quinn frowned at her. "Just how is it that you happen to have a sufficient quantity of such medications to take care of me and all my men?"

Sharaf shrugged again. "Foresight," she said. "Simple foresight. That, and the ingenuity of a biochemical AI-driven organelle built into my pack. From base materials, it's essentially able to make quite complex organic chemicals on demand."

"What's this compound supposed to do and how will you deliver it?"

"Injections, of course," she said. "Just a small, thin needle, nothing too frightening for fighting men such as yourselves."

Quinn snorted. He eyeballed what was left of the squad. "Do I have any volunteers?" he asked.

No one raised a hand. Not even me this time. I had to admit I wasn't in too trusting a mood when I looked at Dr. Sharaf and her kit full of odd amber fluids.

She began building up her first injection as we watched. Contrary to everything she'd said, the needle looked rather large, and the fluid looked like maple syrup to me. It was sort of thick and orangey-brown.

"I thought not," Quinn said. He disconnected one of his gauntlets, rolled up a sleeve and presented his arm to the ghoulish scientists. They administered an injection which Quinn did his best to pretend didn't hurt.

"What the hell?" he complained after ten seconds or so. "Are you drilling for oil there?"

"We've got to get into a vein—deep into a vein."

Quinn frowned and watched them. When they were finally done the syringe was empty. We all watched as she began to prepare the next injection. This time, it was Charlie who objected.

"Hold on a second. Are you using the same needle for all of us?"

Dr. Sharaf shrugged. "I don't have enough disposable needles for the whole lot of us. We must make do."

"That's disgusting," Quinn said, "and dangerous."

"That's true," I said, speaking up for the first time. "If one of us is infected, you'll make sure that we all are."

Dr. Sharaf pouted a bit, but she finally agreed to use one separate needle for Ledbetter, and a second one for the rest of us. She used the tip of a laser rifle to burn off any residue between injecting different people.

When it was my turn, I almost bit my tongue. The process was actually quite painful and extremely lengthy. It felt like a surprising amount of fluid was gushing into my veins.

When it was over, I shrugged down my sleeves, slammed my gauntlets back on, and then picked up my carbine.

"How long does that inoculation last anyway?" I asked her. "For life, I hope."

She laughed at me. "No," she said, "not that long, but hopefully it will keep us stable and healthy until we get out of here—or until we all die."

"An encouraging thought, doctor."

We munched on rations, sipped water, and tapped on the walls until at last, Lt. Quinn came to a decision. We'd been in here something like five hours, and although we clearly had enough oxygen to last a long time, water and food were not in plentiful supply.

"Corporal Tench hasn't reappeared," he said in a glum tone. "I'm marking him down as lost in action. Any objections?"

None of us argued. Maybe he'd freaked out and run off somewhere. Whatever had happened, he'd probably gotten himself killed by now. That didn't seem like Tench, but you never knew how a person was going to react when they were faced with their first killer alien cyborgs.

Quinn decided to attempt breaching the doorway we'd found that was closest to the airlock next. He reasoned that it was possibly less dangerous than the others.

I didn't find his logic compelling, but then, I wasn't in command.

We used the same electrostatic discharge technique to open the door again, and it rolled up with silent, smooth perfection.

Inside was yet another dark, frigid room. We lit up the chamber and aimed a half-dozen laser emitters into it with our fingers caressing the triggers—but we didn't fire. There wasn't anything to shoot at.

Stepping inside, we began to search the place. It was quite a bit different from the other chambers we had discovered thus far. The room was large, dark, and extremely cold.

Unlike all other chambers, it didn't warm up as we spent time inside. It stayed frigid. Lights had come on, and air had begun to fill the space—but there was no heat.

Slowly, very slowly, a bluish light began to filter in from the walls, but the heat never did come on. Soon, we discovered why.

When we reached the back of the chamber, we found nothing but a bank of cylinders. These large, tall containers were made of the same metal as the doors and passages were. Each of the cylinder had an opening that could be triggered exactly as the alien doorways had been.

When we dared to open the first one, again standing in a circular firing squad pattern, the door rose up to reveal no insectile robot or cyborg. Instead, something new and equally terrifying met our eyes.

It was human, we could tell that much—or at least it had been once. A frozen figure was inside the cylinder. His face was twisted up in horror and pain—even agony. The look reminded me of the expression we'd seen back aboard the Teklution ship.

The entire cylinder was filled with a block of ice. Vapor poured off it. I suspected the substance wasn't frozen water, but rather frozen methane.

The figure inside was still visible, as the ice was only an inch or two deep over the face.

"What a way to go..." Quinn said. He reached out and polished a section over the face. "It's a woman, I think."

He was right. We all stared, wondering who she was.

"Probably a crewman from the Teklution ship," I said.

"Yep, that must be it. Well, that proves it. These aliens obviously attacked the Teklution ship, got aboard, and took a few prisoners."

"Either that," Dr. Sharaf said, "or this fool wandered into this complex, just as we've done, to explore it. She was captured and frozen."

"That's possible."

"Out of the way," she said, crowding forward. "I must take a sample."

We watched, frowning, as she stepped up with a tiny electric drill. She bore deeply into the ice until she finally struck the frozen corpse. After nearly a minute of creating smoke and making whirring sounds, she extracted a sample of flesh. She stowed it in a specimen jar tube and packed it away.

None of us objected to this desecration of the dead. After all, we needed information. Dr. Sharaf, as unpleasant as she might be, was probably the one who was going to give it to us.

Chapter 30: Corporal Tench

We moved from metal tube to metal tube after that, finding each of them to contain a frozen human—or at least a humanoid—figure. Several of them seemed like modern people, just like us. They even wore crewman's clothes underneath all that ice.

But when we got to the seventh in the line, we all gasped. The figure inside was different. It was unmistakable.

"What is *that*?" Quinn demanded. "Some kind of a freaking caveman?"

"Look at all that hair…" I said.

"Fantastic…" Dr. Sharaf chimed in. She immediately stepped up with her drill again. Her hands were almost shaking with excitement. "What a find," she said. "It might be Cro-Magnon—or a Neanderthal. Maybe even Homo erectus? This is the find of the century."

We watched in disgust as she performed her ghoulish probing of the frozen corpse.

"If that thing really is some kind of primitive human," Quinn said, "even if it's just from the Bronze Age or something, then this alien base has been here for a very long time."

"I told you that already," Dr. Sharaf said. "We've found evidence before—things like this. Yes, these alien cyborgs… beings, robots, whatever the hell they are, they've been studying us for a long, long time. If they've been visiting Earth to investigate us lately, however… well, we haven't seen one."

"What about UFOs?" Ledbetter asked. "I've always heard about those."

Dr. Sharaf scoffed at him. "Fantasies and scare tactics," she said. "Extraordinary claims require extraordinary proof."

Ledbetter grunted and pointed a finger at the Cro-Magnon, or whatever it was, frozen in the tube in front of us.

"What do you call that, then?" he demanded. "I'd call that physical evidence. I'm feeling pretty convinced right about now."

Most of the rest of us were nodding. Even Dr. Sharaf's one surviving sidekick seemed to be on Ledbetter's side this time, but Sharaf only scowled and kept working her drill.

In the end, we opened up over thirty tubes. We took a sample of each and stuffed them away in Sharaf's backpack—or more accurately the backpack of her overburdened minion. He was serving as little more than a pack mule at this point.

Then, she sealed each of the strange frozen tombs by reversing the process of engaging the strange metal sliding hatches.

"Why would they put this room so close to the entrance?" I asked.

Dr. Sharaf shrugged. "Of course, we can't know their logic, but I would suspect they're somewhat like ants in their thinking. They all look alike, after all. They're quite busy creatures, and they're often ferocious. In fact, calling them something like ants with a metallic exoskeletal structure seems like a pretty apt analogy. I must make a note of that."

She actually did make a note before continuing. "Anyway, in an ant colony, there are worker-creatures that go out and gather. They separate things in their tunnels into a series of chambers on different levels. In fact, the more I think about it, the structure of this entire complex reminds me of an ant colony. It's dug down deep into the earth, and just like their bodies, it's encased in metal. Each of these chambers are significantly separated from all the others."

"Cyborg ants?" Quinn said.

"Yes. Just look at the architecture. Humans generally build quite differently. We tend to construct a series of geometrically identical chambers separated by walls, all on one flat plane. These creatures don't think the way we do. Not at all."

"I guess it does make a kind of sense," Quinn said. "They sure as hell don't look like us."

"Exactly. We must assume that their mentality is just as different as their physiology. Ants..." she said. "Yes. I'm trying to remember what I know about entomology. It's been a long time. But the separation of chambers, these long slanting tubes for passageways, even their physical appearance. Yes, I believe these cyborgs are somewhat ant-like."

"Intelligent ants?" I said. "That's just wonderful."

Then, Ledbetter spoke up again. "They're worse than just giant bugs. These intelligent ants have advanced technology, and they're able to build metal skins for themselves."

"If this is an ant colony," I said. "Then where is their queen?"

They all looked at me. In fact, they stared. No one spoke for several long seconds.

"Let's keep searching for her," Quinn said.

We searched one more chamber, and lost another marine in the process. Lt. Quinn called it quits for the day after that. "You're all getting tired. We'll rest and look around after we've gotten some sleep."

We eyed one another, wondering about the wisdom of this move. Sure, we had air and heat now, but we didn't have much in the way of food—and most importantly, water. That was quickly becoming our number one priority.

"We've spent a solid ten hours inside this alien ant colony, or laboratory, or whatever the hell it is," Quinn said, "so I figure we could all use some sleep. We'll set up a watch of two men and rotate through an eight-hour rest period."

It was hard to sleep on the cold metal floor of the passageway, but we managed to do it. It was too cold to sleep in the freezer room, obviously, and the other chambers were all defiled by large dead alien cyborgs. We had to make do with the slanting passageways of the main tunnel that connected the entire complex together.

It was during the fifth hour, while I was on watch, that something went wrong.

One of the doorways, one of the few that we'd never opened, rolled up silently. The metal melted away into the ceiling without a sound.

I whipped up my carbine, aimed at the opening and shouted for everyone to wake up. They surged to their feet with grunts, groans, and a clatter of weapons.

A shadow was cast from inside the room. Oddly, this chamber, unlike every other one that we'd opened before, was lit inside. There was no sign of depressurization, either. Therefore, we could only surmise that the chamber beyond had air in it as well as light. The distinct lack of a puff of icy gases also indicated that it was about the same temperature as the main passageway.

A shadow appeared. Something lumbered forward out of that passageway. It was an odd, misshapen thing. A strange humanoid that shambled out of the chamber and into the main passage.

The figure was wearing the uniform of a Red Company marine. This was the only reason we didn't fire at it immediately, because the creature itself was quite hideous, even terrifying.

We aimed our rifles at it, shouted, scrambled to our feet and then backed away as it approached.

"It's Tench," Ledbetter said. "It's Corporal Tench."

It was true. Despite his alien demeanor and grotesquely twisted body, the uniform, face, even the stripes on his shoulders were distinctive—it had to be Corporal Tench.

"What the hell happened to him?" Quinn stepped up, aiming his rifle at the shambling unfortunate. "Halt right there, Tench," he said. "Where the hell have you been?"

Tench stood there, laboring to breathe for a moment. Each wheezing effort puffed up his sides more than should have been possible. As each breath was released, his sides shrank back down again. It was kind of like watching a bullfrog in a swamp take in great lungfuls of fetid air.

"I..." he said. "I got lost."

"I should say you did, man." Quinn turned around toward Dr. Sharaf, who was unsurprisingly at the very back of the line of humans. "Doctor, is this why you gave us those injections?"

She nodded her head solemnly. "I didn't know the exact nature of the transformation, but I've heard of such things. I was given a formula, something that can slow the progress of the disease."

Quinn looked from her to Corporal Tench and back again. "Are you saying we're all going to end up like that?"

She shrugged. "Unknown."

"Well, that's just wonderful. If these freaky ant-alien things don't kill us, we're going to turn into freaks ourselves."

"We could always freeze ourselves, sir," Ledbetter suggested. "In those tubes back there—those guys look like they haven't changed at all."

"Thanks for the helpful suggestion, Private. I might just shove you into one of those tubes and try it out."

After that comment, Ledbetter shut up in a hurry.

"I'm sorry, sir," Corporal Tench rasped out. "I was injured back aboard the Teklution ship—just like Ledbetter over there—but I hid the injury. After a while... I started to feel different."

"What do you mean, *different*?" Quinn demanded.

Tench gestured toward himself vaguely. "Like a freak," he said. "Not myself."

"Has your mind been affected as well as your body?" Quinn asked.

"Yeah, somewhat," Tench said. "When I got into that fight with the aliens, when they all rushed us from different directions, I felt an urge to charge at them physically, to take them on hand-to-hand. It was all I could do to control myself. It was a berserker rage."

Quinn squinted at him. He was listening, but I could tell he was taking every word with a grain of salt. "Where'd you go?"

"By the time the fight was over, all of you were looking at the corpses. I stepped out. I went through this door. I found one more of the aliens, but it was distracted. I managed to kill it."

Quinn stepped forward. He grabbed each of Corporal Tench's arms and stretched them out. There were tears, bloody tears, through his spacesuit. "Your spacesuit's ruined, Corporal."

"Yeah," Tench said. "Like I said, I couldn't control myself. I got close to the one in this chamber. I grappled with it. Those spines, those claws… I managed to twist its head clean off, but it tore me up some, too."

Corporal Tench pulled back his sleeves to show what I saw were shockingly large arms. In fact, his forearms looked as if they were twice as thick as they had been before. His fingers, his thumbs, even his wrists had swollen somewhat. Could his bones have thickened? I didn't know.

"The funny thing is," he said. "I've been really hungry, and I've been eating everything I could find."

Dr. Sharaf finally approached. Her curiosity had outweighed her fear. She examined Tench warily. "Where could you have gotten enough food to have grown this much? Assuming your metabolism could even generate flesh like this—it's fantastic."

"I did find something to eat…" he said, trailing off.

We thought about that, and then we stepped into the chamber to look past him. Indeed, we saw what we had all feared might be the case.

A dead cyborg was laying on the floor with its thorny body ripped open. The metal had been torn back to reveal the flesh inside. It looked like Corporal Tench had feasted upon it.

"That is really gross, dude," Ledbetter said.

"I'm out of food, water—everything," Tench said. "I decided to try to come back and rejoin Red Company."

We eyed him uncertainly.

"I'm going to have to ask you to disarm yourself, Corporal," Quinn said.

"Yes, sir," Tench agreed, lowering his rifle to the floor. He also pulled out his pistol and handed it by the butt to the lieutenant.

Lt. Quinn still reached out with a hand and wriggled his fingers. Tench reluctantly took out his last weapon, his combat knife, and deposited it into Quinn's hand.

"We've got something better for you than just rations," Quinn said.

"What's that, sir?"

"An injection," Dr. Sharaf said, shuffling forward with an orangey-brown syringe with a dripping needle, as if she'd known this moment was coming. It seemed to me that she'd loaded up a double dose this time.

When she plunged in the needle and shot goop into Corporal Tench's veins, he howled like an animal from our primitive past.

Chapter 31: A Fortunate Discovery

In the chamber where Corporal Tench had been hiding, tormented by his mutations, we made a fortunate discovery: a source of water. It made sense that the ant-like creatures, being at least partially organic, would need water to survive. We had uncovered their water supply.

"It's quite ingenious, really," Dr. Sharaf explained. "Do you see these tubes here, descending from the surface? I assume they extend all the way up. They're filtering the sparse atmosphere of Eris. It's only about one percent of the density of Earth's, even thinner than the atmosphere of Mars. But it's sufficient."

"Enough for what, Doctor?" I asked, curious.

"Enough to extract water from the air. Water is vital in many ways. With a simple process, you can separate oxygen, hydrogen, and of course, water itself—the essence of life."

"How can there be so much water on this rock?" Quinn demanded. "It's way below freezing out there, and there's no obvious sign of..."

"You forget the geysers, Lieutenant," Dr. Sharaf reminded him. "They proved deadly for a few of our comrades when we first arrived here."

"Oh, right," Quinn said, recalling the incident.

"Yes," Dr. Sharaf continued. "Eris has a heated volcanic core and a significant amount of water deposits, likely brought here by comet strikes in its past. These deposits result in periodic geothermal explosions that shoot hot steam into the atmosphere. This system filters that steam, extracting half-frozen particles from the atmosphere far above, and supplies this installation with air, water, and heat."

"Huh... So, this contraption does all that, does it?" Quinn asked, tapping on the intricate loops of metal tubing.

Sharaf lurched forward and grasped his wrist. "Please, don't!" She was clearly concerned about the delicate nature of the device. "We're all going to have to rely on this equipment for our survival."

Quinn and the rest of us backed away, not wanting to accidentally damage the contraption that provided us with air, water, and heat. The device looked alien and intricate.

"We still need food," Quinn pointed out.

"Yes, obviously," Dr. Sharaf responded. "I suspect it might be behind the last door, the one we haven't explored yet."

There was indeed one final door, located at the bottom of the complex's deepest passage. We had found it hollow upon tapping, but no one had dared to enter.

Sensing another significant ass-kicking might be in our near future, Lt. Quinn instructed us to eat a ration for breakfast, drink deeply from our newfound water supply, and prepare for action. Surprisingly, he didn't order us to venture down the passageway and breach the entrance. Instead, he had us set up an ambush in the chamber with the life-sustaining machine.

"These ants," he said, "they have to come to the water room at some point to replenish their supplies or feed. Instead of hunting them, we're going to trap them."

We set up a watch, and after twelve long hours, our tactics paid off. Three of the ant-like creatures—more than we'd ever faced at once—entered the room.

One came from an unexpected direction—through a doorway we hadn't even known existed. The other two entered through the main passageway, the same path Corporal Tench had stumbled through not long ago.

The fighting was intense. Thankfully, Quinn had positioned us so that there was no risk of accidentally damaging the alien machine even when firing at the front entrance. However, the additional cyborg entering through the side passage posed a challenge, as it was quite close to the machine.

In the moment of the attack, surprise and near panic took over. We aimed our laser emitters at the third creature who was flanking us.

Quinn shouted for us to hold our fire, but his order was difficult to follow in the heat of the moment.

Unexpectedly, Corporal Tench lost control of himself. He charged at the third cyborg and began grappling with it. The two fighters sustained terrible wounds. Tench's thickened hide was punctured by the cyborg's spines, while we repeatedly shot the enemy until it fell.

Sadly, Tench was gravely injured by the time the monster went down. The other soldiers had managed to eliminate the two remaining adversaries who had entered through the main entrance without sustaining any losses. Corporal Tench was the only one critically wounded.

"Do you think he can make it, Doc?" Quinn asked.

Dr. Sharaf shook her head, administered a few more injections, and then solemnly walked away.

Blood was everywhere, and Corporal Tench was dying. He tried to speak to us but couldn't. We offered him comforting words, well-wishes, and hopeful illusions of returning to Mars and Earth. We all knew it was just empty talk, and eventually, Corporal Tench drew his last, rasping breath and died in a puddle of blood.

"Well," Quinn said, gazing down at the body, "at least he redeemed himself. That's a Red Company marine right there. He saved us all in the end. Don't forget it, boys."

We nodded, knowing we wouldn't.

We waited another day and then a third. Nothing came to find us. We began to worry that the aliens had a secondary source of sustenance, or that they were all dead. We considered sending out recon parties to scout the last chamber. But each time this was brought up, Quinn urged patience.

On the third day, a loud scratching sound echoed from the passageway beyond the main door. We grabbed our weapons, wiped the sweat from our faces, and braced ourselves for another desperate battle. After a minute or two of tense silence, the door rolled up, revealing nothing but a dark, metallic, thorny tendril.

"What the hell is *that*?" Quinn asked. "Starn, go take a look."

It was probably the worst order I'd ever received, but I obeyed. I approached the door and peered out, only to see something I never expected: a massive, hulking alien creature, similar to the others but significantly larger.

It was thick and robust, unlike the others who were thin and narrow at the joints, waist, and neck. This monstrous queen alien appeared incredibly imposing.

As the creature spotted me, it laboriously dragged itself forward, barely able to move or fit in the passageway due to its immense size. It was easily five times the mass of any other alien we'd encountered, dragging itself over across the deck like a colossal lobster. It rounded the corner and began squeezing through the doorway, only to be met with a barrage of laser fire.

Every surviving marine unleashed hell on the alien monstrosity. It shuddered, steamed, and hissed, attempting to hook onto us with its long, spiny limbs. It failed to reach us. I suspected it had been weakened by a lack of food and water, as its minions had been unable to bring it sustenance. Driven by desperation, it had emerged from its dark lair in search of what it needed to survive.

Due to its slow pace and immense bulk, we managed to destroy it before it could reach us. As the lifeless creature slumped to the ground, we all breathed a collective sigh of relief.

Chapter 32: Blackwood's Lie

Nearly a week had passed since we'd entered this strange alien lair. We were unable to locate any more enemy ant creatures. They were all dead—if they were really alive in the first place. Regardless, the queen and all her workers had ceased to exist.

I had to wonder how long this colony had survived here on the frozen rock that was Eris, only to succumb to Red Company in the end. Quite possibly, if they hadn't attacked the Teklution ship and suffered losses there, we might not have been able to overcome them. But in the end, Earth's second ship had prevailed, and this alien hive was as dead as the others Dr. Sharaf had spoken of.

Still, that wasn't much solace, as we were pretty much dead ourselves. We had found sources of food: mossy growths, fungus, and disgusting things that grew like bulbous fruits in the darkest corners of the tunnels. We now had air, heat, water, and food—if you could call it that. But we knew we couldn't last forever.

We weren't like these ant creatures. We would go mad eventually, or more likely, long before that, we would start to transform. After all, Dr. Sharaf only had so many precious injections to keep the genetic mutations we could feel itching in our bodies at night from taking over.

I had to wonder if this was how a werewolf would have felt, had such legends actually been true.

As the days wore on, all of us noticed slight, minor differences in ourselves. For me, one of my arms felt unusually strong, stronger than the other. Oddly enough, it was my left arm. I was fairly certain I'd been the strongest man in Red Company since the day I joined up, but now I was more than certain.

Experimentally, I decided to test my bulky arm one day. Wearing a double-layered glove from one of our fallen, I grabbed hold of one of the great queen's hind legs.

I dragged her down the passageway, so she no longer blocked the path that led to the room with food and water. The others, who later noticed my handiwork, were shocked. I didn't tell them I'd done it with a single arm.

Ledbetter confided in me that he had a peculiar new transformation as well. His was quite different, however. It involved his sense of hearing. He claimed he could now hear my heart beating inside my chest, and he complained that it made it difficult for him to sleep at night.

I didn't believe him at first, but after I moved the queen, whose corpse was vast and weighed quite a bit even on Eris, I began to suspect he was telling the truth.

At some point, I realized we were all going to turn into whatever Corporal Tench had transformed into. Perhaps, unlike him, we'd be less able to control our emotions, thoughts, and behaviors—especially after we'd been trapped in these warrens for months—or possibly years.

But fate took a strange turn two weeks after our arrival at the alien warren.

"Someone's tapping at the door!" Ledbetter shouted from the passageway.

None of the rest of us had heard a thing. But, as I said, Ledbetter could hear things.

"Are you sure?" Quinn asked.

"Yes sir, I'm sure. I can hear it."

By this time, Lt. Quinn knew of Ledbetter's superior hearing and had grown to trust it. "All right, company," he said. "This is probably it. Our last stand."

"Why would you say that?" Dr. Sharaf demanded.

Quinn looked at her. "Think about it for a minute, woman. We arrived on Eris and found a single lab buried beneath the ice, right?"

"Don't speak to me as if I'm an imbecile!"

"But you are acting dumb. Do you really think this lab is the only one on the planet? What if this whole rock, every mile or two, has a colony like this one?"

Her eyes grew wide, and she looked quite alarmed. Apparently, this thought had never occurred to her.

It had never occurred to me either. In fact, I was quite happy that Quinn had decided to keep these sorts of dark beliefs to himself until this critical moment.

"Who knows?" Quinn said. "Maybe they have a way of transmitting messages to one another. Maybe the queen next door has been trying to call her sister for weeks, but she's gotten no answer. Now, she's sent her troops to find out what went wrong."

Solemnly, we gathered our force and stood in two ranks. The first rank was kneeling in front, while the second was standing behind them.

We aimed our weapons upward toward the great airlock, waiting for it to open. At last, the external hatch did open. I heard it hiss with the audible escape of gases. We all listened as the air was cycled out, then back in again.

"They're coming," Quinn said in a harsh whisper. "Prepare for depressurization, guys. Faceplates down."

We all snapped our faceplates closed. We polished the tips of our weapon emitters one last time. Our batteries weren't full, but hopefully, we had enough juice left in our guns to finish a few more of these monsters before we were overwhelmed.

It seemed to take forever, but finally, the inner door of the airlock sighed open, and one single laser bolt spat out.

It was Charlie who had fired the shot. Fortunately, his aim was poor, and the bolt only gouged the ceiling, creating a sizzling hole in the metal.

"Hold your fire!" Quinn shouted.

Stepping toward us was Captain Hansen. She was shouting the same thing to her troops.

Both sides were shocked to meet the other. Sergeant Cox led his own fresh squad of marines in Hansen's wake.

The two halves of Red Company surged forward. We clasped hands, hammered backs, smiled, and cheered. Our brothers in arms had come back to rescue us.

"I don't get it, Captain," Lt. Quinn said. "You took off over a week ago. Why'd you come back for us?"

"I didn't," she said, "not exactly." She turned back toward the rear of her squad of troops, "Perhaps Accountant Blackwood can explain."

There he was: a tall, thin, oddly misshapen figure at the very back of the assembly. He was the last one at the airlock and the last one to tentatively step inside the alien hive. He kept his faceplate locked down firmly, breathing only the safe air inside his spacesuit.

Blackwood noticed our stares. He immediately pointed an overly long finger in my direction. "It was him," he said. "He's the reason we came back."

"What?" Quinn frowned, turning to stare at me. "What did Starn do?"

"He met with Yeoman Carter," Blackwood said, "before *Borag* lifted off. She confessed everything. There was contact—physical contact."

"What are you talking about? There wasn't time—" Quinn began, but then Sergeant Cox stepped up, and he gave Quinn a very meaningful stare.

"Could I have a word, sir?"

Frowning, Quinn allowed himself to be pulled aside. The two of them spoke heatedly together for a moment.

In the meantime, Captain Hansen stepped up and examined her first dead ant alien.

"What are these disgusting creatures?" she asked.

We explained in great detail, with Dr. Sharaf taking on most of the burden. She spoke as if she was giving a lecture at a college. Soon, Captain Hansen went from fascinated to bored.

"All right, all right," she said. "So, you got in here somehow and killed all of them. So much for a friendly first-contact scenario."

"Captain," I said, daring to speak to her directly, "why did you come back? I don't quite understand."

"Because you contaminated my yeoman, Private. Once this was revealed, it was too late to quarantine her. Essentially, she had already contaminated my entire ship. We were all declared quarantined at that moment. Therefore, we calculated we might as well come back here and see if any of you were still alive."

"Or better yet," Blackwood said, "if there were any profit-bearing artifacts that could be returned to Mars."

Captain Hansen glanced at Blackwood. "Some of us are very concerned about our finances."

"Someone has to be," Blackwood said. He seemed quite pleased with himself.

Blackwood kept glancing at me, giving me little eyebrow raises and other odd gestures. Slowly, I began to get an idea. Could it be that this was all part of Blackwood's grand plan? Had he lied about Freya and me having somehow fraternized? All that, just so we could get Captain Hansen to turn the ship around and return to pick us up?

It seemed fantastic, but I couldn't think of another explanation. Frowning, I found I didn't like the lie. I didn't like being blamed for the endangerment of the entire crew of *Borag*. But I also didn't like the idea of being marooned here on Eris forever. So, I decided to keep my mouth shut.

By the time Sergeant Cox and Lt. Quinn had finished their discussion, Quinn seemed to be in the same mood that I was. We both stopped talking about why *Borag* had returned.

We took our time after that, showing Captain Hansen around the entire installation, we displayed the bodies, the technology, the devices we'd found, and even, perhaps most shocking of all, the room full of frozen beings from the distant past. Dr. Sharaf showed her the samples she'd taken, all the recordings, the measurements.

Captain Hansen's eyes were wide. "This, plus the alien discoveries... this is going to be worth a fortune if we're allowed to turn these things in to Earth-Gov."

"Don't worry, Captain," Blackwood said. "Fortunes have a way of speaking for themselves."

Eventually, the fresher half of Red Company helped the rest of us, who had gotten rather worn out after spending weeks stuck in this hole. We returned to *Borag*, and there were a lot of examinations, scrubbings, and samples taken by the medical crew.

Eventually, we were released into the ship's general population. This surprised me, as we were still taking Dr. Sharaf's injections to keep ourselves in a normal state. Apparently, between her and Blackwood, the medical people were convinced we were harmless.

It was a real treat to be allowed to lie down on a bunk. A hot shower, hot food, and a real bunk. These things had never been so comforting before.

Our half of Red Company was either dead or exhausted, so Sergeant Cox was left with the job of going down into the alien labyrinth to plunder the place. Our holds were soon filled with strange artifacts and frozen bodies. I noticed that the tubes containing the specimens taken from Earth were carried aboard and stowed away in the deepest freezers in the aft hold.

A few days later, the great ship lifted off again, and we headed back toward Mars. On the return trip, things were a lot more subdued. The officers had been worried about morale aboard the great vessel, but they didn't have to be. Everyone knew we were heading to our home port at Mars, a place of relative freedom and comfort. That was a lot less daunting, a lot less damaging to the average sailor's mind, than was a trip into the unknown.

Perhaps even more important was the simple fact that we all now knew we carried a cargo of true value. Not even the oldest spacers aboard could recall having found anything remotely comparable. Cargoes of titanium, uranium, plutonium, and diamond were all as nothing compared to this alien treasure trove.

When we were about halfway home, Blackwood came out of his lair on the highest decks. "I have good news," he announced over the ship's public address system. "Everyone aboard is eligible for a large bonus, twenty times the amount that was distributed at the start of this mission."

Cheers went up all over the ship. Some people wept. The D-class contracts, they would be able to buy out their indenture status.

Ledbetter grabbed onto me and did a little dance. "We're rich," he said. "We're friggin' rich."

I smiled, but I kept my eyes on Blackwood. His grim visage still filled the ship's screens. He wasn't done yet. Even I knew that in moments like this, he always delivered the good news first.

"However," Blackwood continued, "we have a new contract that everyone aboard must sign in order to gain access to this well-deserved fraction of the ship's profits."

Groans arose from the group at Red Company headquarters. These groans were not as loud as the cheers had been before, but they were significant. Trust was thin in our group.

"Do not be concerned," Blackwood said, "these new contracts are not onerous in nature."

"Yeah, right," Sergeant Cox yelled at the screen.

"But they are… significantly binding, especially in the area of non-disclosure."

Blackwood went on, explaining that the biggest detail of the new contracts was that we weren't allowed to speak of what we had seen on Eris. That if we ever discussed any details of this mission, of its nature, of the events that had occurred, even of the destination itself, we would all be in forfeiture of our shares. We'd lose all our profits, quite possibly our freedom—and perhaps even, we were led to understand, our very lives.

By the end of this little speech, we were somber, yet still we were eager to sign. How could we not be? Except for our bonus prior to this mission, no one aboard *Borag* had seen a serious profit in a long time. This was our chance to get back in the black again, to have a positive net worth. This meant freedom and comfort for all of us, and all we had to do was keep our mouths shut.

The decision was a relatively easy one. I made it in my mind immediately. I planned to sign. Perhaps, I'd even go back to Earth when this was all over with. Who knew?

"And," Blackwood continued, after we'd all digested what had been said so far, "there is one more tiny wrinkle. Hopefully, this will not be a barrier to everyone's happiness and success on this mission, but we shall see. The last stipulation of the new contract, which I urge you all to sign, is that you *must* all sign it. If anyone aboard *Borag* refuses to abide by these terms, the new contract is null and void for everyone."

He let that sink in for a few moments, and our eyes roved. We glanced at one another.

Already, I could tell what we were thinking. Who would it be? There had to be a holdout. Who was going to suddenly become principled or otherwise unwilling to sign? Who was going to figure they could get a better deal? Who was going to blow it for all of us?

Already, my mind had leaped onto the next critical point. I understood now that Blackwood was a genius. By making an all-or-nothing deal, he was putting a fantastic level of pressure upon even the most reluctant. After all, we had about three months to go before we reached Mars. That was a long, long time to live aboard a spacecraft full of people who hated your guts.

After that it took a few days, but eventually, everyone aboard signed. Even the officers who didn't want to. Even the crustiest old cranks who argued we could get a better deal. They were not listened to.

In the end, Blackwood prevailed. The deal was signed, eagerly by some, reluctantly by others—but it was signed.

I wondered how long it would be before someone leaked the information, and the word got out about the alien bases. Could it really be possible for nearly a thousand people aboard a mining rig to all keep quiet, even when they were drunk, even when they were in a narcotic stupor? I frowned, thinking that over. Dr. Sharaf had indicated that in the past, such bases had been discovered, but we had never heard about it. I had to surmise, therefore, that agreements like this had been drafted before, and they'd been successfully enforced. Quite ruthlessly, I imagined.

In every human society, there were always certain facts that weren't allowed to be known. The existence of an alien society that predated mankind's civilization appeared to be one of those truths.

But in order to keep the secret, there must be real authorities, real teeth behind Blackwood and his words. This contract wasn't just something between Interplanetary Excavations and each of us. No, it went further than that. It had to go right up to the governments. The media had to know. To keep quiet about this kind of story, for so long, *everyone* had to know the truth—except the people at large.

Those quick, easy steps of logic led me to the inescapable conclusion that I'd better keep my frigging mouth shut about this voyage. If I wanted to keep my freedom, my money, and my head on my shoulders, I was going to have to keep quiet.

When all the wrangling with the contracts was done, the large ship's displays began to show the growing, rust-orange ball that was Mars. It grew imperceptibly larger with every passing day, and the crew became ever more pleasant to be around.

Freya, in fact, was spending more and more time accompanying me on the mid-decks. We were both allowed to fraternize and attend certain bars and entertainment spots, few and crowded though they were, aboard *Borag*.

She and I had both become somewhat freer with our expenditure of credits, which allowed us to enjoy dates together as we never had. Instead of freebie hikes outside the Martian dome, we were enjoying relatively expensive meals, beverages and even senso-movies in the ship's tiny theater.

In what was perhaps a wise move, Blackwood had allowed everyone's credit limit to rise. We were essentially being allowed to spend some of the money we hadn't yet received, to borrow against our shares of the profits that would come at the end of the voyage.

It was difficult not to partake of this early bounty. I made sure I didn't indenture myself again, mind you. I went nowhere near any gambling casinos, legal or otherwise. But I did my best to entertain Freya, and she was even more successful in entertaining me.

In private, we occasionally discussed matters such as the big lie that Blackwood had told to get Captain Hansen to return to Eris.

"There's no way he could have done it alone," she said.

"What do you mean?" I asked her.

"Captain Hansen has to suspect the truth," she said. "In fact, I don't even think it was Blackwood's idea, necessarily."

"Explain what happened, then. You were aboard the ship. I wasn't."

"Yes, well, we flew for a week or so. I was devastated. Half of Red Company was gone, you included. There was nothing more depressing to contemplate than the long voyage home with men like Lacroix trying to take advantage of me, rather than a gentleman like you."

She smiled, and I smiled back. I didn't bother to mention that this was perhaps one of the first times in my life I'd been called a gentleman.

It was probably the uniform. It both gave women like her a sense that I was honorable, and I couldn't deny that it also had given me something to be honorable about. The marines were good for me, even if the service had been personally costly—in terms of the blood lost.

Freya was talking again, so I tuned back in.

"Anyway," she said, "I went to the captain and then to the other officers, and I tried to urge them to go back. Blackwood took me aside. Maybe that was when he got the idea. He accused me of having fraternized with you and being infected. He claimed I must have been at least exposed to whatever contaminants you'd been exposed to. Of course, the whole idea was preposterous. You never left the Teklution ship. You stayed there in quarantine as you were supposed to."

"I wouldn't exactly call it quarantine," I said. "I was busy fighting these weird creatures."

Freya frowned at me. I hadn't told her too much about that part of our recent ordeal.

There were secrets within secrets in this group. We'd all been sworn to secrecy about the existence of the alien base in the first place, but there was another, deeper layer of secrecy involved. That set of secrets was held by those who'd survived those long days on Eris alone. We were still taking injections concocted by Dr. Sharaf, for instance.

We still had to get a monthly injection to keep our mutations under control. At least we each had our own personal supplies of the medication. But I'd wonder from time to time how many other humans were in the Solar System somewhere taking these same regularly administered injections. It was strange to think about.

So, there was a mutation secret, a Red Company secret shared only with Dr. Sharaf and half the marines aboard the ship, and then there was the ship-wide secret. Everyone aboard *Borag* knew about the aliens we'd discovered, and we all knew what had happened to the Teklution ship.

Lies within lies.

Lastly, as I listened to Freya, I realized there was yet another lie to contend with. This was what I thought of as "Blackwood's lie."

"How could he convince anyone," I asked, "that you and I somehow had physical contact? I was aboard the Teklution ship until *Borag* lifted off."

Freya leaned forward. She lowered her voice as if perhaps someone was listening. I didn't know if they were, so I leaned forward, and I lowered my voice as well.

"There were a couple of workmen, do you remember?" she asked. "Outside the ship?"

"Yes, two dogs were there from *Borag's* maintenance crew."

"Blackwood got hold of the video of those two men when they ran back to *Borag*. He altered the records—the visuals from the ship's cameras, even the logs from when they walked aboard through the aft airlocks."

"So?" I asked.

"He changed everything. He made the video show that it was me and you returning to *Borag*, not two random workmen who had helped cut open the door on the Teklution ship."

"How did he do that? With software?"

"Yeah," she said, "a deep fake. I saw his false evidence. The workmen looked just like us. Shots of our faces were melded in. Even the automatic ID of the radio transponders in our helmets was recorded in the logs—he thought of everything."

I shook my head. "How could he work up something like that so quickly?"

She shrugged. "I think he's a master of stuff like that. What is a ship's accountant, if not a masterful editor of reality?"

I laughed, and she finally smiled and relaxed some as well. We were able to enjoy ourselves after that until the following day when I was called to an urgent meeting at Red Company headquarters.

When I walked in, I immediately knew something was up. This was because I knew all the individuals who were present at the meeting. I knew them very well. They were the survivors, those who'd been abandoned on Eris. Even Dr. Sharaf and her surviving sidekick were there.

"Ah, Private Starn," Dr. Sharaf said. "Of course, you would be among the latest of the late. And where is your closest companion?"

I frowned at this and began to protest on Freya's behalf.

"No, no—not the yeoman girl. I mean—oh, there he is!"

Private Ledbetter was slipping through the doorway behind me. He had a smile on his face that rapidly melted away when he saw the crowd, just as mine must have done. Within moments, his face transformed from congeniality to alarm and concern.

"Come on in, Private," Sharaf said. "Take a seat. We all have some things to discuss."

Here it comes, I thought to myself, the next circle of lies.

We, in a sense, were *Borag's* ultimate secret. We'd all demonstrated signs of infection while we were on Eris. This caused me a pang of worry as I thought about it. I'd been fraternizing quite a bit with Freya lately. What if I had unwittingly infected her? Was she going to need injections someday or be transformed into a hideous monster like Corporal Tench?

I raised my hand. Looking bored, Dr. Sharaf pointed at me. "Yes, yes. A question. Let's get it out of your system."

"Doctor?" I said. "It seems to me quite irresponsible that we've been allowed to have contact with everyone aboard this ship. I mean, aren't we spreading whatever it is we have?"

"No," she said, and she said it firmly. "I've looked into it. I've had discussions. This isn't the first time this sort of thing has been dealt with, as you probably suspected."

"Right…" Lt. Quinn said. "I knew as soon as I saw you were packed up with doses of an antidote to these mutations that it couldn't be the first time the Earth has seen this phenomenon."

"That's right," she said. "We've encountered it before. We've never encountered the aliens in their live and active state, but we have dealt with the infection and the mutations."

"What's the purpose of infecting humans with genetic viruses, anyway?" Quinn asked.

Sharaf shrugged. "We don't really know. It's one of many experiments that they typically performed upon humans. Maybe they were trying to breed us as a form of mutated soldiers. What we do know is that as long as you're taking this compound, it is not possible for you to transmit the disease. You must be fully mutated in order to spread it. That is how Ledbetter and Corporal Tench got the disease in the first place."

I nodded, thinking it over. It did make sense. When I raised my hand again, she pointed me at me with a sigh.

"So… how did the rest of us get infected?" I asked. "I mean, not all of us were torn up by those cyborgs."

"Yes, but we all spent a week living in their complex, drinking their water, eating their strange alien foods. It was a foregone conclusion that we would all contract the disease. Even I have caught a little something."

She pulled her glove off then, and she showed us that she was sprouting an additional finger on her hand. It was kind of nasty to look at. She quickly pulled her glove back on again.

"What's the upshot of all this?" Quinn demanded. "Do we really have to give ourselves these injections once a month for the rest of our lives?"

"For now, yes," she said. "You'll be provided with a year's supply of the inhibitor. Don't lose it. We're searching for a better solution, mind you, but for right now, this medication is all we have."

We all frowned. It was upsetting news. I'd kind of hoped that this was the sort of thing that you would get over eventually, that your body would fight it off. But it wasn't a disease, not really. It was a genetic transformation. Our very DNA had been altered. Honestly, it gave me a chill just to think about it.

After that, she swore us all to secrecy, and handed us each a small satchel containing a year's supply of the drug we needed to maintain our natural states. She left us all with one final warning as well. "None of us shall ever be allowed to return to Earth again, not until we've been declared cured."

"What?" I exclaimed. She was blowing one of my greatest fantasies right then and there.

She smirked at me. "Ah, yes, of course, the Earth man protests immediately. But alas, it's true. We will all be watched. We are all known. Do not even attempt to return to Earth's farthest orbiting space station. If you aren't executed out of hand, you'll be arrested and you'll vanish into some dungeon, never to be seen again."

"Oh, so that's the deal, is it?" Quinn complained. "All the mutants are left out here on the fringe of the fringe, left to eke out lives among the rocks in the icy cold forever?"

"Yes, that's right," she said. "That is our shared fate. And you should all know that I became a mutant over a decade ago."

We stared at her in surprise. We, of course, hadn't known that, but it made quite a bit of sense. In fact, it was doubly obvious now why she had been forced to go on this lengthy mission and why she had had a secret supply of the very drugs we all needed to prevent transformation on her person.

Eventually, the meeting broke up. Those of us who were from Red Company were feeling depressed. We were all trapped in a secret circle. We had survived Eris, but we were cursed.

We moved together as a group to the grungiest, dimmest-lit bar down on the lowest deck. There, we drank until we didn't care about our status as exiles any longer.

Chapter 33: Our Triumphant Return

At long last, the great day came. We arrived at Mars port again, and I can tell you that after a year in space, we wanted to get off that ship pretty damned badly.

Everyone had long ago signed all of Blackwood's agreements, of course. Our accounts were full. *Borag* was not only in the black, but she was also relatively well-off, and everybody was smiling as we arrived at the spaceport and were immediately allowed to disembark. After double-checking to make sure my accounts were indeed brimming with credits, I took Freya to the nicest restaurant in the nicest hotel in Mars City.

We lived it up for several days there. It was almost like a honeymoon.

But then, on the fourth day, I got a call from Captain Hansen herself. "Corporal Starn?" she said.

I blinked a few times. Her words were not quite sinking in. "Uh... yes, Captain?"

"I've talked things over with Commander Kaine. We've come to a joint decision. You are to be given the rank of Corporal in Red Company. I see by your account numbers that you are now able to buy out your own contract should you wish to. There will be no ill feelings if you do. At least half of Red Company has chosen that option already."

I didn't know this. I was quite surprised, in fact. But the more I thought about it, the more I realized why so many had bailed out. Those who had survived on Eris had pretty much had the shit scared out of them. And the rest of them, well, they'd just spent a year in space, and they were not interested in more of that kind of punishment. Maybe they'd sign on with another ship that wasn't quite as unlucky and volatile as *Borag*.

I sucked in a deep breath and heaved a big sigh. "I didn't know that, sir. But you said something about me being a Corporal?"

"That's right," she said. "The job is open, after all. Tench did not survive the voyage. Lt. Quinn has recommended you for the job. But, of course, you will have to sign a new contract to officially gain this new rank."

My head rolled back on my shoulders. What a decision to be faced with. "Can I at least think about it, sir?"

"No," she said. "You can't, because there's something else. I would like you to attend me personally. I'm going back to Interplanetary Excavations headquarters today. Will you meet me at the space elevator?"

I thought about it, and I quickly came to a decision. I figured the very least I could do was one final favor for Captain Hansen. After all, when I'd first met this woman, I'd been a lowly rock-rat with no hope. Now, I was a relatively well-off individual, a self-sufficient worker, a man who could choose among contracts in the future as opposed to being bought and sold on the open labor market.

"All right, sir. I'll be there in five."

I gathered my kit, gave Freya one last kiss, and hurried to the space elevator. To my surprise, Captain Hansen was alone. Not even Blackwood attended her.

Together, we walked toward Interplanetary's company headquarters. I had to wonder who we might meet there. So far, I had never seen a pleasant person inside that building. I probably never would.

When the receptionist showed us into the big office at the top of the towering structure, I was disappointed to see the controller sitting there at his sumptuous desk. When we appeared in the doorway, he ushered out a group of suits who gave us odd glances on the way by.

"So," Captain Hansen said when the door was shut, "the Colonel isn't here to surprise us today?"

"That's right," he said. "Earth-Gov isn't involved in this discussion."

The controller and the captain exchanged pleasantries for a while, and the controller managed to give her thin praise. "You and your crew did well. Unexpectedly well. It was a difficult assignment, but you pulled through."

"Yes, sir," she said. "In fact, I have plans for my newfound wealth."

The controller's eyebrows shot up. "And what might be those plans?"

"I'm considering independence, sir."

The controller laughed. It was not a pleasant sound. "Independence? Not with my ship, you're not."

"Collectively, my top officers and I have the money to buy *Borag*. We also have that option in our contract."

The controller waved his fingers in the air as if an offensive odor was attacking his face. "Come on, Captain," he said. "No one ever exercises those options. They aren't real."

Captain Hansen calmly produced her contract and threw it on his desk. It was a plastic slip of computer paper. It rattled and glowed on the flat surface between the two of them.

"This is a legally binding document, Malkin," she said.

The controller rolled his eyes, sat back in his chair, and laced his fingers behind his bald head.

"Captain..." he said, "let's not become unpleasant. I'm a businessman. People like you and me, we do business together. We know our places. We perform our jobs. We do them well. Now, your job is to go on missions for Interplanetary Excavations until such time as the company decides you're no longer useful—which essentially means no longer profitable."

I dared to glance at Captain Hansen's face. Her eyes were narrowed, but she hadn't twisted a muscle. She wasn't scowling, not exactly. She was just staring flatly, the way one might stare at a worm on the sidewalk.

"You seem quite confident, Controller," Hansen said. "Can you tell me why you think I will not be able to go independent?"

He smiled and nodded. "Yes, I can tell you easily. For example, did you know there's a new fee for docking here at Mars Station? It's quite exorbitant, actually."

Hansen looked at him. "I've heard of no such fee."

"Yes, yes. Look at it—right here." He produced a document and threw it toward her.

"This computer paper," she said, picking it up and staring at it, "it's blank."

"No, no, it's not blank. You see there at the top? That's the insignia of the Mars provisional government. The regulators use that same stationery, you see. And at the bottom, you see where it says 'signed by?' It's already been pre-signed. All I have to do is fill it in."

"Fill it in with what?"

"With a description specific enough to catch *Borag* and maybe a few other ships that I want to."

She stared at the document. "Are you showing me evidence of corruption and regulatory mischief?"

The controller laughed again. "No, I'm showing you how things work around here. Let us understand the Solar System and how it operates. There's Earth, and then there's *not* Earth. That's the first thing you have to understand. Earth is controlled by a series of stodgy old governments. The colonel belongs to that group."

"Controller, I don't see what—"

"Bear with me. Everything else in the Solar System is controlled by corporations. Only companies can operate ruthlessly enough to conquer space, to gather all the riches from the asteroids and the moons and the belts of fine dust. Earth-Gov doesn't like us much, but we bring a lot of wealth back to them. There is a third group, of course. Those saddest of characters we call pirates. You could always join them, but believe me, you're never going to take one of our ships and be able to operate as an independent. You're either with the corporations, or you're against them."

Captain Hansen scowled, giving the man her death-stare. He seemed unaffected.

"Honestly, you should know all this by now, Captain. It's sort of embarrassing that I should have to give you this little speech at this point in your career."

For several long seconds Captain Hansen stood there, as stiff as a rock. Finally, she reached out and snatched her contract back up off the desk. She turned away from the odious man, and I moved with her, accompanying her every step of the way. I now knew why she thought she might need a trusted bodyguard while she faced a snake like this.

"Hold on there," the controller said. "We're not quite done yet. Since you're not going independent, but you are wealthy, and you can certainly buy yourself out and leave Interplanetary. In fact, you can leave *Borag*, and Mars itself while you're at it. Feel free. I'm in no way going to stand against you—but I'm not going to allow *Borag* out of our hands. She's too great of an asset."

"You were telling me in great detail how my ship was a liability just a few months ago."

"That was actually over a year ago," he said. "But never mind. If you wish to remain at your post as captain of *Borag*, you are welcome to do so. In fact, we will offer you a signing bonus."

"I don't want credits," she said. "I want greater freedom."

"Credits *are* freedom," the controller said gently. "The kind that you can actually possess and enjoy. Do you want to hear about your new mission, or are you resigning your captaincy? Those are your two options at this point."

Captain Hansen really was scowling by now. She was angry, and I couldn't blame her. In fact, I wanted to throttle the fat guy behind the desk, but I figured I probably wouldn't make it out of the building alive if I did. Still, it might be worth it…

"I'll take a third option," Captain Hansen said at last. "*Borag* is going back to rock mining until further notice. The ship isn't in debt, and you can't stop me from doing that."

The controller frowned. He thought that over, tapped a few numbers onto his desk, and then nodded, folding up his lips.

"All right," he said. "You're correct. You're completely within your rights to do that, and no one in the company would oppose you—including me. So for right now, go with it. Do whatever you want, Captain Hansen. The outer Solar System is yours to explore and exploit."

Together, the captain and I walked out of that office, and we didn't say a word to each other until we reached the street. Even then, I waited until we were twenty paces away from that building before I spoke to her.

"Captain Hansen," I said, "I'm really sorry about all that."

She stopped, turned, and looked at me. "It's not your problem, Corporal. By the way, are you still a Corporal in Red Company?"

I didn't hesitate for a second. "Yes, ma'am," I said. "I'll gladly accept the promotion, and I'll sign with you for another year."

The captain gave me a slight nod, and she almost smiled.

"That's good," she said. "At least there's one bright spot to this shitty day."

After that, I escorted her back to the space elevator. There, Freya met me. After giving the captain an odd glance, she turned to smile up at me. "Hey, I've got a surprise for you."

"What's that?" I said. My head was full of distracting thoughts.

"I'd love for you to meet my parents."

Alarmed, I turned slowly to face her. She had such a big, happy smile on her face that I couldn't bear to disappoint. So I smiled, too.

"That would be great," I managed to say.

The rest of the evening wasn't the best—but it was better than I'd hoped to experience back when I'd been marooned on Eris.

That night as I lay with Freya, I gazed out through a hotel window with a glorious view. The night sky above us presented a truly mesmerizing spectacle. The great Mars City dome, made of transparent materials, offered a clear and unobstructed view of the Martian heavens. As I stared upward, I noticed the sky appeared darker than it did on Earth. There was also a reddish-brown hue due to the iron-rich dust particles suspended in the planet's thin atmosphere.

The familiar constellations from Earth were still visible, but with subtle differences in their orientations and positions.

Mars' closer proximity to the asteroid belt also offered a chance to observe more frequent meteor showers. Every now and then small rocks burned up while entering the atmosphere, streaking across the sky like shooting stars.

Phobos and Deimos, Mars' two small moons, made their appearance an hour after dusk. Phobos, being closer and larger, appeared as a prominent crescent that moved quickly across the sky, completing its orbit in just eight hours. Deimos, on the other hand, looked more like a bright star that took around thirty hours to orbit Mars.

The most striking feature, however, had to be our fine view of Earth and the Moon. Earth appeared as a bright bluish star, shining with a steady glow, while the Moon could be seen nearby as a much dimmer point of light. Observing my home planet from a distance always felt surreal.

I wondered if I'd ever set foot on Earth again.

THE END

Books by B. V. Larson:

Red Company Series:

Red Company: First Strike!
Red Company: Discovery
Red Company: Contact

Visit BVLarson.com for more information.